EVEN
WHITE TRASH
ZOMBIES
GET THE
BLUES

DIANA ROWLAND

DAW BOOKS, INC.
DONALD A. WOLLHEIM, FOUNDER
375 Hudson Street, New York, NY 10014

ELIZABETH R. WOLLHEIM
SHEILA E. GILBERT
PUBLISHERS
http://www.dawbooks.com

First Printing, July 2012

1 2 3 4 5 6 7 8 9

DAW TRADEMARK REGISTERED
U.S. PAT. AND TM. OFF. AND FOREIGN COUNTRIES
—MARCA REGISTRADA
HECHO EN U.S.A.

PRINTED IN THE U.S.A.

For Cathy, who always knows how to brighten my day.

ACKNOWLEDGMENTS

Huge heaping thanks, praise, and adoration go out to:

My fabulous husband, Jack, for being ten thousand kinds of awesome and for finding a cool and creepy factory for me to tromp around in for location research.

My sister, Sherry, for supporting me and teasing me as needed.

My daughter, Anna, for amazing hugs and kisses.

Dr. Michael DeFatta, for patiently answering gross questions.

Steve Everly, for explaining the role of a probation officer.

Nina Lourie and Nicole Peeler, for daring to read and critique my rough drafts.

Roman White, for support, friendship, and asskickery.

Matt Bialer and Lindsay Ribar, for helping me get to where I am now.

Dan Dos Santos, for my AMAZEBALLS cover art!

And, finally, for my incredible editor, Betsy Wollheim, and everyone else at DAW who has helped make these books a fantastic reality.

Chapter 1

"So you hiding a body in here or sumthin'?"

The speaker gave a rasping chuckle as I pulled open the door of my storage unit, but behind his show of amusement was an avid curiosity that he was clearly desperate to satisfy. His question held a certain irony, considering that he fit the image of a serial killer a lot more than I did. Greasy black hair hung in lank tendrils from beneath a soiled Saints ball cap, his "Stor-This!" t-shirt with cut-off sleeves revealed slender arms with a surprising amount of muscle definition, and he apparently had the nervous habit of biting his nails—so severely that the tips of several fingers bore scabs.

On the other hand, I was the one who had a large chest freezer in a storage unit. Okay, yeah, so maybe that was a teensy bit suspicious. I could practically see the possibilities whirling behind his yellow-tinged eyes. Perhaps I was hiding the body of a past boyfriend? Maybe a parent? *How about a too-nosy storage unit manager?*

"Nah," I replied with a friendly smile. "I won one of those grocery store shopping sprees and didn't have any room back at my house to put a freezer. Didn't want all the stuff I got to go to waste, y'know?" I flipped the lid of the freezer open so that he could see the contents. He peered in, hungry curiosity shifting to disappointment as he took in the sight of several dozen frozen dinners, various plastic containers, and a couple of slabs of ribs wrapped in plastic. Definitely no corpses. Even the ribs were obviously non-human in origin.

"Oh. Yeah, okay. Makes sense." He straightened and stepped back as I placed two more plastic containers in the freezer.

"Made a big batch of soup yesterday," I explained as the hunger nudged at me. It wanted what was in those containers, but I was trying hard to be super careful about not splurging. I knew I needed to ration my supply carefully. I had a nice surplus right now, however, I'd learned from hard experience not to depend on that. "I ran out of room in the fridge at home," I continued, "so I figured I might as well put it out here for later on." I closed the lid, made sure it was fully clasped. "Sorry, no bodies!" I said with a laugh.

His mouth twisted into an answering smile, but it was clear I'd ceased to be interesting now that he knew there was nothing mysterious to be found in storage unit number five-three-four. Good thing he had no idea that the contents of the freezer were far worse than a corpse.

He wandered back up to the office while I closed and locked the unit. There was nothing at all that said I had to show him what was in my unit, but I knew damn well that if I hadn't let him look he'd have probably broken in to satisfy his curiosity, and then I'd have run the risk that the contents of the freezer would be ruined.

The slabs of ribs were exactly what they appeared to be—and from pigs, not humans—but the soup and the frozen dinners contained my very prized stash of about three months' worth of brains.

Yes, human brains.

Hello, my name is Angel, and I'll be your zombie today.

Chapter 2

"I know I'm the one with the so-called iron stomach," I said, "but even I think this is seriously disgusting."

I was under the floor with my head and shoulders in a narrow service tunnel-type thing, just far enough to where I could barely peer around the corner where another tunnel intersected the one I was in. There was a corpse in the tunnel on the left. I couldn't see a whole lot, but I could definitely smell it, even through the protective mask that kept me from choking on the grit and dust. So could everyone else.

"Flashlight?" I asked, reaching my hand blindly behind me. Someone shoved one into my hand, but the light only confirmed what my nose had tried to tell me. He was about ten feet down—bloated up and completely filling the tunnel. Considering that the tunnel was barely two feet across at best, I had to wonder what could have possessed him to try to squeeze through this narrow space. One arm was extended over his head, and the other looked to be wedged tight by his side. A pool of reddish purge fluid extended several inches along the shaft—a disgusting reddish brown discharge from the mouth and nose. A shiver ran through me at the sight of his mangled fingertips and thin streaks of blood along the side of the shaft. He'd done his damnedest to claw his way out or shift position. *Did he suffocate or did he die of thirst?* God, I hoped it was the first.

I worked as a van driver and morgue assistant for the St. Edwards Parish Sheriff's Office which meant I'd seen plenty of death. Most of the time the job was pretty straightforward—someone would die in their home or in an accident, a death investigator and I would come out, the investigator would do his or her thing, and then I would get the body into a body bag and bring it to the morgue where later I would assist the pathologist during the autopsy. It was nasty, smelly, sticky, and sometimes obscene and heartbreaking.

But I loved it. And not just because it provided me easy access to the brains I needed in order to stay . . . well, "alive" wasn't the right word. "Nicely undead"? "Not rotten"?

I shivered again, though this time from cold. It was early December, and while it rarely got cold enough to make a northerner twitch, I'd lived in south Louisiana my entire life, and anything below fifty degrees was unbearably chilly for me. Besides, we had plenty of humidity, which meant it was cold *and* damp. And yes, I was a weenie.

I shimmied my way back out and climbed up through the gap in the flooring. "Look, that whole section is going to have to come apart," I told Derrel Cusimano, the death investigator I worked with. "There's no way I can pull him out. He's stuck." Supposedly these tunnels had originally been used to route steam pipes throughout the decrepit building we were in, but the factory had been retrofitted numerous times over the last seventy-five years; old pipes had been ripped out and new pipes had been laid, carrying everything from water to data lines. Not all of the old pipes had been removed, either, and I had a feeling that was how my dead guy had managed to get himself nicely stuck. I swept my gaze over the floor. Supposedly, sections of the floor had been designed to be easily removed for access to the tunnels, but renovations and construction had covered most of the flooring with tile or linoleum, which meant that getting to the body was going to require some strong hands and possibly heavy machinery. At least it wasn't behind a wall. That would have been a disgusting nightmare.

Derrel let out a sigh. "Well, it was worth a try. Fortunately you could get far enough in to see."

I snorted. "Dude, I don't think you could even get your head in there." I worked with Derrel for at least ninety-nine percent of the calls I went out on, but we couldn't be more different in appearance. He was a former linebacker for LSU. Big, bald, black—a solid wall of meat and muscle. Meanwhile, I was a skinny white chick who had to jump up and down on the scale to get it to register more than a hundred pounds.

He chuckled. "That's exactly why I need an elf-sized partner."

"Yeah, well you won't catch me making toys or cookies." I tried to dust myself off then gave up. This whole place was so filthy I was only rearranging the dirt and sending it up into choking clouds. I wanted badly to put on my jacket, but I didn't want to get it messed up, either from dirt or bodily fluids. "How the hell did anyone know there was a dead guy in there?" I asked.

"This place just got bought, and workmen came in to do some cleanup and construction." He gave a sweeping gesture at "this place." We were in a factory on the banks of the Kreeger River just south of Tucker Point. In fact, the building was literally on the edge of the river, forming part of the seawall, and the straight drop had surprised me when I'd dared to peek out a window. Supposedly, it had been some sort of big-time car manufacturing plant in the 1920s or 30s and had then been any number of other things, including a warehouse, a movie studio, a factory again—this time for military vehicles—and then some sort of shipping facility. It had been rebuilt and renovated each time, which meant that it was now a bizarre mix of old and new, with nothing really fitting together properly and whole areas that didn't seem to connect to anything else. I'd had to walk through a defunct office section to get to this portion of the warehouse, and while nothing about a dead body could freak me out anymore, the peeling paint, abandoned office furniture, and broken windows had given me the godawful willies. I figured if zombies could be real, then there was nothing to say that ghosts couldn't be too.

"Anyway," he said, "the workmen smelled something funny. One of the guys was convinced it was more than just a dead rat and called the cops."

I nodded. There was something about "dead human" smell that was different than "dead rodent" smell.

"Cops could smell it too," Derrel went on, "so they called out Marianne and her cadaver dog. The dog went right to that spot in the floor and stared down at it. Bingo."

"Cool," I said, keeping my voice neutral as I scanned the warehouse for the petite woman and her dog. I spied her sitting on the steps to what had probably once been the foreman's office. I quickly looked away before she could see me looking at her and make eye contact. I wasn't quite ready to talk to her yet. What the hell was I supposed to say?

Derrel frowned at the opening in the floor, seemingly oblivious to my angst about Marianne. "Just wish I could figure out why the hell this guy decided to climb through there."

"Stealing copper, probably," I said.

He turned to me, lifted an eyebrow.

I grinned. "Not that I would know anything about any sort of larceny—" I chose to ignore his amused snort. "—but copper is pretty damn valuable, and I bet this guy was trying to use the tunnels to get into one of the closed-off sections in case there was any scrap metal he could go through."

Derrel pursed his lips and nodded. "It's amazing the things I learn from you."

"I'm full of useless knowledge."

Now was the time for people with more brawn than I to take care of dismantling the floor. I stepped back and found a spot to wait that wasn't in too many shadows, then had to bite back on a squeal as a hand came down on my shoulder. I spun to see Detective Ben Roth standing beside me.

He gave me a grin. "Damn, Angel, when are you going to put some meat on your bones?"

"When you make me a sandwich, bitch," I retorted as I worked to get my pulse under control.

He snorted. "It wouldn't help. I've seen you eat. You must have the metabolism of a goddamn hummingbird." He grinned and patted the spare tire at his waist. "I'm more of a penguin myself. But, hey, this penguin can bench his bodyweight *and* pass the departmental PT test with flying colors."

"*And* eat an entire muffaletta in one sitting," I added.

"I excel at the important things!"

"Yeah, well, I'd kill to have something resembling curves," I said, patting my nonexistent ass. The main reason I could stuff my face all I wanted was because, as far as I knew, I couldn't get fat. And not because of an amazing metabolism, either. Okay, that was probably part of it, but some of it was due to the fact that I wasn't—technically—alive.

He chuckled and dropped his hand, but then his expression grew more sober. "I guess you've heard about Ed?" he asked.

"Marcus told me earlier this week." I did my best to keep my expression neutral with maybe a touch of "damn that's fucked up" in it.

Ben blew out his breath. "I guess I should be glad that we have such a strong lead on who the murderer is, but it doesn't do us much good with him still in the wind."

I gave a cautious nod. "You think maybe he's in the area?"

"Nah. I think he's long gone." He grimaced. "Marcus is taking it hard though."

My gaze drifted to where the deputy stood on the other side of the long room. Marcus Ivanov looked like he'd stepped from the pages of an ad for "Hot Russian Men!" if such an ad existed. Dark hair and eyes, tall with just the right amount of muscle and barely an ounce of spare fat. But beyond the awesome good looks, right now he looked like one would expect a man to look who'd recently found out that his best friend was most likely one of the most notorious serial killers this area had ever experienced: shattered, maintaining a tough façade, determined to get through the whole ordeal with the help of his friends and coworkers.

I had to hide a smile. Deputy Marcus Ivanov deserved an Oscar for the performance he was giving.

Two weeks ago Marcus's best friend, Ed Quinn, had disappeared during their annual hunting trip. At least that's the story Marcus had given the authorities when the two of us returned to town. The reality was quite a bit harsher. Ed was a zombie hunter who'd been methodically hunting down zombies and chopping their heads off. After discovering that Marcus and I were also zombies, he'd tried to kill us as well. I'd saved Marcus's life and defeated Ed . . . and then gave Ed a choice: he could run, or I could eat him. Well, eat his brain. And I probably wouldn't have actually killed him and eaten *any* part of him, but Ed hadn't known that.

Needless to say, he'd decided to run. Marcus and I did our best to make it look like the two men had become separated in the woods, and then we returned to civilization and dutifully reported Ed missing. It probably hadn't been the best possible plan, but it was the best we'd been able to come up with considering the circumstances.

The one part of it that we'd both hated was the fact that a search party would have to be organized, and we'd have to play along with it while money and resources were spent on a pointless search. But at the last minute providence smiled upon us. Before the first man-hour could be wasted tromping through the woods, activity was discovered on Ed's credit cards. Moreover, surveillance video clearly showed him at a local sporting goods store purchasing camping and hunting equipment as well as an eyebrow-lifting amount of ammunition.

At that point the entire thing had been viewed as out of character for Ed, but the authorities had no choice but to simply shrug and chalk it up to a possible early midlife crisis. After all, there was nothing illegal about a grown man suddenly deciding to go on an extended camping or hunting trip. But a few days ago an anonymous caller tipped off the cops that Ed was responsible for the recent series of decapitation murders. Within no time at all search warrants were obtained, and incriminating evidence in the form of bloodied clothing was found in his apartment.

But the real mystery was that Marcus had sworn up, down, and sideways that he hadn't called in the tip. And I certainly hadn't. So who the heck could have known Ed was the killer? And, more importantly, did they know that the victims were zombies?

"It's tough for Marcus," I told Ben. "He's known Ed most of his life. I just hope Ed is really gone." I gave a shudder that I didn't have to fake.

Ben scowled. "Yeah, well I want to catch him before he does it again." He muttered a curse. "It fucking kills me that he was under our noses this entire time."

I didn't trust myself to speak so I simply gave him a sympathetic grimace as guilt curled through me. I'd let him go. And I wasn't so convinced Ed was long gone. I'd scared him off, but I found it hard to believe that he would have picked up and relocated, leaving two "monsters" like Marcus and me to roam free.

Despite my reluctance I found myself looking over toward the cadaver dog and handler who'd been called in to help locate the source of the dead body smell. The petite woman was still sitting on the steps to the foreman's office, her dog sitting patiently at her feet. Part of me wanted to avoid talking to her at all costs, but I knew that was the coward's way out. And while I was really damn good at being a coward, I was trying hard to change my ways. Besides, this woman sure as hell didn't deserve to be shunned by me or anyone else simply because she was Ed's girlfriend, and I knew she was having a tough enough time of it as it was.

Forcing a friendly smile onto my face, I made my way over to Marianne. The sun was low enough in the sky to paint a broad swath of the floor in jagged shadows as it filtered through broken and grime-streaked windows, and I had to shield my eyes from the glare of the sun off the river as I approached.

She looked up as I neared, eyes wary and haunted.

"Hey, Marianne," I said. "Hey, Kudzu," I said to the dog as I scratched its head. It gave me what had to be a puzzled look. Kudzu was a cadaver dog, and I had a feeling I confused the hell out of it. I smelled dead, yet I kept moving around.

"Hi, Angel," the dark-haired woman replied, wariness fading slightly.

"How you holding up?"

"Shitty," she said with a wavering smile. "But at least they seem to be done questioning me."

I gave a grimace of sympathy. "Yeah, Marcus had to go through that as well." It only made sense that, as soon as Ed was established as a suspect, the people closest to him should be grilled in case there was anything they could add to the investigation and search for him. I could only imagine that it was even harder for Marianne since they surely had to wonder if she'd been involved in any way. But apparently she'd requested to take polygraphs and voice stress analysis or whatever the heck was used nowadays in order to prove her innocence, and it had been enough to clear her of any suspicion.

Personally, I was relieved that she didn't seem to be involved. I didn't know her all that well, but from what I'd seen she seemed to be a genuinely nice person. It was bad enough that I'd been snowed by Ed. If Marianne had also turned out to be a zombie killer I'd have been seriously pissed.

A loud crash made us both jump. I spun to see that the workmen had peeled up an entire section of flooring and tossed it aside. "Time for me to get back to work," I said. On impulse I leaned in and gave her a quick hug. "Hang in there. Shit gets better."

She seemed shocked at first, then relaxed and returned the hug. When I released her she gave me a grate-

ful smile. "Thanks, Angel. Maybe we can do lunch or
something sometime . . . ?"

"I'd like that," I replied, only lying a little. I'd feel
much better about hanging out with her once I knew for
certain Ed wasn't lurking somewhere close.

Squaring my shoulders, I made my way back to help
separate the corpse from the wreckage. At least I had the
legendary iron stomach going for me.

Chapter 3

By the time we got the body extricated and into the body bag, the evening sun was busily painting the sky over the highway in brilliant shades of orange and yellow while also making it hard as hell to see to drive. As I got closer to Tucker Point, election signs became more frequent for everything from school board to state senator, including several for the parish coroner, Dr. Duplessis, AKA my boss. Elections were still a few months off, but politics were a spectator sport in Louisiana, and quite a few candidates started campaigning well before qualifying even opened. I'd heard whispers that the coroner might actually face some competition in the next election, but even though it was doubtful there was anyone who could pose a real threat to Dr. Duplessis, he wasn't taking any chances.

I heard my phone buzz with a text message, but I waited until I could pull into the parking lot of an

XpressMart to read it. I wasn't worried about dying in a car wreck, but I sure as hell didn't want to do the same to anyone else.

In the past months I'd developed a much higher appreciation for the value of life.

It was from Derrel. *No rest for the wicked. Just got a call re another death—accidental fall at NuQuesCor Lab. Meet me at front gate.*

Well, it wasn't the first time I'd gone from one death scene straight to another. I knew from experience that I could fit four bodies in the back of the van, though it wasn't pretty. I texted back an "OK", then pulled the GPS off the dash and stuck in the address he'd sent. Hunger nudged at me again, but I was pretty sure this was hunger for real food. At least part of it was, and satisfying that much would help keep the brain-hunger at bay—at least for a few hours.

This whole "controlling my urges" thing wasn't as easy as it sounded.

I killed the engine of the van and hurried inside the convenience store. The girl behind the counter looked about my age, maybe twenty-three at the most, pale-skinned, with hair that looked like it suffered from a distinct lack of shampoo use. She lifted her head as I came in, gave me a vacant look before returning her attention to her phone. A brief wave of sympathy went through me. I'd done more than my share of shit jobs like that. And while there were lots of people who wouldn't see my current job as a step up, I knew there was no comparison.

I quickly grabbed chips and a Coke, giving the clerk as friendly a smile as I could manage while I paid, silently urging her to hurry the hell up, and for chrissakes I'd seen roadkill move faster. She finally managed to fumble out something resembling the correct change, delivering it with the same glazed-eyed, slack-jawed look she'd worn the entire time I'd been in there.

Did I ever look like that? I wondered briefly. Probably so, I thought with mild amusement as I shoved my change into my pocket and hurried out. There'd been plenty of times I'd gone to work high as a kite.

My navel-gazing had me distracted enough that I nearly barreled right into someone about to come into the store.

"Oh, shit, sorry!" I exclaimed.

"Angel?"

As the door swung closed behind me I blinked and focused on who I'd run into. Hispanic, not much taller than me, and a little bit stocky. I didn't recognize him at first, until I realized he was wearing a uniform. Khaki pants, black boots, navy shirt with an insignia shaped like the state of Louisiana with "Agent" and "Probation and Parole"...

Shit. This was my probation officer.

Almost two years ago, while I was deep in my "Angel is a moron with zero judgment" phase—a phase which had lasted for most of my life—I'd made the mistake of trusting my then-boyfriend and had believed that there was nothing shady about a nearly-new Prius that he could get for me for only five hundred dollars. A couple of weeks later I was pulled over and promptly arrested for possession of stolen property, and spent a terrifying three days in jail before making bail. Eventually I was sentenced to three years probation.

I managed an unsteady smile as I clutched the chips and Coke to my chest like a shield. "Um, yeah. Hi, Mr. Garza. How's it going?"

"I'm doing fine," he said. His gaze raked over me, pausing on the insignia on my own shirt. "Still with the Coroner's Office, I see."

For a second I couldn't figure out how the hell he would have known I was working there. I was a low risk offender which meant that I only had to meet with him in person every six months. *Yeah, but I have to turn in those stupid forms*, I reminded myself. Every month, along with a check for sixty-five dollars, I had to give all sorts of details about my living conditions, work situation, and any possible incidents that might affect my probation.

"Yeah. Still with the C.O," I replied. "Two months now."

"That's some sort of record for you, isn't it," he said, mouth curving in a humorless line.

I fought the urge to hunch my shoulders or shuffle my feet uncertainly. "I'm doing a lot better now," I said, possibly a little defensively.

"I see that," he said. "I'm real glad to see it." He didn't look very glad, but then again, I wasn't sure I'd ever seen him smile.

I cast a longing glance at my van. I needed to get going, but I couldn't exactly blow my probation officer off. "Yeah, thanks. I, um—"

"How's the studying going?" he asked, cutting me off.

My response was to blink stupidly. "Hunh?"

"The GED," he said. "It's one of the conditions of your probation, remember?"

"Oh, right!" I said, plastering a smile onto my face. "Sure, it's going just great. I, um, I'll be taking it in just a coupla months. No problem." I kept the smile frozen on my face while inside I cringed. *God damn fucking shithole crapstains!* I'd completely forgotten about that little detail. Since I was also a high school dropout, one of the conditions of my probation had been that I had to get my GED—the General Educational Development test which could serve as a substitute for a high school diploma.

He probably could tell I was handing him a line of complete bullshit. "Do you have a few minutes?" he asked. "There are a couple of things I'd like to discuss with you."

"I can't," I practically gasped. "Sorry. I'm on call, and I just got texted to go pick up a body." I fumbled my phone off my hip and waved it for emphasis.

He pursed his lips, but nodded. "Sure thing. But don't forget, we do have a scheduled meeting next week." He pulled out his phone and scrolled through a couple of screens. "Wednesday. Nine a.m.."

"I'll be there," I assured him, smiling in what I hoped was a confident manner though I had a feeling I looked more manic.

"Good. Please don't forget," he said. "There are some important matters we need to discuss."

"I won't forget," I promised. "I gotta go now!" I ducked around him before he could say anything else and practically sprinted for the van. I had a feeling he was watching me as I drove off, but I was too chicken to look back and see.

Great. My probation officer had "important matters"

to discuss with me. There was no way in hell that could be a good thing.

And the GED . . . ? I groaned as I followed the directions from the navigation system. Sure, I'd dutifully listened to the judge's conditions when they'd been handed down. But, at the time, three years had seemed like such an insanely long time that I didn't feel any sort of rush to get started on it.

And, more importantly, there'd been a little part of me that felt it didn't matter. In three years I'd be dead, or arrested again, or something equally self-destructive. I certainly hadn't been thinking of any sort of future.

But, I realized with a sense of mild shock, it had been close to a year and a half since that arrest. And now I had to learn all the shit from high school that I never bothered to learn back then.

I am so screwed.

It was probably a good thing that the trip to NuQuesCor was somewhat convoluted, forcing me to pay close attention to the GPS, and helping take my mind off my educational shortcomings.

The lab turned out to be not *quite* in the middle of nowhere, but certainly far from anything anyone gave a crap about. It was full dark by the time I pulled up in front of the building, and the only way I could be sure I was in the right place was because of the small cluster of emergency vehicles near the front entrance. A black Dodge Durango was parked next to an unmarked police car, and I saw Derrel leaning against the front grill. As I climbed out of the van he gave me a casual lift of the chin in greeting, then pushed off the Durango and started my way.

"Sorry it took me so long," I said as I yanked the stretcher out of the back of the van.

"Not a problem," he replied. "Crime scene is still taking some pics. Figured I'd meet you out here since getting to where the body's at is a bit complicated. You ever been here before?"

I swept my gaze over the ugly white exterior, only now seeing an unlit sign that identified the place as Nu-QuesCor. Otherwise it resembled little more than a large white brick. A few narrow windows here and there marred the surface, looking out of place and rather pathetic.

"I didn't even know this place existed before today," I admitted.

Derrel's eyes crinkled. "They're one of the top tech employers in this part of Louisiana."

I snorted. "Derrel, up until a few months ago my grandest career aspiration was to get off the night shift at the XpressMart."

He chuckled under his breath. "Well, it's also quite possible that NuQuesCor is the *only* tech employer of any note in this part of Louisiana."

"Again," I said, "minimum wage girl here."

"Not anymore," he said.

"Not anymore," I agreed, somewhat surprised at how certain I was of that fact.

"Good deal," he said. "All right, let's get to it. Oh, and you'll need your badge and ID."

"My badge . . . ?" Grimacing, I returned to the front of

the van and spent a slightly frantic few seconds digging through my belongings. To my relief the badge in question was still at the bottom of my purse where I'd tossed it after it had first been issued to me, along with my Coroner's Office ID card. I retrieved both, then went ahead and grabbed some extra gloves and stuffed them into the side pocket of my cargo pants.

Derrel had his badge clipped to the front of his belt, and I quickly copied him. He gave me an approving smile, then together we headed up the sidewalk to the entrance with the stretcher and the empty body bag in tow.

The inside of the building was a lot more impressive. The double glass doors opened up into a large two-story lobby that looked more like the entrance to a hotel than a lab. Panels of burnished metal covered the walls and the floor was a grey marble with dark black flecks. Off to the left was a shuttered coffee stand along with an assortment of tables and chairs. Beyond that were couches and coffee tables, with an odd sculpture of what I thought might be birds in flight looming over the seating area. A balcony/walkway type thing overlooked the lobby, with a set of curving stairs and an elevator off to the right. And in the center of the lobby was a circular desk, but instead of a concierge it was manned by a security guard who gave us both a tight-faced glower as we approached.

I was asked to produce both badge and ID, which were subsequently scrutinized as carefully as a bouncer would in a college town. For that matter the guard looked like he could totally be a bouncer—tall and thick. Thick neck, thick shoulders, thick arms. Even his nose was thick.

Fortunately my ID looked sufficiently authentic, and I was allowed to continue on to a doorway on the far side of the lobby, this one manned by another dour guard who required us to sign in on a clipboard. I hid a smile at the sight of Deputy Marcus Ivanov's neat signature further up the page. He was busy tonight as well.

We finally passed through the door and entered a stark white hallway with lots of closed doors. No marble back here, just regular industrial white tile that made my shoes squeak. I felt a low hum of machinery and heard the occasional distant beep. The doors all had numbers on them, but no signs or labels to indicate what went on behind them. I also noted that all but a few had specialized locks that required a fob or keycard.

"What's the deal with all the security?" I murmured to Derrel. "Is this a government building or something?"

"Not anymore," he replied, keeping his voice low as well. "Used to be a NASA computer center a couple of decades back, but NuQuesCor took over the building about five years ago. They're private, but they work on some government contracts. From what I gather they mostly do nutrition science, sports supplements, vitamins, and the like. But even though they aren't NASA anymore, they still likely have a fair amount of proprietary information that they want to protect. Hence the security."

"In other words, they're afraid of industrial espionage, that sort of thing?"

"Exactly."

I gave him a doubtful look. "What could an industrial spy want in a nutrition science lab?"

"Well, suppose they come up with low-fat low-sugar

food that doesn't taste like complete ass," he said. "They don't want someone else coming in and stealing it before they can patent it, right?"

"Ahhh, gotcha. It all comes down to money."

He snorted softly. "It always does."

We came out abruptly into another two-story area that appeared to be a lunchroom. By my guess it was in the exact middle of the building to judge by the hallway entrances on all four sides. There was no "hotel lobby" look to this, either. This was more of the plain white décor. Walls, ceiling, even the staircases to my right and left were white. The only deviations from the color scheme were the tables and chairs, all made from what looked like aircraft aluminum.

Yellow crime scene tape had been strung across each of the hallways, and I saw a number of onlookers peering toward the stairs to my left. There, crumpled at the foot of those stairs, was the body.

I figured he was in his late fifties or maybe early sixties. Short grey hair, somewhat aged and lined face. He was dressed in a dark blue uniform that looked to be the same as the one the other security guards wore, though I saw that he was missing a shoe. A trickle of blood tracked from his ear, which I'd come to learn meant a bad head injury. But that was easy enough for me to figure out, since there was another pool of blood beneath his head. From what little I could tell, it looked like this guy had tumbled down the stairs, landing at the bottom with enough force to crack his skull open.

Hi there, darlin'. My name is Angel, I thought. *I'll probably eat your brain sometime soon. I hope you don't mind.*

I held back the snicker and managed to maintain a properly serious expression. I wasn't the smartest chick in the world, but even I knew that laughing at a death scene was pretty uncool.

In the couple of months I'd been working for the St. Edwards Parish Coroners Office I'd probably been on more than a hundred death scenes. Some were tragic and heart wrenching—which was anything that involved kids; a few were truly bizarre—such as the guy who choked to death on a sex toy; but the large majority were simply in the category of "ho hum, another person died and I get to go pick them up."

It wasn't that I was jaded. At least that's what I kept telling myself. But my views of death had certainly come a long way from the screwed up chick I used to be. I mean, I was definitely still a chick, but I wasn't screwed up. Well, not *as* screwed up. Or rather, I was screwed up in different ways.

This death scene looked like it was going to be one of the ordinary ones. No kids, no sex toys, no batshit craziness that I could see so far.

A gangly red-haired man wearing a jacket with *SEPSO Crime Scene* stenciled across the back flashed us a smile. "Almost ready for y'all," he said, lifting the camera in his hands.

"No rush, Sean," Derrel replied before turning to me. "I'm going to go talk to the head of security and see if I can get this guy's personnel info."

"Go wild," I said. Derrel gave me a wink and a smile before abandoning me and heading toward an unsmiling man with a walkie-talkie in his hand, who totally looked like a head of security. Hell, he practically looked like a

Secret Service agent. He wore a black suit and white shirt, with a tightly knotted grey tie that had some sort of boring and forgettable pattern. Dark brown hair was buzzed short enough for the military, and good grief, if his jaw had been any more square it could have been used as a brick. All he was missing was the little ear thingy with the squiggly wire that I always saw Secret Service agents wearing in the movies. He was deep in conversation with a slim auburn-haired woman several inches shorter than he was. If he was dressed like Secret Service, she was dressed like an uptight congresswoman—maroon suit with a fitted skirt, cream blouse, and matching cream pumps that were well within the "I am a woman to be taken seriously!" height range.

The woman walked away before Derrel reached them. I watched as Derrel spoke to the security guy, then they both headed off down yet another hallway, I assumed to get the dead guy's personnel file.

Which meant I was definitely at loose ends until he got back. I made myself comfortable against the wall and took in the general bustle of activity. Detectives Abadie and Roth had their heads close together and seemed to be involved in a serious discussion, though, knowing them, it had more to do with acquisition of Saints tickets than anything to do with the body. A knot of six or seven people stood in the hallway on the other side of the room, held back by the thin, yellow authority of the crime scene tape strung across the entryway. I assumed they were employees who had stayed late. Several of them wore white lab coats, and they all had ID badges clipped somewhere visible. Most of them looked upset or simply curious, but a few looked annoyed and impatient. The woman who'd been speaking to the security guy was talking on her cell phone, and she looked downright pissed. Maybe all of this was disrupting some sort of super important project? That sort of attitude didn't really surprise me anymore. I'd lost count of the number of times I'd been out on a highway to pick up a victim from a traffic fatality and witnessed some irate driver bitching about the fact that the road was closed off while we did our work. Some people were insensitive shits, and that's all there was to it.

Then again, maybe she's fighting with a husband or boyfriend, I told myself. *Or maybe her purse was stolen, and she's calling to cancel her credit cards.* Sometimes people weren't actually insensitive shits and were simply having a bad day. See, this was me trying to be open-minded and understanding.

I looked around for Marcus and saw him near the hallway, across from where Derrel and I had entered, in conversation with a tall and slender blond woman wearing a lab coat. I felt a frown tug at my face as I watched them. This was definitely more than him talking to a possible witness, not with how close they stood or the way she occasionally touched his arm. She looked deeply upset, though, and kept glancing toward the body.

I didn't have much time to wonder about it before Derrel returned from his info-gathering expedition with the security chief guy. As if on cue, the crime scene tech stepped back from the body and gave a slight wave to let Derrel and me know he was ready for us to get on with our part of this whole thing. No one else was allowed to touch the body except for coroner's office people, yet we had to wait until the crime scene folks finished doing all the stuff they did, which meant there was usually a little dance of cooperation when it came to working death scenes.

Derrel and I stepped forward now and carefully rolled the man over so that Sean could snap pictures of the other side of the body as well as the floor beneath him. The dead man's grey uniform shirt had been unbuttoned in the front and sticky pads dotted his torso, left over from the EMTs—the only exception to who was allowed to touch the body, since technically it wasn't a "body" until it was declared dead after the EMTs ran an EKG strip. They'd already come and gone, which was often the case on death scenes. Even unbuttoned the shirt looked overly large on him, and the pants were bunched up beneath his belt. He must have lost a lot of weight recently. Maybe he'd been sick? Not that it mattered now.

"Definitely some serious skull fractures," Derrel said as he ran his gloved fingers over the man's head. Pieces moved underneath the scalp in unnatural ways as he carefully probed the injuries. He glanced up at the stairs, a slight frown tugging at his mouth. "He must have tripped? Somehow he came flying down and smacked his head hard. I'm not seeing any blood anywhere else on the stairs." He glanced up at the tech for confirmation.

"I didn't either," Sean said, "but I took lots of pictures anyway. One of the lab employees who was working late here walked through the room just as the guy hit the bottom. He called nine one one immediately, but . . ." He shrugged.

"But this guy was probably dead within seconds," Derrel murmured.

Sean took one last shot of the man's head and then stepped back. "And that's the last of it for me. Thanks, y'all."

Derrel gave me the nod, and I went ahead and spread the body bag out on the concrete. The man looked like he probably weighed around one-seventy or so—more than easy enough for me to handle when I was "well fed," but it had been about a day and a half since I last had brains, and my strength was about what one would expect from someone my size. In other words, total weakling.

Fortunately, Derrel was willing to help without me having to ask. He grabbed the dude under the shoulders, I grabbed him under his knees, and together we got him into the bag with a minimum of fuss. A smear of blood lingered on the tile, and I saw that it had seeped into the grout, making a stain. That'd be a bitch to get out.

Derrel tilted his clipboard toward me so that I could jot the dead guy's info onto the toe tag—Norman Kearny, age sixty-three—and then I snapped the rubber band around the big toe of the foot that was already shoeless. I did a quick search of his body for valuables, finding only a watch; no wallet or jewelry. After removing the watch and dropping it into a property bag, I retrieved the wayward shoe from under the stairs and stuck that in the body bag as well. It was probably stupid, but I had a feeling that if the shoes were separated they'd never get paired up again, and they'd be doomed to wander the world alone forever.

I started to zip the bag closed and paused. I was fairly brain-hungry right now. I wasn't ravenous or anything, and I hadn't reached the point where I was starting to smell or skin was peeling off, but my nose for brains always got better the hungrier I was. And with this guy having a fractured skull, I should've been able to smell his brains quite clearly. Hell, my stomach should have been yelling at me to pry the broken pieces of skull apart to fish a handful out and cram it into my mouth right this instant.

But as far as my nose was concerned, there was nothing of interest within the man's head. *Which is probably a good thing,* I decided, *since treating the guy's head like a popcorn bowl probably wouldn't go over well.*

Hiding a smile at the thought, I finished zipping the bag closed, then got it onto the stretcher and belted into place. I felt someone come up beside me, but I didn't need to turn to see who it was.

"You hungry?" Deputy Ivanov murmured.

"Fucking starving," I replied just as quietly. "It's been slow at the morgue, so I'm trying to go longer between meals." My lips twitched. "And somehow last night I burned off a whole lot of brains." I gave him a sly, knowing look, but frowned as sudden worry struck me. "Why? Do I smell?"

He started to shake his head, then shrugged. "Nothing anyone would notice. I ate this morning, so my senses are probably being overachievers."

I gave him a light elbow in the ribs. "You don't have to lie. A good zombie boyfriend tells his zombie girlfriend if she's starting to rot. Just like you'd better tell me if I have spinach in my teeth."

He grinned. "Or if your skin starts peeling off?"

"Exactly! That'd be as bad as having my skirt caught up in my underwear!"

He leaned close. "I made a new batch of pudding this morning."

I gave him a sidelong look. The pudding in question was nicknamed "foreplay"—and was heavily spiked with pureed brains. "Are you hoping I'm hungry or horny?"

"I know you're both," he said with a wink.

"So, who was the blond chick you were hugging?" I asked. I think I even managed to do so without sounding jealous. Well, not too jealous.

Amusement lit his eyes. "That was Dr. Sofia Baldwin. I've known her since high school."

"Uh huh," I said, giving him a mild stink eye. "And did you ever date her?"

He grinned. "Yes, and before you get too green-eyed, she dumped me."

I gave a sniff. "Well, either she's an idiot, or I have yet to discover your horrifying flaws."

He lifted an eyebrow. "Or both."

"Hmmf. We'll just have to see. Now get out of my way, I have a corpse."

He stepped aside. "I'll call later."

"Yeah, well, we'll just see if I answer."

His low chuckle followed me as I pushed the stretcher down the hallway.

The security guard pulled the lobby door open for me and gave me a slight dip of his chin in greeting as I passed him. I gave him an appropriately sober nod in return. The scent of his brains swirled briefly around me, accompanied by a jab of hunger that reminded me I needed to eat soon unless I wanted to start falling apart.

I continued on outside, shoved the stretcher into the

back of the van, and then climbed into the driver's seat. Screw this whole rationing crap. Especially if there was any chance I was starting to smell. *That* was one thing I was super paranoid about. The bottle of brain-chocolate smoothie in my lunchbox was only partially thawed, but I went ahead and downed what I could. By the third gulp the hunger faded away to be replaced by a lovely feeling of warm energy.

It wasn't until after I'd put the half-full bottle back into my lunch box and started the van that it occurred to me:

If I'd been able to smell the live guard's brains, why hadn't I been able to smell the dead one's?

Chapter 4

The question continued to tumble through my head as I headed to the morgue. My cell phone rang, interrupting my train of thought, but I didn't even need to look at the caller ID to know who it was.

"I almost didn't answer," I said with a smile.

I heard Marcus laugh. "You know you can't resist my charms."

"Don't flatter yourself, cop-boy," I warned.

"Okay, how about if I remind you to be careful."

I sobered. "I'm being careful. I promise. And you as well." *Be Careful* had become his mantra in the past couple of weeks. Both of us were hyper-aware that the threat of Ed still hung over us.

"I am," he said. "But that's not the only reason I'm calling. I didn't get a chance to talk to you at the scene, but my uncle's having a get-together tomorrow, a casual

cookout sort of thing, and I was wondering if you'd like
to come with me."

"Your uncle the zombie?" Marcus's uncle, Pietro Ivanov, had been the one who'd turned him after Marcus
contracted rabies from a raccoon. The rabies had absolutely nothing to do with the zombieism, except for the
fact that, apparently, rabies was almost always fatal once
symptoms began to appear. Marcus hadn't even considered that he could be at risk and hadn't bothered to seek
treatment for the rather minor bite until it was too late.
Conveniently, Pietro also owned several funeral homes,
allowing him to keep them both well supplied with
brains.

"That's the one," he said.

"Um, sure thing," I said.

"You don't sound very excited."

Okay, so I was pretty transparent. Either that or he
already knew me damn well. Or both.

I took a deep breath. "Well, you're asking me to meet
a member of your family. And that's kinda nervous-
making, y'know?" Something else occurred to me. "And
on that note, who else will be there besides your zombie
uncle?"

"Just a couple of people. A family friend or three.
Don't worry about them. This is mostly for you to finally
meet Pietro."

"Uh huh. Yeah, nothing at all to be nervous about.
We've only been dating a couple of weeks. Shouldn't this
wait until the three-month mark or something?"

He chuckled. "Stop it. He'll love you."

"That's not really the point," I replied. Okay, it *was*
kinda the point, at least to me. I really doubted that I was

the kind of girl parents always dreamed their son would bring home.

I heard him sigh. "Look," he said, "I know it seems like things are moving really quickly, but I think it's important that you meet my uncle, especially with all this stuff about Ed going on. I promise, he's not going to eat you."

I made a face at the phone. He didn't get why I could possibly be utterly terrified of meeting his family, even it *was* only his uncle. But at this point I knew I wouldn't be able to make him understand.

"Okay. Fine."

"Great! Call me when you get off work tomorrow. We'll drive over together."

"Can't wait."

"Liar," he said, then hung up.

I continued on to the morgue. The Coroner's Office building was damn near the exact opposite of NuQues-Cor. Two stories, wood and brick exterior, lots of windows, and attractive yet subtle landscaping. This facility was fairly new, and one of the main goals had been that the design not be stark and scary but as warm and comfortable as possible. Made perfect sense to me. Hell, if nice carpet and neatly trimmed shrubbery helped people deal with the loss of a loved one, I was all for it.

The morgue portion of the building was on the far back end and wasn't quite as warm and welcoming. The general public never saw this entrance, where the bodies went in for autopsy and came out on their way to the funeral home. Just one more step in the machine of death. Even when it was necessary for next of kin to identify a loved one, the death investigators preferred to use pictures instead of having them actually see the body. Much less traumatic for everyone involved.

The back parking lot was empty except for my piece of crap little Honda parked on the far side of the small lot. I glanced at my watch. Nine p.m. Marcus's warning remained foremost in my mind. I made sure to do a careful scan of my surroundings before I parked the van as close to the building as I could. My nerves hovered on a knife's edge as I pulled the stretcher out and swiped my ID card at the door, and I didn't relax until I got myself and both bodies safely inside with the door closed behind me.

The scent of the morgue surrounded me like an old friend. An old, dead friend who'd been steeped in formalin and cleaning products. I wasted no time getting the bodies into the cooler and properly logged in, as well as the property from the security guard recorded and deposited into the small safe. Then I breathed a sigh of relief, returned to the outer office, and plopped myself down at the computer. Yeah, some people might think it was weird that I enjoyed the peace and quiet of the morgue, but I was probably the last person to be freaked out at the thought of sharing a room with dead people. Besides, I didn't have a computer at home, and this was a helluva lot easier than trying to use a computer at the library. Most of theirs were ancient and slow, plus I hated having to wait my turn and then having my time limited.

I could use the morgue computer 24/7, and all I had to do was put up with the way the place smelled.

I diddled around for a little while looking at funny pictures and reading some local news online, then got down to the business at hand: figuring out what I had to do to take, and pass, the GED. After about half an hour I had the information I needed as far as how to schedule a test, but I also had a fairly solid idea of what sort of stuff was on it—and how much of it I didn't know. *But unless I want to spend the rest of my life on probation, I don't have much choice, do I?*

With reckless disregard of Coroner's Office resources, I printed off stacks of practice tests and study guides, gathered it all up and then headed for the door. I knew how I'd be spending the rest of my free time.

I yanked the door open, then let out a choked cry as a masked someone dressed all in black shoved me hard in the chest. I staggered and landed in a sprawl on my back as papers went everywhere. I began to scrabble back to my feet, then froze at the sight of the gun pointed at me.

"Get up," the man holding the gun ordered.

At first I thought that my attacker was Ed. It was the fact that he didn't instantly shoot me that gave me the first clue that it wasn't. I was pretty sure Ed wouldn't be giving me any more chances to get the drop on him. But then the oddness of seeing someone in a ski mask in south Louisiana threw me so badly that I damn near forgot there was a gun pointed at me and instead I mentally flailed for some logical reason he could be wearing a ski mask. Okay, so it was a little chilly, but a ski mask was a bit of overkill, wasn't it? Or maybe it was one of those baklava thingies. *No, not baklava—that's some sort of Greek pastry. Shit. Focus, Angel!*

My pulse thudded as I scrambled to my feet. About three feet separated us. Could I take him? I was somewhat well fed on brains, but not tanked all the way up and certainly not overloaded to the point where I had super zombie speed. He looked pretty well built—taller than me by a good bit and broad-shouldered. On the other hand I knew what it was like to get shot. While I was trying to stop Ed from killing Marcus and chopping off his head, Ed had shot me twice in the chest—an experience I really had no desire to repeat, 'cause, yeah, it hurt.

But if this wasn't Ed, who was it and what the fuck was going on?

"The body," he said, with a jerk of the gun toward the hallway. "Open the cooler and give it to me. Or I kill you," he added, tone so even that I had zero doubt that he would.

A thousand scenarios flashed through my head of me fighting him off, but I discarded them as quickly as they crowded into my skull. I wasn't fast enough right now to get to him before he could shoot me, or strong enough to fight him off even if I could. And while I didn't really fear getting shot—or rather, I didn't fear *dying* from being shot—it would slow me down enough that I might not be able to stop him from taking the body he was after, in which case I'd have been shot for nothing. Besides, I knew there were security cameras covering the parking lot and the door to the morgue. I didn't *have* to get shot. The evidence of this guy forcing his way in would be on that tape. Or hard drive. Or whatever it was that security cameras used now. And if I *did* get shot, I'd have to go out to the van to get one of my brain slushies out of my cooler. That would be recorded. Plus, I'd have to clean up the blood before anyone saw it to avoid having to explain how I could be shot and yet not have any gunshot wounds. Oh, and I didn't have a change of clothes . . .

Much easier to simply avoid the whole "getting shot" thing.

Taking a deep breath, I turned and walked down the hallway to the cooler, my shoulder blades prickling the entire way. After punching in my code on the touchpad, I pulled the door open and stepped back.

He didn't take the bait. "Bring the body out," he said in a low pleasant voice, as if he was offering to carry my groceries for me.

I couldn't help but scowl. If he was going to steal my body, why did I have to do all the work?

"Which body?" I asked. "I picked up two tonight."

"Kearny."

Stepping into the cooler, I was briefly tempted to give him the wrong body, but then figured that he'd surely check. This guy was cool as ice and wouldn't be fooled that easily. Besides, the body of the guy we scraped up out at the factory was already pretty damn smelly, and he'd be able to tell even without opening the bag.

I gave the appropriate body bag a yank and hauled it out onto one of the gurneys, then pushed it out and into the hallway. "What now? Do you want me to bring it to your car for you?" I couldn't quite keep the obnoxious out of my voice.

He surprised me by chuckling. "Now that would be rude of me," he said. "To the door will be sufficient."

Scowling, I went ahead and pushed the gurney and its cargo to the door.

"That's good enough," he said. "Now if you'd please turn around and face the wall."

My pulse jumped as I met his eyes. There was nothing there—no emotion or stress. If he wanted me to face the wall so that he could shoot me in the back of the head, then there was a good chance I could actually die from that, especially since there was no one around to give me enough brains to help me survive that sort of thing. No, my body would be found by Nick or whoever was coming on in the morning, and they'd assume I was dead-for-real. I'd probably be autopsied and all that shit. And, godalmighty, would I be aware of that? Or would I wake up, starving and willing to attack anyone nearby, such as Nick or, worse, Dr. Leblanc?

All of this flashed through my mind in less than a second. I shook my head, a stiff little motion. "I'd rather not," I managed.

He let out a dry chuckle. "I'm not going to kill you. But I do need to slow you down." With his free hand he pulled a pair of zip ties out of a back pocket.

Nope, still didn't trust him. I had to at least try to take him out—

"Don't try it," he said, voice low and thick with warning as he lifted the gun and sighted it on my forehead. "Shooting you would be messy and more complicated than this needs to be. But if you force my hand, I'll do what I have to do."

Gulping, I nodded, then turned around. *He's not letting me see his face*, I told myself. He wouldn't do that if he'd planned on killing me. Still, I breathed in shallow pants as he pulled my arms behind me and cinched my wrists together with the zip ties.

"Down on the floor," he ordered. I numbly complied,

and a few seconds later he'd secured my ankles the same way.

With that taken care of, he ceased to pay any attention to me. With a fluid motion he picked up the body bag and slung it over his shoulder, then was out the door. I craned my head around and caught sight of a dark-colored car, but the door swung closed before I could make out any details.

Taking a deep breath I yanked hard at the zip ties holding my wrists, hissing at the flare of pain that lanced down my arms as the plastic snapped. I might not have been juiced up enough on brains for super speed, but I had no problem burning some up to get out of the zip ties. The ankle ties were no trouble either, though I saw that the plastic had cut my wrists. A thin trickle of blood made its sluggish way down my hand. For an instant I thought about hurrying out to the van to slug down enough brains to heal that crap up, then abruptly thought better of it.

No, if I had no marks, then no one would believe that I'd been tied up.

With bloody wrists and a pissy attitude, I grabbed the phone on the desk and dialed 911.

Chapter 5

"What do you mean, there's no surveillance video?" I demanded.

The chief investigator, Allen Prejean, gave me a sour look. "We've been having technical problems with the system," he said in a tone that made it sound as if it was my fault. It didn't take a lot of smarts to figure out that he didn't much like me. Allen was in his mid-thirties with a significant beer belly, a smoker who sneered at exercise and defiantly proclaimed his love of fried foods. Yeah, sure, I'd been well on my way to killing myself with painkillers and alcohol, but he wasn't much better off, in my opinion.

I scowled and sat back in the seat, crossing my arms defiantly over my chest. My wrists had been bandaged but they didn't hurt. They were mostly just numb—one nice benefit of being a zombie. On the other hand, the hunger was once again poking at me.

We were in the conference room of the coroner's office, along with two deputies, Detectives Ben Roth and Mike Abadie, Captain Pierson, who was the head of the Sheriff's Office Investigations Division, my partner, Derrel, and the Coroner himself, Dr. Duplessis.

Apparently the theft of a corpse by a masked gunman in an unmarked car was a big deal. Or maybe it was the fact that no one seemed to believe me.

Dr. Duplessis tugged at his bow tie as a frown touched the edges of his mouth. The bow tie was his "signature look" which, I was told, he always adopted when it came time to start campaigning. I thought it made him look sort of goofy, but for all I knew this was part of some grand strategy to make him seem approachable and interesting. Then again, now that I thought about it, that made sense. Without the bow tie, the coroner looked like pretty much every other politician—clean cut, charming smile, dark hair with a touch of grey at the temples. In other words, boring.

He gently cleared his throat. "Angel, I'm sure that whatever happened was very traumatizing. The fact that there's no corroborating video is certainly troubling, but that simply makes it even more vital that you be as honest with us as possible about the incident. Are you absolutely certain you didn't stop anywhere on the way back to the morgue? Perhaps you left the door unlocked?" His mouth curved into a serious frown. "If you lost the body somewhere along the way, we need to know now so that we can take the appropriate steps to recover it."

"I am being honest!" I said, fighting back the horrid lump in my throat. Taking a deep breath, I set my hands on the table. "Look, I swear, I made it back here with both bodies safe and sound. I brought them in and put them both in the cooler. I did some work on the computer, and when I tried to leave, a guy with a gun and wearing a ski mask forced his way in and told me to give him the body or he'd shoot me. I asked him which one. He asked for the security guard by name—Kearny—and I got that body bag out for him. He tied me up with zip ties and then left with the body bag in a dark-colored car. I shimmied to the desk and managed to cut through them, then called nine one one." I gave the coroner a pleading look. "Why can't you just believe me?"

His lips pressed together, and I didn't need him to answer me. I knew why he couldn't trust me. I was a felon and former drug addict. High school dropout. My word wasn't exactly dipped in gold. And even I could see how a story about a very polite masked gunman—and, really, what the hell was up with that?—could be somewhat beyond belief.

I swallowed hard, then fixed Allen with a hard look. "How long has the surveillance been messed up?"

A muscle in his jaw twitched. "A couple of days, to judge by the recorded data."

"And how many people know about this?"

He flicked a glance around the room. "Probably no one. I do only because we tried to access the recording from tonight and couldn't."

A tiny bit of tension left my body. "Then why the hell would I make up a story like this if I knew that the surveillance video would prove me wrong?"

The sour expression on Allen's face deepened, but I could see I'd scored a point. And to judge by the nods of others in the room, I wasn't the only one. The mood in the room seemed to shift, to my intense relief.

Ben cleared his throat. "Angel's not stupid. And right now we have no other information. I say we go on her statement unless and until we get any reason to think otherwise."

I shot him a look loaded with gratitude. A hint of a reassuring smile twitched the corner of his mouth, just for an instant.

Dr. Duplessis sighed and sat in the chair at the head of the table. "This whole situation is distressing. After consideration, I'm inclined to believe that Angel was the victim of a prank—some sort of frat boy hijinks—since I find it hard to believe that there could be any nefarious purpose to stealing the body of an elderly security guard." He shook his head while I gritted my teeth. Frat boy hijinks? There wasn't a university within fifty miles of Tucker Point.

"Right now, I'm grateful that no one was hurt," he continued, giving me what was probably meant to be a warm and caring smile. And perhaps it really was, but I was too wound up at the moment to believe it.

Captain Pierson gave me a measured look. "How about if Detective Roth and I speak to Miss Crawford on our own for a few moments." He glanced to the coroner. "To get a coherent statement without so many onlookers, you understand."

Dr. Duplessis seemed only too pleased to be given an excuse to leave. "Yes, of course. Let's all clear out and let the police do their job."

Within a minute the room had emptied—with Derrel giving my shoulder a comforting squeeze and a worried look on the way out—leaving only the three of us. I trusted Ben, but the captain scared the crap out of me, and not only because I had no doubt that he knew my criminal history. He had ice-blue eyes that seemed to take in everything, and I had a feeling he wasn't the type who could be misled easily, if at all.

He took a seat across from me and laced his fingers together on the table. "Miss Crawford, I want you to tell your story again, please. With your permission, I'd like to record your statement."

"Yeah. Okay."

Ben pulled out a small digital recorder and set it on the table. "S-E-P-S-O case number twelve dash four nine six three one," Ben rattled the words out. "Detective Ben Roth and Captain Jeffrey Pierson interviewing Angel Crawford." He gave me another slight smile, then sat back.

"Miss Crawford," Pierson said, "please tell us in your own words what happened tonight."

I did. Again. Detailed the whole goddamn thing, the whole three minutes of it—or however long it lasted. And then Pierson asked me to go through it again, but this time he kept stopping me and asking me to clarify points, or he'd repeat parts back to me to make sure he had it right. Sometimes I had to correct him. By the fourth or fifth time I went through it, I was absolutely certain that I'd changed my story or was starting to imagine parts of it. And I was hungry. Oh fucking lord, was I ever hungry. Why the hell hadn't I chugged some brains before calling 911? Why on earth had it mattered that I not heal up the cuts? It sure hadn't helped them believe my story. I kept my hands clasped in my lap since I was terrified that my fingernails would start falling off, just from the stress.

"Look," I finally said, "I think it's important that this whole thing seemed . . . professional."

Pierson lifted an eyebrow at me. "Professional body-snatchers?"

I fought back the urge to scowl at him. "No. I mean, the guy wasn't nervous at all. He was calm and cool, and the whole thing seemed almost rehearsed. I mean, with how smoothly he pulled it off." I shrugged. "He was waiting for me, and if the fucking cameras had been working you could have seen that. I came straight from the death scene, so somehow he knew I was heading here with the body. He didn't have long to prepare, and it was fucking flawless."

Ben tapped his chin. "Tell us again what he said."

God. This would be like the fourth or fifth time. "He said, 'The body. Open the cooler and give it to me or I'll kill you.' But he said it super calm-like. I mean, like he was asking about the weather."

"Did he have any sort of accent?" Pierson asked.

I thought for a second. "No. No accent at all."

Ben let out a soft snort. "Well, that in itself tells us a lot in these parts."

"Right," I said, straightening. "He didn't sound like he was from around here."

Ben jotted some notes onto the pad in front of him. "You said he wore a mask, but is there anything else you can tell us about him? How tall was he? Eye color? Build?"

I rubbed at my eyes. "Um, his eyes were dark. I mean, not blue. I guess brown or dark hazel? And he was taller than me, but that doesn't take a whole lot. Well built. I mean, like definitely in shape. Not pudgy."

Ben scraped his chair back and stood and motioned to me to do the same. I complied, and he stuck his finger out in a fake gun. "About my height? Or taller?"

"Taller, definitely."

Ben looked over to the Captain, who stood without asking. He was at least a head taller than Ben. "His height?"

I felt self-conscious as all hell, but I went ahead and stood in front of him. I didn't ask him to pretend to hold a gun on me though. That would have just been weird as shit.

"Not quite as tall as him," I told Ben, returning to my side of the table. "About somewhere in between."

"All right then," he said with a smile. "It's a start."

I didn't think it was much of a start, but I wasn't about to say anything.

Pierson leaned forward and clicked the recorder off. I looked up at him warily.

"Thank you, Angel," he said, surprising me with the use of my first name. "We appreciate your help."

"Do you believe me?" I asked him bluntly.

He pushed his chair back in. "I do not believe you are attempting to deceive me," he said with a tight smile, then gave Ben a nod before moving to the door. But he stopped with his hand on the doorknob and turned back to me. "One more question, if you don't mind."

"Yeah?"

"You didn't say anything about being afraid that he would shoot you," he said, tilting his head slightly. "Why is that?"

"I, um, was just shocked more than anything." A cold hard knot began to form in my belly. I wasn't stupid—I could see how my apparent lack of fear could possibly be read as my being somehow involved.

"Of course," he said. He gave me an understanding smile, but it didn't reach his eyes. "It's a good thing you were able to keep calm. The last thing any of us want is another body."

I gave a stiff nod. I didn't really trust my voice at the moment.

Pierson opened the door, but before he could exit Marcus slipped in and made a beeline for me. "You okay?" he said, gaze sweeping over me as if to check for himself that I was free of pesky bullet holes. "I just heard about the holdup."

"I'm fine," I said, feeling absurdly self-conscious. I thought for an instant he was going to lean in and kiss me, but he apparently thought better of doing so in front of the others. Instead he simply gave my arm a squeeze. Over his shoulder I could see the Captain eyeing him with a slightly narrowed gaze. But to my relief, Pierson continued on out, with Ben right behind him. "I'm fine," I repeated as the door swung shut. "It's cool."

"Good to know," Marcus said. He gave a sigh of relief, then pulled me into a hug. I allowed myself to relax against him. "You need to eat more," he murmured. "Weird shit is going on, and now's not the time to be at less than full strength." He pulled back and held my shoulders while he looked intently into my face. "I know you're trying to ration your supply, but I can always help you out if you get into a bind."

"I know. I was just about to. And you're right." He'd always been more than willing to share, but I'd decided shortly after we started seeing each other that I would only hit him up for brains if I had no other choice. I didn't want to be dependent on him—or anyone. "Look," I said, "there was something weird about that dead security guard."

"Weird how?"

"Well, he had a fractured skull, and I was pretty hungry, but I couldn't smell his brains."

A frowned tugged at his mouth. "Are you sure? Maybe it wasn't fractured enough for you to be able to tell."

I shook my head. "It was fractured. Trust me. I could see pieces moving around under the scalp. And back at the lab I was hungry enough to smell brains in living people." Hell, I still was. The little bit that I'd chugged in the van had been more than used up during this whole incident.

The troubled expression on his face deepened. "I don't know, Angel. You shouldn't let yourself get so hungry—it affects your thinking and judgment."

I tamped down my growing irritation. "Yeah, I know that, but it wasn't so bad before the holdup. I had some in the van on the way over. I think stress burned a bunch up."

He shoved a hand through his hair. "The only reason I can think that you wouldn't be able to smell the brains is if he was a zombie. But that's not possible. He was definitely dead-for-real. The paramedics ran a strip on him and everything."

"How do you know he wasn't a zombie?" I asked. "I don't think that the EKG strip showing he was dead is enough proof he wasn't. When you were shot I'm pretty sure you didn't have a heartbeat." Or maybe he did, I thought, suddenly unsure. It wasn't as if I stopped and checked. Ed shot Marcus right in the head, and as soon as I scared Ed off I grabbed Marcus up and hightailed it back to my car where I proceeded to stuff him full of brains. Thankfully it worked.

"I'm simply saying that I think it's more likely your sense of smell was off." He gave me a smile that was probably meant to be reassuring, but he was seriously misjudging my mood and the day I'd had.

I pulled back from him, narrowed my eyes. "Seriously? My sense of smell was off? Marcus, are you fucking kidding me? I was just held up at gunpoint. Some mercenary motherfucker stole the body, and now I'm telling you that there was something weird about it. Why the hell won't you believe me?"

"I'm sorry." He grimaced. "You're right. I guess I was really wanting this to be something random—"

"You weren't here when I was describing this guy and what he did," I said, planting my hands on my hips. "Dude, it wasn't just some random asshole grabbing a body for shits and giggles. This guy was some kind of fucking pro. He fucking zip-tied me!" I held up my bandaged wrists for emphasis.

He took a deep breath. "Okay. I'm sorry. Then there must be some explanation." Yet there was still a flicker of uncertainty in his eyes. "I won't say that I know everything about zombies but, the thing is, a fractured skull is pretty minor for one of us. And his body would have started rotting while it worked to fix up the fracture. Does that make sense? He was just . . . a corpse."

Reluctantly, I nodded. "Okay, so maybe not a zombie.

But there was still something wrong with his brain. I *know* that." Maybe the guy had cancer? But, no, I'd seen—and smelled—cancer-ridden brains before.

"I believe you," he said. "I swear. And my uncle is the person to ask why that might be." He smiled and squeezed my shoulders. "So it's a good thing we're going to see him tomorrow, right?"

I heaved a sigh. "Right. I'm really looking forward to it. Can't wait."

He laughed, pulled me into a hug. "You're a shitty liar."

"Don't know why. I've had tons of practice."

Chapter 6

Marcus insisted on walking me out to the parking lot, which was more than fine with me. I retrieved my lunchbox and purse from the van and slugged down the rest of the brain smoothie as I walked to my little Honda Civic. By the time I reached my car the cuts on my wrists had healed up, and my mood in general was much improved.

My dad's truck wasn't in the driveway when I got home. I sat there for a minute without getting out of the car while I looked at the house and considered my options. Dad and I had spent the last two weeks getting the house cleaned up a bit, though there was still a long way to go. The crushed beer cans "paving" the driveway had taken three full days to rake up and get into bags, and I'd borrowed a weed whacker from Marcus and managed to tear through about a quarter of the overgrown weeds in the side yard before running out of the string. It's also possible there'd been plenty of string left and that I quit and ran shrieking when I uncovered a snake that was in the process of eating a mouse.

The first thing I saw was that the bags of crushed cans were gone from the porch. I had zero doubt that Dad had taken them down to the recycling center to see what cash he could get for them. Probably a decent amount, considering how many we'd had. However, I also knew that the recycling center closed at six, and it was almost midnight now.

Dad didn't have a job. And I was pretty sure he wasn't out buying groceries, not at this hour.

I silently measured my exhaustion level, then sighed, backed out, and headed down the highway. I didn't really expect to see his truck at Pillar's Bar, but I was a bit surprised that it wasn't at Kaster's, his usual hangout. *Of course he knows I'll be looking for him.*

I finally spotted the beat up truck at Puzzles Bar. I almost didn't see it, and if I hadn't been looking hard I certainly wouldn't have spied it parked all the way in the back and tucked behind the dumpster. I pulled into the lot, but once again, didn't immediately get out. Should I even go in and confront him? Or, maybe not even confront him, but. . . .

Shit. I squeezed my eyes shut and rested my forehead on the steering wheel. This was going to suck no matter what I did. I could ignore the fact that he was drinking — ignoring it was what I'd pretty much always done, 'cause, godalmighty, it was so much easier and less stressful and less painful.

But that's what I've always done. Hey, Angel, how'd that work out for ya?

Sighing, I turned off the engine and got out of my car.

Either way this was going to suck, but this way I was in control of the suck.

At least that's what I told myself.

The interior was lit primarily with various neon beer signs and the two TVs positioned at either corner of the long bar. It wasn't a big place. It didn't need much more. The bar itself was about twenty feet long, but there was only room for four tables beyond that. This was the sort of place you went by yourself, when all you wanted to do was sit and drink and pretend to watch TV.

Dad saw me pretty much as soon as I saw him. I watched the emotions crawl across his face—shame, anger, defiance, resignation. Hell, it was like the stages of grief.

I plastered a smile onto my face and headed toward him. The smile caught him off guard; it was clear he was expecting me to be pissed or resentful. And I was, but I wasn't about to show it.

"Hey, Dad," I said as I slid onto the stool next to him. "Saw your truck as I was driving by and figured I'd come in and say hi."

He looked confused, but only for an instant. He wasn't stupid by any stretch. "Yeah, right. You saw the cans gone, you knew I had money. How many bars you check before y'found me?"

I shrugged. "Five. Maybe six."

He lifted his beer after a second's hesitation, took a defiant gulp. "So what now. You drag me back home like a fucking kid?"

"I'm not your enemy. And I'm not your jailer. I can't make you come home, and I can't make you stop drinking." I shrugged. "I just want you to know I'm in your life no matter what."

He set the beer down, scowled at me. "Where'd you learn to fight so dirty?"

I grinned, then nodded to the bartender. "Coke, please."

Dad scowled, rolled his eyes, pushed the beer away. "Larry, give me the same."

We sat in silence for a while, drinking our respective non-alcoholic drinks. It wasn't exactly a companionable silence, but it wasn't quite hostile either.

"I dunno what to do, baby," he said after a while. "I didn't wake up this morning and decide to go cash in the cans and then go get a drink." He muttered a curse. "Damn it, I went to cash in the cans, and I was gonna buy a new damn lawnmower, surprise you."

I had to smile. I believed him. "Those fuckers are expensive now."

"More than I expected. I mean they had some cheap ones, but I'm too old and tired to be pushing a lawnmower around, and I was hoping to get a self-propelled one." He scrubbed a hand over his face. "So I left the store and instead of just going home and thinking about it, I decide I'm pissed and I need a drink."

"Yeah," I said. "I know what that's like." I didn't bring up the possibility of rehab. We'd talked about it. He'd even agreed to do it, but we couldn't afford it. That was it, plain and simple. Rehab was expensive, and Dad didn't have health insurance. And don't get me started on the state-run facilities. The only other option was AA. I wasn't a big fan of the preachiness of Alcoholics Anonymous, but at least it was affordable. Not that he'd gone to a meeting yet.

"I'm sorry I'm such a piece of shit, Angelkins," he

mumbled, gazing with hound dog eyes at the bubbles in his Coke.

"What do you want me to say to that, Dad?" I said, showing a bit of my anger for the first time. "That's such a bullshit statement. You want me to feel sorry for you? I feel sorry for you the same way I feel sorry for me. We both got fucked in a lot of ways, but at the same time we fucked ourselves. Or do you just want forgiveness? 'Cause, to be honest, if all you want is forgiveness you gotta know that I sure as shit wouldn't be here right now if you didn't have it."

My dad blinked at me. "I ain't near drunk enough to handle how much you've changed."

"Me neither," I said fervently. "C'mon, I'll take you home. You can call one of your buddies to bring you back for the truck in the morning."

To my relief he didn't protest, though I'd been pre-pared to give him the speech about how he'd been ar-rested not long ago for domestic violence, and he didn't need a drunk driving arrest on top of that. He silently paid his tab and then followed me out to my car, and as soon as he was in, he tipped back the seat and closed his eyes. I was pretty sure he wasn't really asleep, but I didn't mind. In fact it made for an easy way out of any need to come up with conversation. The domestic violence arrest had been for him beating the crap out of me, and even though we were both working hard to put things back together, there were still plenty of raw spots.

He opened his eyes as I stopped the car in front of the house, confirming my suspicion that he'd simply been avoiding the need to talk to me. I followed him up the steps and inside. We'd come a long way toward getting the house fixed up and cleaned up, but we still had a long way to go. The broken window in the front was still held together by duct tape, the furniture looked like yard sale rejects, and the carpet held numerous stains from who the hell knew what. But there was a lot less clutter, and I was trying my best to not let the dirty dishes go for more than a couple of days.

"I'm going to bed," my dad mumbled, heading for his bedroom. I simply nodded and headed to my own, wishing the wounds between us could be healed as easily as the cuts on my wrists.

My dad was still asleep when I got up the next morning—not surprising since I popped awake at eight frickin' a.m. despite my intense desire to sleep as much of the day away as possible. Or at least until eleven since I wasn't back on call again until noon.

I stared at the ceiling for a while, hoping to fall back asleep, but instead my mind decided to go racing around the whole business about me needing to pass my GED, and I eventually gave up and got out of bed. After taking a quick shower and pulling on cargo pants and a coroner's office shirt, I crept out of the house, closing the door quietly behind me as I tugged on a jacket. Things were a lot better between my dad and me, but old habits of tiptoeing around him died hard.

The closest bookstore was in Tucker Point, and the only reason I knew how to find it was because about a month ago an elderly patron had been found dead in one of their reading chairs; and apparently had been dead for a few hours before employees realized that he hadn't turned a page in the book in his lap in quite some time.

The woman behind the counter had pitch-black hair with a bright blue streak in it along with pierced lip, eyebrow, and nose. But the greeting she gave me was warm and friendly. I managed a smile in response, feeling absurdly like an utter imposter. When had I last been in a bookstore with the intent of actually buying a book? Had I ever? *Now that's pathetic*, I thought with a sigh.

"Can I help you find anything?" she asked with a bright smile.

"Um, no, just looking," I mumbled, then hurried toward the back of the store. Almost immediately I began to regret dismissing her help, since I didn't have the faintest idea where GED study guides would be. And if I went back and asked now, I'd look like a double dumbass, since not only could I have asked when I came in, but also because I needed to take the GED in the first place. Yeah, I knew I was being a moron, but hey, I wasn't famous for being rational.

It took close to ten minutes of wandering, but I finally found a section that had guides for all sorts of tests—most of which I'd never even heard of. MCAT, LSAT, GMAT . . . ? I finally spied the GED guides near the bottom. But, good grief, there were so damn *many*. I stared in dismay at the two full shelves.

"This series is a good one," the clerk said from beside me, startling me thoroughly. She gave me a nice smile as I recovered my composure, then reached to tap the spine of a blue and white volume. "It has good explanations of the procedures, the instructional sections are clearly written, and it's reasonably priced."

"Um. Thanks," I said, trying not to flush in embarrassment.

"You getting it for a relative or a friend?" she asked.

I realized suddenly that she could tell I was ashamed of my need to take the GED and was trying to give me an "out." To my surprise I relaxed and found myself smiling.

"No, it's for me," I said. Screw it. It was stupid for me to be embarrassed or ashamed. Okay, so I'd dropped out of high school. At least I was trying to do something about it now.

Her smile widened. "That's awesome. I took it about eight years ago." She chuckled. "That's how I know that one's a good study guide."

"You were a dropout?" I blurted, then grimaced and shook my head. "Sorry, that's none of my business."

"It's cool," she reassured me. "But yeah, I was a weird kid. Was bored with school so I dropped out halfway through my senior year." She rolled her eyes. "Dumb move since there are a lot of universities that won't take the GED and make you go to a junior college for a year or two before you can apply to transfer." Then she shrugged. "Not the end of the world, though. Just took me a little extra time to get my degree."

I managed a weak smile. University? Hell, I just wanted to avoid going back to jail.

"You ready to check out?" she asked. "Or do you want to browse some more?"

"I think this is enough for now," I said. Cripes, when was the last time I'd read a book? I was such a painfully slow reader that it felt like it took me forever to get through a novel. By the time I got to the end I'd damn near forgotten what happened in the beginning.

She didn't seem at all fazed by my response and simply

headed back to the register with me trailing along in her wake. As she rang up my purchase my gaze wandered over the displays, then paused on the stack of newspapers as the headline caught my eye. "This too, please," I said, snagging a paper and setting it on the counter.

She added it to my total, and in short order I was heading out to my car. As soon as I was in and had the door closed, I pulled the newspaper out and read the lead story as quickly as I could, all the while feeling as if I'd swallowed a rock.

Coroner's Office Loses Dead Man

Sheriff's office personnel are investigating the loss of the body of an accident victim late Wednesday night. A coroner's office morgue assistant, Angel Crawford, was responsible for picking up and delivering the body to the morgue, and later told sheriff's office investigators that the body was stolen from her by a masked gunman. However, an unnamed source at the coroner's office has stated that there is currently no evidence to support her claim, and the working theory is that the body was either lost or stolen while in transit from the accident site to the parish morgue. Crawford, a high school dropout who is currently on probation for possession of stolen property, has worked at the St. Edwards Coroner's Office for less than three months. The name of the accident victim is being withheld at this time.

My hands were shaking by the time I made it to the end of the article. Could they have possibly made me

sound any worse? The coroner had made a neutral statement about the incident still being under investigation
and how grateful he was that no one had been hurt, blah
blah blah . . . but nothing about believing my side of the
story. Betrayal curdled my gut. I also had a pretty dark
suspicion that I knew who the "unnamed source at the
coroner's office" was. Allen Fucking Prejean. Not that it
mattered. *And even if I do pass the GED and get off probation, I'll still always be a felon, and I'll still always be a
high school dropout.*

I did not—did NOT—want to go in to work and face
anyone with a pulse, and it took every fucking ounce of
carefully scrounged discipline to actually turn the car in
the proper direction and head to the coroner's office. But
I also didn't plan on budging from the morgue itself. *If I
even have a job still*, I thought miserably.

I'd hoped to slip in the back unnoticed, but my heart
sank at the sight of Derrel leaning against the hood of
his Durango by the back door. It was clear he was waiting for me. *He's going to break the news to me that I'm
fired, or suspended, or some shit like that. Hell, maybe I'll
even be arrested for filing a false police report, and my
probation will get revoked.* Oh yeah, there were all sorts
of shitty things that could happen now.

I parked my car on the other side of the lot and mas-
ochistically made myself walk to him. He wasn't smiling,
but he didn't look angry or upset, which I kinda
thought—or at least hoped—he might look if I'd been
fired.

"You saw the newspaper?" I said as soon as I was
close.

"I did." He pushed off the truck and suddenly enveloped me a hug that made my ribs creak before releasing me. "Angel, you're not going to lose your job."

"You don't know that," I replied, doing my absolute best to keep my voice from shaking. I thought I was successful, but Derrel was more than perceptive enough to know how upset I was.

He let out a soft sigh. "Look, I know what you're thinking. You just got your life back on track, and now everything's about to be yanked away. But you have something now you didn't have before."

"Jeans that don't have a rip across the ass?"

A smile twitched across his mouth. "Well, yes. But you also have a cadre of people who have your back. If—and it's a big 'if'—you lose your job here, we'll find you a job. Maybe even one that doesn't require you to dig through dead bodies."

But that's the part of the job I need, I silently wailed, but I put on a brave face and the smile that Derrel was expecting. "Thanks. I appreciate that."

He leaned back against the truck again and lowered his head to peer at me. "Not to be too nosy, but that was your first offense, wasn't it?"

I heaved a sigh. "Yep. I guess that's why I managed to slide by on just probation."

A frown creased Derrel's broad forehead. "Why didn't you plead eight-nine-three or eight-eight-one-point-one?"

I gave him the blankest look I possessed. "Dude, I have no idea what you're talking about."

The frown progressed to his mouth. "Your attorney should have pled you eight-nine-three, which, in Louisiana, for certain offenses, allows you to expunge it so it

doesn't show on your record, as long as you keep your
nose clean afterwards."

I snorted. "My attorney was a public defender who
was so hungover he couldn't even remember my name.
And I'm pretty damn sure he didn't even read my file
until about five minutes before I went before the judge."
I grimaced and tugged a hand through my hair. "I wonder if I can go back and get it changed."

Derrel shook his head slowly. "Doesn't work that way.
Only way for you to get your record cleared now is a
pardon. Sorry."

"What, you mean like from the governor?" I gave a
low bark of laughter. "I doubt the governor will give a
crap about a skank who got caught with a stolen car."
Then I yelped as Derrel smacked me on the side of the
head. "Ow! Hey!"

"Stop calling yourself names," he said with an accom-
panying dark glower. "There are plenty of people in this
world who are willing to do that for you. Don't make it
easy for them."

I rubbed my head, scowling. "Okay, okay."

He grimaced. "I feel responsible that all of this happened. I should have come back to the morgue with
you." He looked truly upset, and I was reminded for the
zillionth time that this man, who looked like he could
still play linebacker without breathing hard, had the gen-
tlest soul I'd ever encountered. No wonder he was so
damn good at dealing with the bereaved.

I shook my head firmly. "Derrel, I've been to the
morgue at night a zillion times. And if you'd been here
he probably would have shot you." I stepped back and

made a show of sizing him up. "Though he might have had to use several bullets."

On impulse I gave him a quick hug, though my arms didn't come anywhere close to reaching all the way around him. "It's cool, big guy. And if you keep that shit up I'll start crying, and then I'll have to kick your ass." I gave him a mock-fierce look that was as much an attempt to cheer myself up as him. "And don't you think I can't! I play dirty."

He grinned. "I know. It's why I like you so much."

Chapter 7

The rest of my shift was blessedly uneventful. No deaths, no autopsies, and at five p.m. I quickly changed into the clothes I planned to wear to Pietro's and drove to Marcus's place. I sure as hell didn't want him to pick me up at my house. My dad still had no clue who I was dating, and I intended to keep it that way until the right time to break it to him that I was dating the cop who'd taken him to jail for domestic violence.

In other words, never.

Marcus greeted me with a smile and a kiss. He didn't seem annoyed or upset, which told me that he hadn't seen the article. And I didn't feel like bringing it up and putting a damper on the rest of the day.

Fortunately—or unfortunately—the whole prospect of meeting his uncle was more than enough to distract me.

"Would you please calm down?" Marcus abruptly said after we were well on our way.

I stopped jiggling my leg, clamped my hands together, and gave Marcus an overly wide smile. "I'm calm. Totally calm. Like ice."

He reached over to give my hand a squeeze. "Angel. It's going to be fine. I promise. My uncle's pretty damn cool." He smiled. "He puts up with me, doesn't he?"

I snorted. "Yeah, like that's hard." I glanced his way. "So, is he your dad's brother or your mom's? What's the rest of your family like?"

"He's my dad's older brother—both adopted. The rest of my family is great. Mom, Dad, my sister, and before you ask, no, they don't know I'm a zombie. My uncle's the only one who knows."

"A sister? Younger or older?"

"Older," he replied. "By about ten years. She works up in Boston." He smiled proudly. "She's brilliant. Masters in Modern Lit and going for her Ph.D."

"Have you thought . . ." I stopped, tried to figure out how to ask what I wanted to ask without killing the mood. "Never mind."

"What?"

I grimaced. "Um, well, this has been on my mind ever since I found out how old Kang was." Kang had been a mortuary worker at Scott Funeral Home, and was the first zombie to give me some pointers for how to exist in my undead state. He'd looked like he was in his early twenties, but had actually been closer to eighty—that is, until Ed killed him and chopped off his head.

A shadow passed over Marcus's face, and I instantly regretted bringing the subject up. "You're wondering how I'm going to someday fake my death and start over somewhere else?" he asked.

"Well, jeez, it sounds so depressing when you say it like that."

He let out a breathless laugh. "I have thought about it . . . and my answer is, 'I don't know.' I figure I'm probably all right for another ten, maybe fifteen years before I have to start wearing makeup or dying my hair grey or something to look older. That's what my uncle does."

"How old is he?"

Marcus pursed his lips in thought. "Sixty-ish, I guess? Something like that. He said he got turned about thirty years ago, and so far he's managed to get by with hair dye and a little bit of makeup that makes it look like he has more wrinkles than he has." He shrugged. "Anyway, I'm not going to make any decisions about what I'm going to do any time soon."

"Makes sense. Sorry."

"Don't be sorry, Angel." The smile he gave me was tinged with sadness. "You're still getting used to all of this. I've had six years to adjust."

I sat back and watched the scenery of forest, swamp, and small towns go by as I thought about what he'd said. How long would it take me to adjust? And what did that even mean? Was I still essentially human, but with a weird disease? Or had I been changed so thoroughly that I was something else entirely now?

"Are you ever mad at me for doing what I did?" he asked, breaking the silence. "I mean, turning you into a zombie."

"Seriously?" I asked. "Hon', I'd be dead, remember?"

"I know, but—"

"Stop it," I said, cutting him off. "No, I'm not mad. It's never even occurred to me to be mad. It's not just that

I'd be dead, but look at me—I have a job, and I'm not a complete fucking loser anymore."

"You were never a loser," he said.

I let out a rude snort. "Now you're just spewing bullshit. Trust me, I was. I'd given up and didn't give a shit."

"You're not one anymore," he said.

"I damn well try at least." And that really was the biggest change, I realized. I cared about my "loserness" and did what I could to fix it. Some things could never be fixed, though, only lived down. I was a convicted felon, my dad was an alcoholic, and my mom had gone to prison for child abuse and then committed suicide while incarcerated. *Don't give a shit* had been my mantra for the last several years, which I'd pulled off by neglecting and abusing myself far more than my mother ever had. I couldn't go back to that uncaring attitude now. Not and survive. Maybe that was why that article stung so badly. I *did* give a shit, and it pissed me off that anyone might still think I didn't.

I snuck a glance at Marcus. He had a lazy smile on his face as he drove, clearly in a good mood. I couldn't bring myself to tell him about the damn article now. *Let's get through this party thing*, I told myself. An hour or so of making nice, and then I could get back to what passed for normal in my life.

I had the first inkling I might be in over my head when Marcus made a turn in to a subdivision and had to stop at the guard gate to show his ID. A short ways past the gate I got a good look at the type of houses in here. Nothing less than two stories, and all big enough for my dinky house to fit into them half a dozen times over. Pristine yards, expensive cars, and the occasional jogger wearing an outfit that cost more than my car. I knew that Pietro Ivanov was, as Marcus put it, "filthy stinking rich," but I was only now beginning to realize what that meant.

After a few turns we pulled up to a three story—well, "mansion" was really the only word that worked. Pale grey brick, three stories, columns in the front, exquisite landscaping including trees near the front door that were shaped into spirals. But that wasn't the worst part. The worst was that this was clearly not going to be "just a few people." The broad circular driveway was already packed with cars, and the street had at least a dozen more lined up along it.

I gave Marcus a panicked look. "I thought I was just meeting your uncle and a couple of others?"

He winced. "I guess my uncle invited some more people over."

"Some?" I cast a frantic gaze over the ten or so cars in the driveway alone.

He gave me a sheepish smile. "He did say it was a cookout. And he likes to have a big crowd." He paused as he scanned the line of cars. "Looks like he invited my folks over as well. There'll probably be a number of associates and family friends . . ." He trailed off at the aghast expression on my face.

I stared at him. "Did you know this was a possibility?" He didn't have to reply; the guilty expression on his face told me everything. "You *knew*. And you didn't warn me? Marcus, how could you do this to me?"

"Angel, relax. I knew you'd get nervous if I told you that you might be meeting my whole extended family—"

"For good reason!" I wailed. I looked down at what I was wearing. I'd dithered for over half an hour on my clothes and had ended up with my nicest pair of jeans, a plain black sweater, and black boots. But the jeans were pretty low cut, and the sweater was a bit tight on me. Fine for meeting a zombie uncle, but ... parents? I could lie to myself and say that I looked fashionable, but I was fairly certain I looked more skanky than vogue. I flipped the visor down to quickly peer at my reflection. Being well fed on brains was making my hair grow like crazy, which meant I had about half an inch of dark roots at the base of my bleached blond hair. Which made no sense to me at all. How could my hair grow if I was dead? I scowled as I swiped at my eye makeup in a doomed effort to make it look less whore-ish.

"Angel, you look great. Please stop worrying."

I gave up on my makeup and settled for wiping away smudges. "Yeah, whatever," I muttered, unable to hide my anger and hurt. "I guess I'm pretty much screwed now anyway."

He opened his mouth to speak, then shook his head and closed it. I started to get out of the truck but he reached out and caught my arm in a gentle grip. "I'm sorry."

I responded with a sour glare. He sighed and released me, but I didn't make another move to get out.

"I'm sorry," he repeated. "I was trying to protect you ... keep you from getting uptight—"

"Uptight?"

He winced and lifted his hands in surrender. "Wrong word. Um, nervous, ill at ease." He groaned and ran his hands through his hair. "Shit, Angel. I guess I was hoping that if I could avoid telling you about my parents maybe being here, that by the time we got here and you saw them you wouldn't have time to get upset." He exhaled. "It was a dumb, dumb plan. I'm sorry. Will you please go in with me?"

A weird feeling of betrayal swam through me, and I had to fight for several seconds to get past it. "Don't ever do that to me again, okay?" I finally said. "I don't like surprises, let alone being blindsided."

"I won't. I swear."

He looked so damn forlorn and upset that I had to sigh. "Fine. Let's go meet your family."

I tugged my sweater down and my jeans up as we walked up to the house. For the first time in my life I was glad that I had hardly any boobs at all. At least I could maybe get by with just "skanky" instead of "skanky whore."

"Wait," I said. "Do your parents know about me?"

He gave a noncommittal shrug. "I might have mentioned you to them earlier this week."

"Great," I muttered. What sort of image would I have to live up to?

Marcus gave my hand a reassuring squeeze as we followed a path of granite paving stones around to the back yard. A hum of conversation and low music greeted us as we passed through a heavy iron gate. I plastered a smile on my face and hoped that I looked more friendly than manic. At first I didn't think there were as many people as I'd originally suspected. It certainly didn't seem crowded. But then it sank in just how enormous the back yard was. Easily bigger than the house and front yard and driveway combined, though it was broken up into sections which disguised how huge it was, somewhat. Whoever had designed the landscaping had interspersed hedges, garden plots, and fountains to form areas for people to wander, or sit and talk with at least the illusion of privacy. I counted three gazebos, two koi ponds, and half a dozen outdoor heaters—useful since there was a bit of a nip in the air. Oh, and at least forty people.

A "couple of people" my ass, I silently grumbled. There were a few faces I thought I recognized, and I had another rude jolt when I realized it was because they were politicians. A couple were clearly local, such as the Sheriff and the mayor of Tucker Point. But I was almost positive one of the men was a U.S Senator. He'd been involved in a sex scandal a few years back, and his picture had been all over the news.

Pietro is rich as hell and has a ton of connections and influence. Yeah, no reason at all to be nervous.

I didn't have long to wait before the frenzy of attention started. Well, frenzy wasn't really the best word, though I definitely felt like a tasty juicy fishy in a school of sharks. Did sharks have schools? Or was it some other word? Well, whatever it was, I was certainly getting sized up. Every person in the backyard seemed to be giving me the *Who the hell is that?* eye.

Marcus gave everyone he saw nods and smiles and kept a firm grip on my hand as he steered me toward a couple seated in one of the gazebos. They looked up as we approached, and it was clear from the delight on their faces that these were his parents. One look at Marcus was enough to confirm it. He looked like the perfect combination of them both. He'd gotten his height, build, and rugged good looks from his dad—a seriously handsome man, with brown-hair, blue-grey eyes, and a friendly, easy smile. If I was into older men I'd have been drooling over Marcus's dad.

And, for that matter, if I was into older women I'd have done the same for his mom. Marcus's dark hair and eyes had clearly come from her, a curvaceous woman who was nothing short of stunning. She had to have been in her fifties, but she carried her years with effortless ease.

Marcus greeted them with smiles and hugs, then he pulled me forward. "Angel, these are my folks, Nathan and Morena."

His mom gave me a warm smile. "So nice to meet you, Angel! Marcus has told us a bit about you."

I wanted to give Marcus a panicked *What the fuck have you told them?* look, but I managed to resist the urge. I didn't think he'd regale them with stories about my former drug addiction, my felony record, my alcoholic dad . . . so what the hell did that leave? My sparkling personality?

I managed to keep my own smile in place. "Nice to meet you, too." There, that was safe enough, right? God, I sucked at this.

"Marcus says he met you at work," his dad said. "Are you a cop also?"

"She works for the coroner's office," Marcus explained, saving me from hysterical laughter. "We get to see each other over dead bodies." He grinned. "Romantic, right?"

His mom chuckled. "Sounds like you're pretty tough," she said with a wink.

"Um, I dunno about that," I said. "More likely I'm just

sick in the head," I added, then instantly regretted it. *Nice*, I thought with an inward cringe. *Just come right out and tell them that their boy is dating a whacko.*

But the Ivanovs seemed to have a generous sense of humor. "Then you're probably perfect for Marcus!" his dad announced.

We sat with them for a short while, making light conversation. I expected to remain a nervous wreck but his folks were so damn nice and genuine that it was impossible not to relax and simply enjoy myself for a few minutes.

Marcus glanced at his watch. "I hate to ditch you," he told his parents, "but I think it's time for me to hunt down Uncle Pietro."

His mother gave Marcus a light kiss on the cheek. "We're going to be heading back to Lafayette soon. You're still coming this weekend?"

He smiled and gave her a hug. "Absolutely."

"It was lovely meeting you, Angel," his mom said to me with such warmth that I was pretty sure she actually meant it and wasn't just saying it to be polite.

"You too," I said, meaning it as well.

Marcus gave my hand a gentle tug, and we headed toward the house. "Your parents seem real nice," I said.

He smiled. "They rock. I'm damn lucky."

We entered the back door of the house and passed into a kitchen so large that I wondered if whoever cooked for Pietro ever got tired simply walking from one end of the room to the other. I was used to fancy houses so I managed not to gawk too much. After all, rich people died just as often as poor people. But Pietro clearly had *a lot* of money. Everything was oak and marble.

Everything. I couldn't even figure out where the fridge was.

Marcus turned to me. "Would you mind waiting here for just a minute while I hunt down my uncle?"

I minded a lot since the last thing I wanted in the world was to be abandoned in the middle of someone else's house where I knew pretty much no one, but I wasn't about to admit that. "Nah, that's fine. I'm a big girl." I even flashed him a wide smile so that he'd believe it.

And apparently he did, damn it. With a parting kiss he was off, leaving me to fidget and pray that I wouldn't have to talk to anyone before he came back.

So of course, that wasn't going to happen. Marcus hadn't been gone more than five seconds before a slim auburn-haired woman came into the kitchen. She gave me a tight, polite smile before heading straight to one of the oak walls—which she then opened to retrieve a bottle of wine. *Okay, fridge successfully located.* I'd have never found that thing on my own.

The woman turned with her bottle, walking with enough care that I suspected it wasn't her first. But she paused as she neared and raked an unsteady gaze over me. "We could be twins," she announced.

I blinked in confusion until I realized she was wearing jeans, black sweater and boots—same as me. Except on her it looked like the perfect definition of "elegant casual." Then again, *her* clothing probably hadn't come from the outlet mall.

"Though I don't think I could pull off that hair color," she added with a twitch of her lips.

I fought the urge to reach a hand up and smooth down my perpetually frizzy, overbleached hair. Leaning back against the counter, I did my best to give off an *I don't give a shit* attitude. "Yeah, it's a personal statement thing," I replied, copying her smirk. *Personal statement?* I sighed inwardly as soon as the words were out of my mouth. That was the best comeback I could come up with?

She let out a snort, then held up the wine. "You drinking?"

"Nah, not right now," I said. Or ever. Drinking alcohol would only make me rot faster while my zombie-ness cleaned up the damage it did. "But don't let me stop you. Knock yourself out."

She gave me another once-over, then apparently decided I was boring her. She rolled her eyes, turned without another word, and tottered off to the backyard.

I barely had time to breathe a sigh of relief before a tall blond woman in a black dress and burgundy jacket entered the kitchen.

"Did a redhead in a black sweater come through here?" she asked me, her forehead puckering into a worried frown.

"Yeah," I said. "She grabbed a bottle of wine from the fridge and headed out back."

She heaved a sigh and leaned against the counter. "Good. Maybe she'll get drunk enough that she'll forget to chew me out tomorrow." I must have looked baffled because she straightened and shrugged. "Sorry. That's my boss, Dr. Charish. She's been on my ass wanting me to explain my requisitions in painful detail, which slows down my actual work, which means she then gets on my ass about not getting my project reports in on time."

I recognized her now. This was the chick that Marcus

had been talking to at the lab. And the redhead was the uptight-looking woman who'd looked so pissed off when we were picking up the body.

"That sucks," I said, since I had no idea what else to say.

"Don't mind me," she said with a small smile. "I'm just venting. I've learned ways around Dr. Charish's craziness." Then she tilted her head. "You must be Angel!" she said. "Nathan and Morena said that you'd come inside. I'm Sofia." She gave me a warm smile and shook my hand. Her grip was cool and firm—one of those perfect handshakes that made me think she had to do a lot of meet and greet type bullshit at her job.

"Yeah . . . that's right. Yes, I'm Angel. Nice to meet you." I decided to play dumb about knowing who she was. "Are you one of his cousins?"

Amusement lit her eyes, though she didn't laugh. "No, I'm just a family friend. I've known Marcus since high school. Have you two been dating long?"

"Not really," I replied. "Only a couple of weeks."

"Well that explains why we haven't heard much about you," she said with a light chuckle. "Though he does tend to stay pretty private." Her lips twitched. "It says quite a bit that he brought you around to meet us so soon."

I gave a weak laugh in response. "Well, we've actually kinda known each other for a while. I mean, we just weren't dating is all." Crap, what had he told them about how long we'd known each other?

Sofia tilted her head slightly. "Ah. That makes more sense. So, tell me about yourself, Angel. Where did you go to school?"

It took everything I had to not pretend I heard Marcus calling for me or my phone ringing. I fought to keep the smile on my face, but I was pretty damn sure it looked sickly. "I, uh, went to East St. Edwards high school."

Sofia waited a beat as if expecting me to say more, then seemed to realize that I was finished. "Of course. Any plans for college?"

A sick tightness began to form in my stomach. *You don't belong here* was the clear message. "Um, not right now. Just working, y'know." The last thing I wanted to tell her was that I hadn't even graduated high school. But hey, I was studying for my GED at least. Or rather, I was about to start studying for it. Any day now.

She took a sip of her drink. "Of course. There are some great online courses that are pretty affordable and don't eat up too much time. That's how Marcus is working toward his masters."

I blinked. "Masters? Oh, I, um, didn't know he'd gone to college." Here I was thinking he was just a cop. He had a degree? Why hadn't he ever told me? Trying to protect my feelings again?

What the hell did he see in me?

"He has a bachelors in sociology. But he figures that with a masters he has a better chance of going federal."

"Federal?" I asked weakly.

She smiled at me over her glass. "Federal agent. FBI or DEA. That sort of thing."

"Oh," I managed. "He . . . never told me that."

Marcus came back then, and I nearly seized him in relief. "I see you've met Sofia," he said, then surprised me by giving her a kiss on the cheek. "You're looking as sharp as ever," he told her.

"And you as well. I was just getting to know your new girlfriend."

"Well, I hate to interrupt, but I need to steal Angel away from you to introduce her to Uncle Pietro."

Sofia's eyes crinkled in what looked like amusement, then she gave me a polite smile and turned away. Marcus tugged me toward the stairs. He glanced over at me as we climbed. "You all right?"

I plastered on a smile. "Sure thing." I wasn't about to tell him that I was suffering from a crisis of inferiority because I was an uneducated doof, and that I was feeling more and more like I didn't deserve to be with him. "I'm peachy keen," I added for good measure.

He didn't look convinced, but luckily for me there wasn't time for him to pry more details out of me. At the top of the stairs we proceeded to the room at the end of the hallway. I wasn't sure what I was expecting. A sitting room or maybe an office. Something that looked a bit like the room Marlon Brando sat in during the beginning of *The Godfather*. It was my dad's favorite movie. I *knew* that room.

This wasn't that room. Not even close. Oh, there was a big ol' oak desk and leather chairs and that sort of thing. But one wall was taken up by an enormous TV, along with consoles for several different video game systems. Opposite that was a smaller desk with a computer and flat screen monitor. Every bit of wall space that wasn't taken up with TV, windows, or door, was filled with bookcases all chock full of books. All kinds—hardback, paperback, non-fiction, fiction, mystery, sci-fi—all precisely shelved and, as far as I could tell, alphabetized.

I pulled my attention away from the intimidating

number of books. In a chair by the window was a man who I could only assume was Uncle Pietro. To my relief, he looked *exactly* how I'd pictured him. Stocky and swarthy, dark brown hair with a scattering of grey, and dark eyes that seemed to crackle with intelligence. I found myself discreetly peering to see if I could detect any evidence of hair dye or makeup but quickly gave up. Whoever did his work was damn good. As far as I could tell the man really was in his sixties.

He stood when we entered and came over to give Marcus a warm hug. "Good to see you, my boy. Very glad you could make it." He then turned to me. "And you must be Angel. I've heard a bit about you." But before I could respond he glanced to Marcus. "Close the door, please. Then we can talk."

That wasn't encouraging. Looked like I was in for another third degree on whether Marcus could do better than me.

Pietro turned back to me and gestured toward a chair. "Please, make yourself comfortable."

I didn't want to sit in the chair, mostly because I wanted to sit next to Marcus. Not to be all publicly affectionate with him, but because I was really fucking needing some reassurance at this point, and a simple hand-holding would have suited me just fine. But I went ahead and sat in the indicated chair, then realized that Pietro probably knew exactly what he was doing and had wanted me separated from Marcus so that he could get a better idea of what kind of person I was. *A nervous wreck*, I thought with a silent sigh.

Marcus closed the door and took the chair next to mine. Still too far apart for me to reach out and take his hand or anything, at least not without me looking like a complete spaz. Which I probably already looked like. Yes, my self-esteem was currently hovering somewhere below rock bottom.

I expected Pietro to sit on the edge of the desk, thereby allowing him to loom over us, or at the very least take the seat behind the desk so that he could be more boss-like. But to my surprise he pulled a third chair over so that we formed a circle. Or a triangle. A circular tri-angle.

He glanced at the door as if to verify that it was shut, then picked a remote up from a side table and turned on some sort of vaguely familiar classical music. "The speakers are pointed so that it's louder by the door," he explained to me. "Makes it pretty much impossible to eavesdrop on us from there." He set the remote down and then leaned back in the chair. I tried to hide how freaked out I was at the sudden display of security. "So, tell me, Angel," he said. "How are you adjusting to being a zombie?"

"It's fucking weird," I said, then flushed at my complete lack of couth. "Sorry, sir, I mean, it's pretty odd, but I think I'm getting a handle on it."

The smile he gave me was almost friendly. Almost. "I don't mind an f-bomb, Angel. Especially considering that you saved Marcus from the hunter."

At first I thought he meant a deer hunter, and it took me a couple of seconds of mental floundering to figure out what the hell he was talking about. Hell, I was a red-neck. Of course I'd think of deer hunting first. "You mean Ed?" I asked, just in case.

"Yes. The zombie hunter." He shifted, crossed one leg

over the other. "I confess I was less than thrilled when Marcus told me he'd created a zombie. There are sustainability issues, you understand."

I knew I looked perplexed. "You make it sound like he put me together in his garage," I said. "And no, I don't understand. What are, um, sustainability issues?" Hell, they already knew I was uneducated. What, I was going to lower their opinion of me?

"I'm referring to how to keep our population fed without resorting to means that would draw attention to us."

"Oh, you mean how to get enough brains," I said. Why the hell couldn't he have *said* that?

Pietro tipped his head in a nod. "Precisely. You are a new zombie, which means that your need is somewhat higher. You probably consume, what, a full brain a week? Perhaps a bit more?"

"Yeah, sounds about right," I said. Hey, look at that, something resembling some answers. "You saying I won't always stay this hungry? How long does that last?"

"About a year. It will gradually taper off a bit to where, with normal exertion, you'll be able to make a brain last about a week and a half. But, this still means that the average zombie needs about forty brains a year." He gave me a sardonic smile. "I'm sure you can see why our population needs to be strictly controlled." He met my eyes, and I had zero doubt that he would have preferred that my population had been controlled, perhaps even before I'd been made a zombie.

Well, fuck him and fuck this whole thing. I leaned back and crossed my arms over my chest. "Yeah, well, you're stuck with me now," I said with a tight smile. "And I guess you're all right with Ed taking a bunch of y'all out?"

He frowned. "We don't kill our own. There are plenty of others willing to do that for us—and Ed is a perfect example."

Marcus cleared his throat softly. "Angel, Ed's not the only zombie hunter out there."

Pietro waved his hand dismissively. "Doesn't matter. There are ways to deal with these hunters."

"Is that who you think stole the body?" I asked. "Zombie hunters?"

Pietro's eyebrows drew down in a frown. "What body?"

"Angel was held up at gunpoint last night," Marcus quickly explained. "They took the body of a man who was killed in a fall out at the lab where Sofia works."

Pietro pursed his lips. "Very mysterious. But unless the victim was a zombie, I can't see why you'd think hunters would be involved."

I silently bristled at both his "you silly idiot" tone and the fact that, apparently, Marcus hadn't talked to Pietro about the body. *So why was it so goddamn important that we come see his uncle so soon?* I cast my mind back over our conversations. As far as I could remember he'd definitely given the impression that the body theft was the big reason why we needed to see him.

Or maybe I was reading more into it. Maybe Marcus was more worried about Ed. I knew I was stressed and on edge, so it was more than possible that I was being overly sensitive.

"I couldn't smell his brains," I said. "I was hungry, and he had a significant skull fracture."

Pietro's mouth curved into a slight frown. "And so you automatically assume he was a zombie? I know the procedures for this sort of thing . . . didn't the paramedics run an EKG strip on him?"

"Well, yes but—"

"With only a skull fracture he would still have heart-beat, though very slow," he said, and this time there was no mistaking the trace of patronizing sneer in his voice.

I shot a look at Marcus, but he remained silent, a pained look on his face. He met my eyes and gave a slight shrug that was clearly meant to convey "I told you so."

Anger and betrayal swept through me, and I had to bite the side of my tongue hard to hold back the urge to either cry or shout a bunch of curse words. "Right. Then I'm not really sure why I'm here," I managed.

Pietro said nothing, but the look in his eyes echoed my sentiment. Marcus cleared his throat. "Angel, you're one of us now. That's why you're here. We're mostly worried about Ed and whoever else he might be working with."

I took a deep breath to get my ragged emotions under control. "What about the other zombies in the area? Have you warned them about Ed?"

Pietro nodded. "The ones who are in our circle know."

"Your circle?" I echoed, frowning. "What does that mean? Are there others?"

Marcus reached and patted my leg. "He means we've contacted everyone we know for certain are zombies." He gave me a reassuring smile, but an uneasy knot remained in my gut.

But I also knew that I'd be wasting my time and breath if I started asking more questions. "Gotcha," I said instead and did my best to smile.

"Very well," Pietro said, standing. "Then we should

rejoin the party." He looked my way as I scrambled to my feet. "Unless there is anything else you wish to discuss?"

I shook my head. He didn't really want to discuss shit with me.

"Very good." He beckoned to the door, and I made my escape.

We didn't stay much longer. Marcus's parents had already left by the time we came out of the meeting, and the last thing I wanted to do was talk to anyone else who wanted to pin me down and ask me about my education and career goals. My goal right now was to stay alive, to survive. Pietro pulled Marcus aside at one point, and I escaped to the bathroom, lingering in there long enough, hopefully, to avoid having to talk to too many people, but not so long that people would wonder if I was sick. Or, I realized later, doing drugs.

Unfortunately, as soon as I came out of the bathroom I damn near ran smack into Sofia in the hallway.

"Angel, I'm so glad I ran into you," she said with an earnest look. "I think we got off on the wrong foot earlier."

I fixed as polite a smile on my face as possible. I wasn't going to make any sort of scene or be a bitch. At least that's what I told myself.

"No, not at all!" I replied. Hell, I might have even gushed it. "Don't be silly. It's *fine*," I insisted.

She shook her head. "No, I mean it. I spend most of my time in a lab which means my social skills sometimes leave a lot to be desired. And I realized that I probably . . ."

"Made me feel like an inadequate moron?" I finished.

She flushed. "God. Yes. I swear it wasn't my intent."

I wasn't sure if she really was as remorseful or uncomfortable as she appeared to be, but I went ahead and took satisfaction in it anyway. "It's cool. I know what I am."

Sofia smiled uncertainly, clearly not sure how she should take that. "Oh. Okay, well, again, I'm sorry."

I gave a stiff nod. "Sure. I'll even accept it." I folded my arms over my chest. "Thing is, you're right. I don't have shit in the way of education. I had a crap family life, and there was no one to tell me to finish school and go on to college or any of that stuff. And there sure as hell wasn't anyone to help pay for it. But it doesn't matter. I'm working to improve myself, and I don't need anyone telling me that I need to do it. Just me." And my probation officer. But I didn't plan on adding that little detail.

She blinked, silent for several seconds, then smiled in the first unguarded expression I'd seen on her. "Now I'm wondering if Marcus is good enough for you."

"I think we're more than good enough for each other," I said.

She dug in her purse and fished out a business card. "Look, here's my contact info. Maybe we can meet for coffee or something someday? Start over and get off on a better foot?"

Not in this lifetime, I thought, but I simply nodded and took the card. "Sure. I, uh, hang on." I dug in my purse for a scrap of paper and scrawled my number on it, all the while wondering why the hell I was giving her my info. I really didn't want to have happy girl-chat funtime over lattes, but it probably would've been insanely rude not to reciprocate.

Thankfully, Marcus rounded the corner at the end of

the hall and spied me. "Hey, I've been looking all over for you," he said. "You ready to go?"

"If you are, sure," I said instead of the "fuck yeah!" I wanted to say. I flashed a polite smile to Sofia. "So nice talking to you." Then turned and walked off with Marcus without waiting for a response.

I held off until we were back in the truck before turning to Marcus. "Have you asked Sofia what she knows about that security guard who died?"

"I did," he said, then glanced at me with a smile. "I promise, I did."

"And?"

"She didn't know him. It's a big lab. Lots of people work there. Sorry."

I gave a stiff nod in response. "What was all that business about with your uncle?" I asked as soon as we were back in his truck.

"What was what all about?"

Oh, I was so *not* playing that game. "Why'd he have to talk to you again?"

Marcus gave my knee a squeeze. "Just some family stuff. He was asking me how school was going and when I was going to graduate. Stuff like that."

He was lying to me. I couldn't explain how I knew, but there was something about his answer that was off. Maybe they did talk about school, but there was more.

"You never told me you were going for your masters," I said, deciding to change the subject for now. "Where'd you go to college?"

"University of Louisiana, Lafayette. Started out as a criminal justice major then switched to sociology."

"So you always wanted to be a cop?" I asked.

"Actually, I was going to go to law school," he said with a self-conscious shrug while I blinked in amazement. "But then my mom developed breast cancer, and I decided to stay closer to home and put off law school. Joined the sheriff's office and been there ever since."

"Sorry about your mom," I said, uncertain what else to say.

He gave me a smile. "Thanks. She's good now. They caught it early, and she's been clean for seven years."

"Why are you going for a masters? Or are you going to go to law school now?" Was that the same as a masters? I didn't know much about how all that worked. I sure as hell wasn't ever going to go that route.

"My uncle's idea, actually," Marcus said. "He thinks I should eventually go into politics, and he thinks going federal could be a good start."

"Oh. Okay." I paused. "Is that what you want to do?"

I wasn't surprised when he shrugged. "Sure, I guess. I mean, I can't see staying a cop for the next twenty years." He glanced my way. "And, as my uncle pointed out, I have certain skills and abilities that could come in pretty handy in federal law enforcement."

Do you do everything your uncle says? I thought, but bit back the urge to say it out loud. I was silent for several minutes while I turned the events of the evening— hell, the entire past couple of days—over in my head. I also considered everything that Pietro had said, but also things that hadn't been said.

"Why didn't you tell your uncle about me thinking the guy from the lab was maybe a zombie?" I finally said. "I felt like an idiot in there."

He sighed. "Angel, I'm sorry. I knew what his reaction would be. I was really hoping you wouldn't bring it up."

Well you could have fucking told me that, I thought but, once again, held it in.

We were almost back to his house when I turned to him and asked, "Why was it so important that I figure out the whole zombie thing on my own?"

"Excuse me?"

I took a deep breath, trying to figure out how to say what I wanted to say. "Okay, so you made me a zombie, and then left the brain smoothies for me at the ER, and got me a job, and then left a note telling me to give in to my cravings."

His forehead puckered into a frown. "Right."

"Why couldn't you just tell me, 'Hey, this is what happened, and you're a zombie now, and this is what you need to do'?" I knew what the answer was, but I wanted to hear him admit it.

A pained look flashed across his face as he pulled into his driveway. "Angel . . . you were a mess. In *so* many ways. Making you a zombie wasn't just about saving your life. It was about . . . about getting you to get control of your life again." He looked over at me. "And it worked. Right?"

"Oh, I don't deny that. But I want to make sure you understand what you did. Yes, you had the best of intentions, and yes, it all turned out well and yes, you saved my life in a number of ways. But you basically put me in a rehab program against my will." He opened his mouth, but I held up my hand. "Hang on. I'm not saying what you did was wrong, and I'm not mad about that. I swear, I'm not."

"Then what are you mad about? Because, you sure seem mad."

I shook my head. "I'm not mad. I promise. But I want to be sure of one thing."

"And that is?"

I met his eyes. "That you never pull that sort of 'I know what's best for you' bullshit on me ever again."

"All right," he said.

I shook my head. "No, I don't think you get it. You do it a lot. I mean *a lot*." His forehead puckered and I plowed on. "You didn't tell me that your parents might be there because you didn't want me to get upset. You didn't tell Pietro about the body because you knew he'd dismiss it, but then you didn't bother telling me that you hadn't told him, which basically left me out in the wind." His face was stony, and I clenched my hands together to keep them from shaking. "Marcus, I really like you, but I don't need a babysitter. Or even if I do need one, I sure as hell don't want my boyfriend to be one. Does that make sense?"

"It does. It won't happen again," he said, but there was a weird note to his voice.

"Okay, so . . . tell me what you're thinking."

He shut the engine off but didn't make a move to get out of the car. "I . . . I've been trying to figure out a way to tell you this all night. Just haven't been able to figure out how."

The knot in my belly started to come back. "Tell me what?"

He lifted a hand and scrubbed it over his face. "Shit. I got called in to Major Hall's office this afternoon. He asked me if you and I were dating."

"Okay," I said, frowning. "Why on earth would he care if you and I were dating?"

"Apparently it matters if we're dating because . . . well, because you're a convicted felon, and I'm an officer of the law."

I could only stare at him for several seconds. "Wait," I finally managed. "You mean, I'm not allowed to date you?"

He wouldn't look at me. "Well . . . as long as you're on probation, yes. It's in our policy manual. I knew about the regulation, but it never occurred to me that it would apply . . ."

"So we have to break up," I said, though my voice sounded strained in my ears. The knot in my belly was thick and hard, but at the same time I had a kernel of relief in there which made me feel instantly guilty. Did I *want* to break up with Marcus? I didn't think that was true, but at the same time I'd been feeling like things were going awfully fast. But it pissed me right the hell off that it wasn't my choice to make.

Marcus shook his head and finally met my eyes. "No, see, the Major didn't say flat out that we had to break up. He just said 'if the higher-ups find out.'" He gave my hand a comforting squeeze, while I did my best to keep my expression even. "Anyway, I've figured it all out."

"You've figured it out?" I echoed. Had he listened to anything I'd said earlier?

"We simply need to tone it down in public. Be 'just friends.'" He flashed me a warm smile that left me cold. "I figure we cool it off for a little while, and then when I stop being on their radar, we can pick it up again and . . .

be discreet." He leaned over and gave me a quick kiss on the cheek. "Don't worry. It's going to be fine."

I stared at him for several seconds. "Do I get a say in this?"

A puzzled look swept over his face. "Of course. But I figured you'd be less than okay with being told we had to break up."

"You're right, I am less than okay with it. But didn't you hear anything I was saying before about not babying me?"

His mouth tightened. "I'm not babying you. I'm simply finding a way for us to be together—"

"Yes, you found a way, you made this decision that we'll have to sneak around. You didn't even think to talk to me about it." I could feel myself scowling. "I dunno, maybe, just for a change of pace, we could try communicating and talking shit out?"

"Since when are you the expert on relationships?" he said. He clamped his lips shut and shook his head. "Shit, I shouldn't have said that. I'm sorry—"

"No, you shouldn't have," I replied, fumbling for the latch on the truck door. "Fuck you, Marcus. Just because my last relationship was shit doesn't mean I don't know what a good one should be like. I don't deserve this." I managed to get the door open and practically slid out of the truck. I started toward my car, but a second later Marcus was out of the truck and in front of me.

"Angel, I'm sorry. Don't go like this."

"Get out of my way, Marcus."

He lifted his hands but didn't step aside just yet. "Angel, please. I shouldn't have brought your ex up. It was shitty of me. Now please, come on inside."

"I need to go home and check on my dad," I said, then took a deep breath. "Look, I've had a really horrible couple of days. I don't want to fight or anything anymore. Please let me go home, okay?"

He sighed and stepped out of my way. I started to move past him, then paused and quickly kissed him on the cheek. "I like you. I do. But I want you to like me too, and I'm not sure you even know who I am."

"Angel—"

"We'll talk tomorrow, okay?" I said, cutting him off.

His eyes were shadowed as he nodded. He turned away and headed to his front door while I continued to my car. As I drove off, I checked my rear view mirror and saw that he was watching me leave. But for the first time in ages I didn't feel shitty or guilty about leaving someone I cared about behind.

Now if I only knew what that meant about me.

Chapter 8

Dad wasn't home when I got there, and I sure as hell wasn't in the mood to go looking for him. I *was* in the mood to go straight to bed and try and forget the past couple of days and, shockingly, I actually fell dead asleep about three seconds after I climbed under the covers.

I woke up sometime after nine in the morning, and even though I hadn't managed to develop amnesia to block out the last forty-eight hours, at least I didn't feel like hammered shit. After checking the driveway to make sure that my dad had come home at some point during the night, I took a quick shower, pulled on my work clothes and a jacket, then slipped out and headed on in to work. I stopped at an XpressMart for a fine, nutritious breakfast of Coke and a cherry Hubig Pie—because every morning should start with deep-fried pastry. But while I was on my way out, I paused to take a closer look at the newspapers for sale by the door. Once again there was an article on the front page about the body theft, and a quick skim confirmed that I was still being painted as a completely worthless human being who was clearly far too irresponsible to be trusted with such an important job, and why hadn't the coroner fired me already?

I didn't purchase the paper. I had no desire to read any more of it. I continued out to my car and, as I drove, did my best to soothe my soul with the classic goodness of a Hubig Pie.

My phone beeped with a text message when I was less than a mile from the office. Anxiety slashed through me, and for an instant I was absolutely certain that I'd been fired and this was the office letting me know I didn't need to bother coming in today.

But no, it was just Derrel texting me an address and asking me to hurry and get the van. Stupid relief swam through me. *They wouldn't fire me with a text message*, I scolded myself. At least I hoped not.

I made short work of exchanging my car for the van and continued to the address of the death scene as quickly as I could without breaking any laws. The address seemed vaguely familiar, but I couldn't immediately place why. The most logical reason was that I'd picked up another dead body somewhere around there, but even so, there was something about this particular subdivision that nagged at me. At any rate, it distracted me from thinking about my growing "fame."

The cars lined up along the street told me that this was a crime scene—and not just a "might possibly be one" either. Two crime scene vans, three marked police cars, and at least that many unmarked . . . yeah, this was something big.

Derrel was waiting for me as I got out of the van. "Murder?" I asked him as I walked to the back and pulled the doors open.

"Yeah," he said, his tone oddly subdued.

I paused with my hand on the stretcher. Derrel didn't get upset easily. Or rather, he didn't show it very often. "Is it a kid?" I asked. "Please tell me it's not a kid."

"No." Pain filled his eyes. "No, it's Marianne."

It took me a few seconds for my brain to click into gear and figure out who the heck Marianne was, but when the sound of the barking dog finally penetrated . . .

"Oh, god," I breathed, all thoughts of the stupid newspaper article flying out of my head. Marianne, who ran the cadaver search dog whenever we needed help finding a body. Marianne, girlfriend of Ed Quinn. He'd used that dog's ability to help him locate the zombies that he would later hunt down and kill. That's why the address had seemed familiar. I knew this neighborhood because one of Ed's victims had been found only a couple of streets away.

"How?" I breathed. "Do they think it was Ed?"

Grief had carved furrows into Derrel's face, and I realized that he'd quite possibly been working with Marianne for as long as he'd been an investigator. "He's the primary suspect," he said, voice gravelly. "Though there aren't any witnesses at this time." He exhaled. "Anyway, I just wanted to prepare you. I know that you and Marcus and Ed had all been friends for a while before . . ."

I nodded, not feeling a need to finish his sentence, *before Ed inexplicably disappeared during a hunting trip with his best friend, Marcus.* It hadn't been at all inexplicable to me, mostly because I'd been the one who'd told him that if he didn't run I would kill him and eat him. Not necessarily in that order. To my credit, this had been after he'd shot me and Marcus with the intent of then chopping our heads off. I wasn't *that* much of a meanie pants.

But why would he come back and kill Marianne? I pulled the stretcher out and maneuvered it up to the house, past the unusually somber paramedics and cops. Marianne might not have been a cop or EMT, but she'd worked with them for long enough that she was definitely considered one of them. In fact, the law enforcement and rescue community had rallied around her in a touching and awesome display of support after Ed's shocking flight.

She was lying on her back in the middle of her living room, arms and legs splayed as if she'd tripped and fallen backward. Her eyes were open, and her face seemed calm, but a thin line of blood tracked from the bullet hole almost perfectly centered in her forehead. I swept a glance around the room, oddly puzzled. The house was neat and clean, comfortably furnished with a few knick-knacks on high shelves. An upright piano rested against one wall. A vase on a side table was filled with flowers. Nothing seemed out of place. No sign of struggle. Then again, if it had been Ed, she'd have let him in, right? But why would he kill her?

Detective Abadie had his head down while he made notes in a steno pad. He glanced up as I entered and gave me a slight nod—a far cry from his usual lip curl coupled with mild disdain.

Sean and another crime scene tech were still taking pictures of the body, so I positioned myself by the wall near Abadie.

"Do you think Ed did it?" I asked him under my breath.

His mouth tightened. "We have no suspects at this time," was his gruff reply, but the grim set of his eyes told me all I needed to know.

I swallowed. "Does Marcus know?"

Abadie gave a short nod. "He's on his way, though he won't be allowed behind the tape." That made sense considering how close he and Ed had been. Abadie gave me a sudden narrow-eyed look as if wondering if it was wise to have me picking up the body since I knew both the victim and Ed. But then he must have realized that pretty much everyone here knew them, so tossing me out would be pointless.

The crime scene techs finished their pictures. Derrel and I moved forward together as if we'd choreographed it and carefully turned Marianne over so that Sean could photograph the back of her head and the other side of her body. Derrel slipped paper bags over Marianne's hands and taped them around her wrists with surgical tape, just in case she had any evidence on her hands or under her nails that could lead to a suspect. Finally we picked her up and placed her in the body bag. I zipped it closed, clasped the buckles of the straps that held the bag in place, and clenched my jaw against a wave of utter helplessness. Why her? Why the hell would anyone want to kill Marianne?

I began to wheel the stretcher out when Abadie stopped me with a hand on my arm. "Angel . . ."

I gave him a questioning look.

"I don't know if you read the newspaper," he said, "but—"

"I saw it," I said with a sour twist of my mouth.

"It's bullshit. Try not to let it get to you too badly. They're only writing crap like that because it's election season, and they're trying to stir up some controversy."

I opened my mouth to say something, then closed it. Then tried again. "I thought you hated me."

His lip curled with mild disdain. "I don't *hate* you. I just don't like you. Big difference. But I do hate assholes, and that reporter is an asshole. Airing your shit in the paper like that is bullshit."

I fought for a smile, but it wasn't happening, so I settled for a nod. "Thanks." And then, because I had absolutely no idea how the hell else to respond to all that, I simply nodded again and continued on out with the stretcher.

Marcus pulled up as I reached the van. I yanked the back doors open and slid the stretcher in, then turned to him as he leaped out of his car and jogged up to me, agony written across his features. "Angel, it is true? Is Marianne . . . ?"

"Yeah," I said. "It's her. I'm sorry." I didn't know what else I could say that could get rid of the grief on his face. And I didn't know how much was for Marianne or for the thought that Ed had done this.

He gave a shuddering sigh and sank to sit on the curb, burying his head in his hands. "God damn Ed," he said hoarsely. "I swear I'll kill him if I ever see him again. She didn't deserve this."

I slowly closed the van doors, then leaned back against them. "Why do you think it was Ed?"

He lifted his head, gave me a perplexed look. "What are you talking about? Angel, who the hell else could it have been? We know Ed went off the deep end."

I frowned but didn't argue the point. Marcus wasn't in any state of mind to listen to anything right now. But for some reason I couldn't wrap my head around the idea that Ed had "gone off the deep end," at least not to such a degree that he would start killing non-zombies. And a single gunshot to the head? If he'd killed her because he was crazy, wouldn't it have been a lot more violent? Wouldn't there have been a fight, or struggle, or something?

But those arguments could be raised another time when the emotional wound wasn't quite so raw. For now I kept my mouth shut, sat down on the curb beside him, and put my arms around him while he wept on my shoulder.

Chapter 9

The autopsy of Marianne was brutal. Not the actual procedure, but the general mood of the room. There was none of the usual joking or conversation that usually helped lighten the atmosphere. The humor that we used as a self-defense against the horror of what we had to do was gone. In some ways it was worse than when we had a kid come through.

Also, we had several observers, which further dampened the mood. Detective Abadie was present since it was his case, but Captain Pierson was also there, silently watching from a discreet distance away while Sean, the crime scene tech, took numerous pictures.

I'd been working with Dr. Leblanc, the parish forensic pathologist, for about two months now, and I prided myself on the fact that I was getting to the point where I could almost anticipate his needs, like a well-trained surgeon's assistant, or some shit like that. Not that I knew crap about surgery—only what I'd seen on TV—but in those shows there was always some nurse or whatever standing right beside the doctor while he snapped out things like, "clamp!" or "scalpel!" Of course, considering how much the reality of police work and death investigation varied from what I'd seen on TV, there was every chance that the medical shows I watched were just as inaccurate.

I didn't hand instruments to him or anything, but I knew his routine—which helped keep me from dropping things or doing anything equally idiotic with people watching.

"Why are they all here?" I murmured to Dr. Leblanc at one point.

He breathed a soft sigh. "It's going to be rather high profile since the number one suspect is her boyfriend—"

"—Who also happens to be the number one suspect in the beheading murders," I finished for him.

He nodded gravely and bent back to his examination. Together we removed the bags from Marianne's hands and allowed Sean to take detailed pictures of them. I didn't see any sign that she'd clawed or scratched anyone, but Dr. Leblanc still took scrapings from beneath the nails, and then clipped the nails and collected them in a small paper envelope. I assumed it would be sent to the DNA lab to be compared to whatever suspect they came up with. Ed most likely. Did they even have his DNA to compare it to? I worried over that for several minutes until I finally realized it was a stupid thing to worry about. Let the detectives figure out how to handle that detail.

It was my job to cut the heads open on bodies, but Dr.

Leblanc assisted on this one since Marianne had been shot in the head. My respect and admiration for him soared as he carefully walked me through the process of doing it in a way that preserved the evidence of the bullet wounds in the skull. I was insanely aware of the presence of watchers, but somehow Dr. Leblanc made it seem as if I was doing him a favor and completely in control, instead of having to be, essentially, told step by step what to do. It didn't even bother me that I kept having to pause so that Sean could take pictures of the wounds.

I gently tipped the brain out and set it in the bed of the scale, then returned to the now-empty skull.

"The forehead wound is definitely the entry point," Dr. Leblanc said in a normal voice, gesturing the observers over. "See how it's concave on the inside of the skull?" He pointed to the beveled edges, while Sean took more pictures.

"Like when you shoot a BB through a glass window," I said, then flushed, certain I'd said something moronic.

But Dr. Leblanc gave me an approving smile. "That's exactly it," he said. "Don't ever believe someone who says they can tell from the exterior which are the entry and exit wounds. You almost always have to examine the interior of the skull."

My flush turned into a glow of pride. I stepped back to give Sean more room to take his pictures, then moved on to help finish up the rest of the autopsy. By the time it was time for me to sew up the Y-incision on her torso, the others had all filed out. I finished up in peace while Dr. Leblanc wrote up his notes, then I carefully put her back in the body bag. After I closed up the big plastic bag that contained all the organs the pathologist had removed and cut samples from, I set that in the body bag as well, between her legs. *That's one brain that I won't eat*, I decided as I wheeled the body back to the cooler. There was no way I could eat someone I'd known and liked.

Dr. Leblanc was ready and waiting for me when I returned to the cutting room with the next body of the day: a twenty-something man who'd most likely died of a drug overdose. Those still gave me a chill whenever I had to deal with one. *There but for the grace of god go I* and all that shit, though I rather doubted that god had anything to do with me being turned into a zombie. Though, if I hadn't been turned that night, I would've definitely died. I'd already been high as a kite when my would-be rapist had slipped Rohypnol into my drink. When I'd fallen unconscious and started having trouble breathing, he'd panicked and was on his way to take me out to the swamp to dump my body when he took a curve too fast and wrecked his car. Either the drug overdose or my injuries would have been more than enough to kill me if Marcus hadn't seen the crash and decided on the spot to do the only thing that could possibly save me.

I got the body of the overdose victim onto the table and prepped while Dr. Leblanc made his initial observations and jotted notes on his pad. I stepped back as he picked up a scalpel off the sideboard, but to my surprise he extended it to me, handle first.

I automatically took it, looked stupidly down at it, then back up to him. "Um. You're kidding, right? You want me to cut him open?"

"You can do this, Angel," he assured me. "You're a tough, no-nonsense chick with an iron stomach. You've watched me do it a few hundred times. Now, cut that body open."

I made a face. "Why can't I just stick to cutting heads?" I said. I might have whined a little bit.

Dr. Leblanc chuckled. "Because I'm lazy."

"Hardly!"

"How about, because you're fully capable of doing it, therefore you should."

I scowled down at the scalpel in my hand. The pathologist had been dropping hints for a while now that he would soon start having me participate more in the autopsies—a statement I hadn't really understood until now. "I'm fully capable of doing many things that I probably shouldn't," I said.

A smile quirked his lips. "I trust that you have the judgment to apply proper discretion. Besides, what you really are is fully capable of being more than a simple morgue tech. There are some agencies where the morgue assistant—or the diener—does almost all of the work of opening the body up and pulling the organs out, whereupon the pathologist simply comes over and takes a look and cuts his samples off." He gestured to the body lying on the metal table. "A bit more training and you could probably get to that point."

I stepped grudgingly up to the body. "Okay, so maybe you *are* being lazy."

He chuckled. "Curses! Here I thought I was being convincing in my mentor persona."

"Nope. I see right through you," I replied, but the truth was that any time Dr. Leblanc made one of those comments it warmed my crusty little soul more than I could have ever explained. More than anyone else in my life, I felt that Dr. Leblanc truly thought I was smart and had potential.

"Dieners make more money," he added with a sly wink.

"Well why the hell didn't you just say that to begin with?" I replied, raising the scalpel.

I found myself wincing as I pressed the scalpel into the skin, which was a bit silly since I was used to cutting the heads open. That involved slicing the scalp from ear to ear over the top of the head, peeling the scalp back, and then taking a bone saw and cutting the top of the skull off, thus exposing the lovely, luscious brain.

Yeah, so it probably wasn't lovely and luscious to most people. But ever since I'd been turned into a zombie the sight of brains got my mouth watering as much as fried pickles and a roast beef po-boy did.

Following Dr. Leblanc's murmured instructions, I made two incisions from the outer edge of the collar bones to the middle of the sternum, then carefully sliced the rest of the way down the torso.

"Be careful not to nick the bowels," he cautioned as I maneuvered the scalpel around the belly button. "That's never fun."

I gave a short little nod as I crept the scalpel down the abdomen at a snail's pace. A lesser man than Dr. Leblanc would have snatched the blade from me in frustration at how slow I was going, but he didn't seem to have the slightest bit of impatience. I fucking *adored* Dr. Leblanc.

I finally pulled the scalpel free as I reached the pubic bone. "Holy shit," I said. "I just cut someone open."

"That you did!" he said, giving me a pat on the back. "Next thing you know you'll be doing surgery."

Snorting, I handed the scalpel back to him. "God help anyone who has me as a surgeon."

He quickly filleted the flesh back from the ribs, then stood back while I took a pair of pruning shears and crunched through ribs and sternum to remove a large triangular section of ribs. "I'll give you a pass on the surgeon thing for now. But only for now." He glanced up at me. "I didn't go to med school until I was in my late thirties. And I wasn't even the oldest in my class."

"Uh, I think I should get through the GED first."

"Fair enough. How's that going?"

"All right," I said, but apparently I didn't sound very convincing. He cocked an eyebrow at me. "Okay, I only recently found out that passing the test is one of the conditions of my probation," I continued, wincing. "Which means I get to see if I can make up for five years of being an ignorant slacker in a little over a year."

He shrugged as he pulled the lungs out and set them on a cutting board. "I have the utmost faith in you. And what will happen if you fail? Do you truly think you'll be tossed in jail, or isn't it more likely that your probation would simply be extended until you pass?"

I let out a gusty sigh. "Well . . . it would most likely be extended. Which means I'd keep studying and try again."

"Ah, that's my girl," he said. "You're too tough to let a little setback like that defeat you." He met my eyes. "Not that I think you're going to fail, mind you. You've done a good job of surviving these past few months," he said. "You've turned your life around in ways that you probably never imagined."

"I had some help," I said, managing a weak smile. "I mean, I don't think I could have done it on my own."

"Perhaps," he said. "But I think you're past that now. You don't need help surviving, do you?"

I started to protest, but then I had to stop and consider. "No, I think I have that much down pat. But at the same time it would really suck to not have people around who have my back, y'know?"

He smiled, gave a nod. "Yes, we all need that. However, I believe it's time for you to take the next step."

I gave him a blank look. "Er, what would that be? You mean learning how to cut bodies?"

He chuckled low. "That's a start, but I'm talking in more of a metaphysical sense." He set the scalpel down, crossed his arms and leaned back against the sink. "You've spent this time surviving. But that's just existing. You can do more. Now it's time for you to *thrive*."

I didn't even know how to respond to that. Finally I said, "Okay."

We continued the autopsy, but I found myself thinking about what Dr. Leblanc had said. He was right, and in more ways than he probably knew. I had the potential to live a very long time. Was I going to stay an uneducated goob forever?

I guess that's up to me.

After I finished cleaning up I swiped the brain of the overdose guy and stuck that container in the cooler in the trunk of my car while retrieving my other container—the one that held my actual dinner. It, too, contained brains, but they were cleverly mixed in with broccoli and stir fry sauce and various other stuff that made the whole thing that much more yummy. Sure, I had no trouble eating brains straight-up, but making the whole thing somewhat gourmet not only made it easier to hide but also kept me feeling more, well, human.

Nick came in as I was finishing eating. There were three of us morgue tech/van driver types, and Nick had been the one who'd trained me. He only topped me by a couple of inches, and in some scenarios could possibly be considered good-looking. He had nice hair and green eyes, but those tended to be offset by the fact that he always seemed to be smirking. He could be a smarmy little shit at times, but every now and then a glimmer of "Nice Nick" peeked through.

He gave a glance to my almost empty container. "Smells good. You cook?"

I gulped down the last pieces, then snapped the lid back onto the container and stuffed it down into my bag. "Sorta. I just throw a bunch of veggies into a pan with some tofu. Add rice, maybe some sweet and sour sauce."

Nick made a face. "Tofu. Gah. Give me real meat any day."

I hid a smile as I gathered up my things. If he only knew. Yet as I left the morgue and headed up to the main building a thought occurred to me that made me stop and laugh.

Nick was grossed out by tofu, but not at the fact that I was eating my dinner not twenty feet from a cooler full of dead bodies.

I grinned and continued on. *We're all monsters here.*

Chapter 10

It was tempting to sit back and consider Dr. Leblanc's words to me and daydream about doing more with my life, but right now finding out about the stolen body was a shitload more important. As dorky as it sounded, my fucking honor was at stake, and unless I got this shit figured out I was going to have a helluva hard time having any sort of decent future.

Therefore, I headed straight for the investigator's office. Derrel was there, painstakingly pecking out a report on the computer. He gave me an absent-minded wave with barely a glance up from the screen.

"Angel, why can't you be more like Nick?" Derrel said with a black scowl.

I could only stare at him for several breaths before I found my voice. "Wh-what? Why do you say that?"

He gave a *hmmphing* sound. "Because Nick is a god-awful fast typist, and Allen has managed to convince the little shit that if he types up all of Allen's reports it'll improve his chances of getting a promotion." He lifted his head and grinned at me.

I returned the grin with relief. "Well, I can't type, but I can be more of a suck-up if you want."

Derrel shuddered. "No, please don't change a damn thing. I've already had to fight off a hostile takeover from Monica."

"A what?"

"Monica wanted to change the shifts so that she was paired with you. I told her to back the hell off. You're stuck with me, chick."

I plopped into a chair. "I'm glad to know you love me so much. Now I need you to prove your love by helping me out with something."

Derrel clicked on something on his screen, then gave me his full attention. "You want to know everything there is to know about the victim from the lab."

"Am I that obvious?"

"Nah. I just know how I'd feel if someone pulled that shit on me." He gave a rude snort, shook his head. "Frat prank? I don't know about that."

"It wasn't a frat prank," I said. "Derrel, that was no college punk. I know the cops have no reason to believe me, but I'm not making this up."

"I don't believe for one second that you're making any of this up."

"I know, and you have no idea how much that means to me," I said earnestly. "Here's what I was thinking: The dude who wrote that damn article was getting off on how horrible it was for the family when the remains of their loved ones weren't cared for and guarded properly.

But . . . has the next of kin for poor Mr. Norman Kearny shown up?"

He leaned back, laced his fingers behind his head. "Y'know, funny thing, that. I've been trying to track them down, and it's looking more and more like Mr. Kearny didn't have any. Next of kin, that is. Widower, no kids as far as I can tell. Not a peep from any of his coworkers, either."

"There's something weird about this whole thing," I insisted. "There has to be a reason that asshole stole that body."

"I'm with you, Angel, but I don't think there's much doubt that this victim was simply a security guard who tripped on some stairs. I have all of the background checks and info that the lab had on file, and it all says that this guy really was Norman Kearny."

"Well, what if the personnel file was tampered with?"

He cocked an eyebrow at me. "You don't think that's veering hard into conspiracy-theory territory?"

I made a sour face. "I know how it sounds, but I think that there has to be some sort of *thing* going on for it to be worth holding me up at gunpoint to steal the body."

Derrel grimaced. "True. Unfortunately I have no idea how we could find out if the personnel file was altered. If we still had the body we could run the prints or check dental records, but . . ." He spread his hands and shrugged.

I sat up straight. "Derrel, I'm fucking brilliant."

He gave me an amused smile. "Well, I've known that for a while, but what makes you think so?"

"I put his watch in the property safe," I said with a grin. "We can have that fingerprinted."

He nodded slowly, an approving gleam in his eye. "That could work, since we don't have the actual body to verify the prints." He glanced up at the clock on the wall. Two p.m. "I have court in half an hour, but I'll talk to the folks in Investigations in the morning."

"I could take the watch over there now," I said, probably too eagerly.

He smiled. "Impatient much?"

I didn't smile back. "Derrel, there are people who think I was involved. My name is plastered all over the paper, and I'm really afraid I'm going to lose my job." I gulped. "And I really need this job." My voice cracked on the last part, and I wasn't even trying to be dramatic.

His expression softened. "I know you do. And I'm sorry you've had to go through all this. I just . . . I don't want you to get your hopes up too far about that watch suddenly answering all the questions."

I nodded stiffly. "I know. But it's worth a shot, right?"

"Right." He gave me a kind smile. "I'll go get that watch out of the safe for you. Let me know what you find out."

Derrel retrieved the watch in its plastic bag for me, then left to go to court. I sat in the office, dithering and angsting for several minutes while I wondered whether I was truly being an overly paranoid idiot with my conspiracy theory. Finally I sighed, picked up the phone and put in a call to Detective Ben Roth, relieved that it was his case. At least he consistently treated me like a person—unlike some of the other detectives at the sheriff's office. If this had been Abadie's case, I'd have probably chickened out.

"Detective Roth," came the gruff answer a few seconds later.

"Hi, Ben," I said, "It's Angel Crawford. From the Coroner's Office," I added, suddenly paranoid that I was totally imagining any sort of rapport we might have had.

"Hiya, Angel!" His gruff tone shifted to something much brighter. "What can I do for you?"

"Well, I'm wondering if you can humor me on something."

"Only if it's naughty," he replied with a laugh.

"Not in the way you probably want," I said, also with a laugh. "Can I come by your office? This may take some explaining. It has to do with the body theft."

"Yeah, sure thing." He gave me some quick directions to where his office was, and then I hung up and drove the van the half mile or so to the building that housed the Sheriff's Office.

His door was open when I arrived. His office was the size of a broom closet, barely big enough for a desk, a filing cabinet, and an extra chair. The desk itself had a computer and a phone on it, and every other square inch was covered with stacks of paper and files. A cork board on the wall behind him had a picture of Ben and a blond-haired man holding several speckled trout, as well as another of him with the same man, arms around each other's shoulders and holding up beers. Around the edge of the corkboard were a number of newspaper clippings of what I assumed were cases that he'd closed. A framed photograph was wedged between a pile of papers and his computer monitor, again of the two men.

I tapped lightly on the doorframe to get his attention. He pulled his gaze from his computer and gave me a wide smile. "Angel of Death!" He chuckled and motioned to the chair in front of his desk. "Come on in, have a seat."

I closed the door behind me, then sat. His eyes flicked briefly to the closed door, but he didn't comment on it. I fidgeted for a few seconds while I tried to think of how to explain my theory. "Is that your brother?" I asked with a nod toward the framed photo, seizing on the first piece of conversation I could think of.

Ben smiled, shook his head. "Nope. My boyfriend."

I blinked in surprise. "Oh!" I paused, fumbled for something to say that wouldn't make me sound like a jackass. "You're, um . . . No one gives you shit about that around here?"

He chuckled. "They're welcome to try. I'm sure some shit is said behind my back, but no one's been dumb enough to say anything to my face or to Neil. I bring him to all of the departmental gatherings that spouses or girlfriends are welcome at, and so far everyone's been cool."

I found myself grinning. Ben might have a teddy bear exterior, but there was a hard glint in his eye right now that told me he would seriously fuck up the first person who dared mess with someone he cared about. "I'd like to meet him someday," I said.

Ben gave a slight nod. "That can be arranged. So, what's going on?"

"Okay, here's the thing," I began. "I know there are people who think the loss of that body was some sort of fuck up on my part—"

"I don't believe that," he interrupted, eyes narrowing.

I gave him a weak smile. "Thanks. But the other theory

is that it was some sort of stupid prank, and I honestly can't believe that it was anything of the sort."

He leaned back in his chair, nodded. "I can tell this is bugging the shit out of you."

"It is, and not just because my name is being dragged through the mud," I said. "Look, there's something weird about the guy who died. I know that on paper he looks like a nobody, but there has to be something else about him." I set the bag with the watch on his desk. "I took this off the body when I first bagged him up. I was hoping to see if it could be fingerprinted . . . to see if the dead guy really was this nobody security guard everyone thinks he is."

Ben picked up the bag and peered at the contents. To my surprise a grin spread across his face. "I love it. A goddamn conspiracy theory." He looked back up to me. "I'll take it over to the lab right now." He stood up. "Wanna come with me?"

"Sure!" I said. I *loved* forensics and CSI and all that shit. There was no way I was going to turn down a chance to see the inside of a crime lab.

The crime lab was in a building adjacent to the Investigations Division, joined by a covered walkway. Upon entering I found myself in a cramped room with a single desk covered in piles of paperwork and one other door that had the kind of key card lock that we used at the coroner's office. A middle-aged Asian woman with hair cut in a short pixie style sat behind the desk. She gave Ben a nod of greeting and me a somewhat inquisitive look. I could see her taking note of the coroner's office insignia on my shirt and some of the doubt in her eyes faded.

"Morning, Tracie," Ben said. "Is there anyone around

who isn't too busy and could do a quick processing of a piece of evidence for fingerprints?"

"No such thing as a 'quick processing,'" she admonished. "And there's also no such thing as 'isn't too busy' around here. We do have a backlog of cases to work, you know."

He gave her a placating smile. "Sure, but I'm always super nice to y'all, and deserve to be bumped ahead of those other rude bastards."

She snorted, but went ahead and picked up her phone and punched a button. "Hey, Detective Roth is here and wants to kiss your ass because he needs something done right damn now. You want me to tell him to get screwed?"

I blinked in surprise, but Tracie caught my eye and winked. "Gotcha," she said into the phone, then hung up. "Sean said you'll owe him lunch," she told Ben, "but he'll come do it."

"Perfect," he said. "He can put it on my tab."

Less than a minute later the red-haired tech opened the secured door. "Oh, hi there, Angel. Hi, Ben. Come on in. This is just one item, right?" He gave Ben a look filled with distrust. "Not like the time that you had fifty-three beer cans?"

Ben groaned. "I swear, that wasn't my fault."

"Of course not," he replied with a roll of his eyes. "Come on in and let me take a look at what you have."

We dutifully followed him through the lab and, much like my first tour of the coroner's office, I was disappointed to see that there was no neon or chrome or anything else cool and slick. Nothing but cramped offices and aging lab equipment. We eventually came to a large room that had four large tables in it, all covered with a ridiculous number of bags or boxes with "Evidence" stickers on them. Sean stopped at a table that actually had some clear space on it, then yanked a pair of latex gloves from a box near the edge and tugged them on. Ben set the bag with the watch in front of him, and I watched impatiently as Sean carefully opened the bag and peered inside.

"Okay, I'll stick it in the fuming chamber, and we'll see what we come up with," he said.

"Fuming chamber? What's that?" I asked. I knew I risked looking like an idiot, but I was also wildly curious about how all of this forensic stuff worked. Even if there wasn't any chrome or neon.

Luckily Sean didn't seem to think it was a dumb question. "Superglue fuming. All you need is an airtight tank, some heat, and a few drops of Superglue." He lifted the watch with a gloved hand. "See, fingerprints leave stuff behind—traces of amino acids, proteins, fatty acids. That stuff reacts to the fumes produced when Superglue is heated, and a sticky, white material forms that clings to the ridges of fingerprints, making them visible." He turned and started walking. "Here, I'll show you."

I followed him eagerly into an adjacent room. A metal table dominated the center of the room and along one wall were a series of glass-doored chambers of varying sizes, from about a foot high to stretching from floor to ceiling.

"These are fuming chambers," he explained, carefully opening the door of one that was only about a foot high. He carefully hung the watch from a metal hook, then opened a small plastic tube and squeezed the contents into a metal tray at the bottom of the chamber. After closing the door of the chamber and locking it, he punched some buttons on the front. "Now the chamber will heat up to release the fumes, which will settle on any fingerprints that might be on the watch," he explained. "And when it's done the chamber will vent the fumes safely away." He gave me a wry smile. "That's a vast improvement over the technique we used to have to use, which was basically a fish tank."

I watched, fascinated as a mist slowly filled the chamber. "How long does it take?"

"About five minutes, but then you have to wait for it to vent. Like I said, much better than the fish tank method, where we basically had to yank the cover off and run to keep from inhaling toxic fumes."

A short while later the lights turned green, and Sean carefully removed the watch. He peered at it through a magnifying glass, nodding.

"Well, there's a beautiful print on the watch," he said, to my delight. "I can definitely run that through AFIS."

I watched in rapt fascination as Sean proceeded to powder the print, pull it off with a piece of sticky paper that I learned was called a lifter, photograph the print that came off onto the lifter, and then transfer the digital image into a computer. From there he pulled the image of the print up on the screen and began marking the enlarged print with red dots—which he explained were "points"; places where ridges ended, came together, separated, or simply made dots.

It looked awesome and, at the same time, tedious as hell.

"Who is this guy supposed to be again?" Sean asked as he submitted the fingerprint with all its marked points into the database.

Ben glanced down at the file. "Norman Kearny." He rattled off the date of birth and social security number. "He should have prints in the system since all employees at NuQuesCor have to get a background check."

Sean tapped a few more keys. "Yeah, here are his prints." His eyes flicked back and forth on the screen, then his forehead puckered in a frown. "But the print on the watch doesn't match them."

An electric thrill ran through me as Ben let out a low whistle. "Angel," he said, "I'm damn glad I humored you."

I managed a weak smile.

Sean glanced over his shoulder. "Now we simply have to find out who it *does* match."

"And where's the real Norman Kearny?" I added.

Ben grimaced. "Damn good question."

My patience had a hard time enduring all the waiting that was apparently a big factor in crime scene forensics. I fidgeted while things flashed on the computer screen. I could only assume *something* was happening.

After about ten minutes my wait paid off. "Well, that's odd," I heard Sean murmur.

"You got something?" Ben asked, leaning forward to peer at the monitor. I did too, though all I saw was two big fingerprints with a bunch of dots all over them. I had no idea what any of it meant.

"Well, I think so," said Sean. "I mean, this sure as hell looks like a match." He continued to click things. "I have well over ten points matched already. As far as I can tell this is your guy."

"Great!" Ben said. "What's so odd about it?"

Sean leaned back in the chair and shoved both hands

through his hair. "I saw the body on the scene. He looked like he was in his sixties at least, right?"

We both nodded, but a knot began to form in my gut.

"Well, just for starters, the guy who matches that print would be forty-three years old."

Ben shook his head. "That has to be a typo."

Sean pivoted to a different computer. "Nope, his other records also have that same date of birth."

"Maybe he looks really old for his age," I offered. "Or perhaps the print is from someone else. I mean, maybe someone grabbed the watch or something."

Sean shrugged. "It's possible, but that's not the only thing that's fucked up. Take a look at this guy's name."

Ben and I leaned in to read the name off his screen.

"That's impossible," Ben blurted while I could only stare.

I'd wanted some sort of confirmation that the guy was a zombie, but this didn't make any sense at all. The name that matched the fingerprints was Zeke Lyons—who'd been decapitated by Ed Quinn about a month ago. He was a zombie. But he was a *dead* zombie. How could his prints get on that watch?

"There's a mix-up with the evidence," Ben said, shaking his head. "This can't be the watch of the guy who died out at the lab."

I finally found my voice. "Sean, you have the pics you took out there, right?" At his nod I continued. "Can you pull those up and see if it's the same watch?"

Sean switched screens and a few minutes later pulled up a file containing all of the crime scene pictures he'd taken. Ben and I watched silently while Sean scrolled through, finally clicking on one that showed the watch on the victim's wrist. He zoomed in.

"It looks like the same watch," Ben admitted. "But that could still be coincidence."

"Sean, can you pull up one you took of his face?" I asked.

Sean flicked a glance over his shoulder. "I can ... and I can also pull up a driver's license pic of Zeke Lyons."

"This doesn't make any sense," I breathed as I looked at the side by side pictures.

"It must be the guy's dad or something," Ben said, deep frown on his face.

My throat was dry as I pointed to the screen. "Look at that thin scar on the side of his chin. Same on both. And the mole on his temple. It's the same guy ... but a lot older."

Ben sat back heavily. "Angel. I take back what I said about being glad I humored you. How the hell do I explain this to my rank? How can this guy be dead ... twice?"

I spread my hands in helpless defeat. My thoughts whirled madly as I tried to make sense of it. I was right about him being a zombie, but ... how could he have survived having his head chopped off? And why did he look so much older? And why did he seem to be dead after falling down the stairs?

What the *fuck* was going on?

Chapter 11

I drove straight from the crime lab over to Marcus's house, pushing my poor little Honda to the limits of its endurance and risking more than a few tickets. His truck was in his driveway when I pulled in, but there was another vehicle beside it—a dark blue Mazda with a long yellow scratch on the driver's side near the back, as if the driver had misjudged the turn around one of those stupid posts at the drive-thru. Not that I'd ever done that or anything. But I didn't recognize the car, so even though I was dying to talk to him I figured it would probably be best if I actually knocked on the door and waited, instead of the usual barge-right-in method that I'd developed over the past couple of weeks. Hell, I was practically living there most of the time anyway. About the only times I stayed at my own house was when Marcus worked night shift, since it felt sort of weird and creepy to be sleeping in his house when he wasn't there.

I shifted impatiently from foot to foot while I listened for noise inside. A few seconds later I was rewarded with the sound of footsteps and then Marcus opened the door. He gave me a puzzled look and stepped back. "Hi, Angel. Why didn't you just come on in?"

"I saw the car," I explained as I entered. "I wasn't sure who it was, and I didn't want to—" I stepped around the corner to the living room and stopped at the sight of Sofia sitting on the couch. "—barge in," I finished, briefly flustered. But it only took an instant to see that if they'd been up to something they'd have had to be ultra-fast dressers. Plus, Sofia looked stressed and upset, and I realized Marcus had lines of tension around his eyes.

"I'm glad you're here," Marcus said with a quick kiss. "There's some weird stuff going on."

"No shit," I said as I moved to the couch and dropped down onto it. "But, um, I need to talk to you about . . ." I fumbled for some euphemism I could use for zombie stuff and failed. "About pudding," I finally blurted, then mentally cringed. *Pudding*? That was the best I could do?

A smile twitched across Marcus's face. "It's all right, Angel. Sofia knows we're zombies."

"Oh." A weird ache of disappointment swam through me. This was the one thing that I shared with Marcus that I'd figured someone like Sofia couldn't, since she wasn't one of us. And yet . . . she *did* share it—and clearly accepted Marcus just fine as a zombie. *What does that leave for me?*

I did my best to swallow back the ache and put on a nonchalant smile. "Okay, well, that makes things easier," I said. "I just found out that the guy who died at your lab really was a zombie." I shot Marcus a quick *I told you so!* look.

Sofia let out a small gasp. "Are you certain?"

"Then how could he have appeared so dead?" Marcus asked, frowning. "Angel, how can you be so sure?"

I perched on the edge of the sofa. "Because the weirdness isn't just that he was a zombie. It's that this was one of the zombies that Ed killed."

He blinked. "That doesn't make sense. What do you mean?"

I quickly told them about the fingerprint on the watch and getting the ID, as well as the comparison of pictures and the matching scar and mole. Marcus still looked dubious, but Sofia clenched her hands together and hunched her shoulders.

"This explains so much," she said, voice unsteady. "He must have been after my research." She lifted her eyes to Marcus. "Pietro needs to know this. I *know* someone's been looking through my files. Somehow one of the other zombie factions found out. I . . . I need protection."

He moved to her side. "We'll keep you safe, Sofia. Don't worry."

I frowned and held up a hand. "Hang on a sec. Could someone please explain to me what the hell is going on? What research? What 'zombie factions'?"

Sofia took a deep breath and straightened. "I've known about the zombies for several years, since shortly after Marcus was turned. Pietro came to me with the offer to fund research in the hopes that I could either find a cure for it or find a way to manufacture a food substitute that would remove the need to consume human brains."

"Is there a cure?" I asked, though I immediately wondered if I'd want it. As weird and gross as the whole zombie thing was, there were definitely some advantages.

She gave a sad shake of her head. "There's no way to remove the parasite without killing the host."

"Wait," I said. "It's not some sort of virus?"

"No, and I'll explain why," she said, her face abruptly growing more animated. Clearly this was a subject that excited her. "You see, viruses infect to reproduce, whereas parasites infect to get a home, freeload, and live out their lives. For the zombies that you see in the movies, yes, a virus makes sense, because they're mindlessly going around trying to bite more people to propagate the infection. But with you—the *real* zombies—the goal seems to be the host's survival, and it's pretty much hijacked your entire body to make sure of it."

"Okay," I said weakly. Then I grimaced. "No, wait. I'm still confused. A parasite . . . like tapeworms? How is that different from a virus?"

She grinned but it wasn't amusement at my ignorance. This was obviously her turf and a topic she relished. "Here's the thing," she said. "Parasites and viruses share some basic traits—they both need to infect a host and use its resources to survive and reproduce, but their global outlook is very different. A virus's business model is based around hijacking your cellular machinery and completely depleting any and all resources it can get its grubby hands on, until the host is either dead or its immune system manages to kick the infecting virus out." She paused, tilted her head. "Or into hibernation. A lot of viral infections are actually permanent; our immune system just gets used to them and forces them into retirement or hibernation, like chicken pox, herpes, warts, and hepatitis."

I shuddered. "Seriously? I had chicken pox when I was a kid. You're saying I still have it?"

She chuckled. "Actually probably not anymore, now that you're a zombie. But I'll explain why that is in a second."

"Don't feel bad, Angel," Marcus said. "I've been through the same Zombie 101 class. Luckily, Sofia does a great job of making it understandable."

"If you say so," I said, trying not to sound too doubtful.

Sofia didn't seem to notice. "First let me explain viruses," she continued. "Success, to a virus, is making a gazillion infectious copies of itself and making its host as infectious as possible, whatever the cost. Absolutely nowhere in this business model is there any accountability or design to save the host resource. It banks on having an inexhaustible supply of hosts available to infect. Keeping the host alive and happy just isn't in the sales pitch." She paused. "I like to compare a virus to a bad company that sets up shop in a third world country to make, say, shoes. After the third world country is raped of every resource the company can get its grubby hands on to build the factories and shoes, the people are starving, and the land has been strip-mined, the company at no point goes, 'Hmmm, maybe we should fix this.' Instead it pats itself on the back for selling lots and lots of shoes, packs up, and sets up shop all over again in a brand new third world country. This exploitive business assumes there will always be an inexhaustible supply of new countries to inhabit and strip-mine."

I mulled that for a few seconds, shocked to find that I actually understood what she was saying. "Right. And we're not like that. We don't try and infect everyone we come in contact with."

"Exactly!" she said, bringing her hands together. "But there's even more to it than that. Your form of zombie-ism actually benefits you in many ways."

"Like the healing up and super-strength and stuff?" I asked.

She gave a nod. "It would be a lot of evolutionary leg work and a *lot* of extra genetic programming to turn a virus into something that would consistently benefit its host. Each change in behavior would mean a genetic change . . . but here's the thing: Because viruses use the host's resources—machinery and energy, they don't actively select against mutation. This is because there is no loss to the virus in letting itself just mutate; it's only wasting its hosts' resources, not its own. So, although useful mutations are selected for, the bad mutations aren't necessarily selected against."

I could feel my eyes beginning to glaze over. "And this means . . . ?"

Sofia smiled. "It means that there's pretty much no way a virus could do what your zombieism does."

"And a parasite could?"

"Right!" She gave me a probing look. "Are you ready for phase two of my lecture?"

"Sure, why not," I said, settling into a more comfortable position on the couch. "Maybe some of this shit will be on the GED."

"Somehow I doubt that!" she said with a wry grin. "All right then: a parasite needs the host to live long enough for it to successfully complete its life cycle; grow, reproduce, et cetera. Parasites use the host more like an environment, rather than a stopover factory. A parasite needs to inhabit and use its hosts' resources, but," she paused, "and here is the big 'but': It needs the host to survive. If the parasite manages to kill the host before it—the parasite—completes its life cycle, it fails. After its life cycle is over, it can kill the host all it wants, but not before."

"Like . . . tapeworms?" I asked again.

"Better. See, it's pretty clear to me that this parasite has a long life cycle. Longer than a human's, which is why it's in its best interest to regenerate the host." She held up a hand. "But, of course, not at the risk of its own well being. We're talking about a parasite here, after all, not a charity."

I sat up straight. "Oh! I get it! It heals us up when it has the brains, and it lets us rot when it doesn't."

She clapped her hands. "Yes! Regeneration when there is food available, and sacrificing the host—the rotting—when it's hungry."

"That's so cool," I breathed. "And disgusting."

Marcus laughed. "All right, Sofia. Now tell her about the mold."

I shot him a frown. "Mold?"

Sofia let out an exasperated sigh. "Not mold—fungus." She looked back at me. "And here is where I will explain how it's not like tapeworms, where a dose of the right kind of meds would clear it right up."

"Go for it," I said lacing my fingers behind my head.

She launched herself to her feet and began an excited pacing. "Well, the first thing I looked at was how a new zombie is made." She glanced up at Marcus. "Marcus and Pietro were able to give me a fair amount of information about the process, and it's clearly not spreadable through a casual bite."

"It, um, takes a bit of mauling," Marcus said. He didn't look at me, which was a relief for me. I didn't want to think about the fact that he'd obviously had to do that to me to make me a zombie.

"Right," Sofia said. "It takes a bit of doing to get the parasite to spin off an infecting spore and get it into the bloodstream of the new host, which is why it can't be transferred via a simple blood transfusion or organ donation." She looked at me with a slight frown. "Are you sure you want to hear the rest? It might be a bit unsettling to hear what happens when the parasite sets up shop."

At this point I wasn't at all sure I wanted to hear the rest, but I sure as hell didn't want to look weak in front of this woman. I felt inadequate enough, thank you very much. "I'm cool," I said with a smile I didn't feel. "Lay it on me."

She took a deep breath. "Here goes. Once the victim has been bit, the infecting spore has access to the bloodstream and through the bloodstream the lymphatic system. From there it hits the immune system and pretty much takes over. It can now tell the host what it's allowed to fight off infection-wise, and programs the immune system to think that the parasite is a friend. So, once the immune system is under the control of the parasite, it's free to roam without it getting harmed or having the host get sick.

"It next travels through the human body, using the bloodstream and lymph system, to every organ and tissue type. At each new stop, it sets up a satellite colony that adapts and mimics the organ, and it makes sure to take over shop and do any necessary repairs. This is the initial colonization—setting up satellite colonies in every organ and making sure the organ is running smoothly, and also setting up a repair shop, so to speak." She gave Marcus a meaningful look. "Which is why you didn't die of rabies."

He gave a short nod.

Sofia's attention came back to me. "And is why you most likely don't still have the chicken pox virus in you, or even if you do, you don't have to worry about it coming back to haunt you in the form of shingles."

She was right. I wasn't ready to hear this. "In other words, this zombie parasite is all through me?" I asked, swallowing hard.

"Yes. Even the brain. I'm still not sure of the exact mechanism by which it crosses the blood-brain barrier—it might simply force its way in, since it has control of everything else. But the good news is that it doesn't kill anything." She gave me what was probably meant to be a reassuring look. "What it does is head for the hunger center and gets itself hardwired in." She shrugged. "And there are probably all sorts of specialized cell-cell junctions, so no way is it getting ripped out of there. Even under the worst circumstances, it's wedged into the brain tight. And now that the satellite colony in the brain is set up, the infection is complete."

She leaned up against the edge of the love seat and crossed her arms over her chest. "There's more, I'm sure. Communication among the colonies, and how it manages to mimic host tissue so extraordinarily well. I mean, you have to really *really* be looking to see something's amiss."

Okay, so it looked like I was stuck being a zombie. "What about the brains? Why does it make us crave brains?"

"Prions!" she said with a proud smile. "And this is the basis of what I've been working on for the past several years. Prions are indestructible—they're basically immortal proteins. Your parasitic zombie colony uses the prion proteins as building blocks and for fuel. The best part is, every time the host eats brains, the parasite has a brand new fuel supply. And, since it has its own personal hardwire into the host's brain, it can tell it to go and get more brains whenever it's running low on prions. If the host can't find any immediately, the parasite takes a couple of actions. The first is, it reinforces its presence in the brain and probably takes resources from elsewhere. Now, as the colony starves and has to start shutting down sections, the first systems to go are the host maintenance—hence the decay and dropping bits and pieces. After all, it's not altruistic."

"Of course not," I said weakly.

"Since the prion building blocks it uses are indestructible, the colony is fine at first, but the host tissue degrades, except for the brain—which the parasite still needs to function so it can make the decaying body try to get *more* brains ... until it eventually runs out of steam and the host and parasite die."

I was silent for a couple of minutes after she finished. I didn't understand all of what she'd said, but I got the basic gist: I couldn't be cured, and there was something in human brains that this parasite needed. "And you make fake brains?" I finally asked.

A mild grimace passed over her face. "I'm trying to make a substitute, but it's proving difficult to isolate exactly what the parasite utilizes."

"But she's close," Marcus said. "And when she gets there, it's going to change everything for those of us with the zombie parasite."

I opened my mouth to say that I could see a lot of problems as well, but then closed it. Marcus obviously adored his uncle, and probably wouldn't take too kindly to me pointing out that Pietro was unlikely to simply give these artificial brains away. Plus, if it suddenly became easy to feed zombies, why not make everyone a zombie? That was a weird and rather horrifying thought. The parasite seemed relatively harmless as long as it was fed, but how did we know it wasn't controlling us in some other way that we couldn't sense?

"Sounds cool," I said instead. "But now that I've had the biology lesson of a lifetime, can you explain how the hell Zeke—whose head was chopped off, by the way— showed up at y'all's lab and looking about twenty years older than he did before?"

Fear returned to Sofia's face. "I don't know," she said as she sank to sit on the love seat.

"Then maybe you can tell me about these 'zombie factions' that you mentioned earlier," I said, looking back and forth between the two of them.

Marcus scowled. "There are other zombies out there who don't agree with the way Pietro wants us to stay organized. Sofia's research isn't complete, but it still represents years of work. If the others get their hands on it, they could conceivably find another neurobiologist to finish it, and then basically corner the market and control the distribution."

"Well, are you going to try to tell me that your uncle *won't* control the distribution?" I said in thinly veiled exasperation. Sofia looked abruptly stricken. Anger flashed across Marcus's face, but I bulled on. "Tell me the truth—do you think he intends to give these fake brains away—to everyone? Even the ones who aren't in his 'circle'?" I made air quotes with my fingers.

A muscle in his jaw twitched. "No, of course not, but he wouldn't be exorbitant about it. He's invested a lot of money in this, you know. And he's not going to take advantage of the others of our kind."

"Yeah, okay," I said. "But you're convinced that any *other* group of zombies would?"

His scowl deepened. "It's certainly possible. I believe that Pietro is best positioned to organize an effective and fair distribution."

Your uncle is a goddamn mobster, I wanted to shriek, but I kept it in. Marcus was clearly in no mood to see any other point of view. Just how deeply did his loyalties to his uncle run? How far would he go to make Pietro happy? And why? Was it simply gratitude for saving his life?

"Okay, that's cool," I said as lightly as I could, adding a smile to go along with it. His expression cleared somewhat, which told me that he was apparently buying my abrupt capitulation. *He's underestimating me*, I realized with a strange sadness.

"Anyway," I continued, "the guy was dressed as a security guard." I shifted my attention to Sofia. "If he really was working for some other zombie faction," and good grief but I felt stupid saying that, "how could he have known about your research?"

She swallowed nervously, flicked a glance to Marcus. "That's a damn good question," he said, his mouth curving downward into a dark scowl. "Hardly anyone knows that Sofia's working on this, which means that there's a leak or mole somewhere."

"Erm, okay," I said. Did he know how ridiculous this all sounded? *Then again, the simple fact that we're zombies is pretty damn ridiculous*, I reminded myself. Why *not* have some sort of spy vs. spy intrigue between the various zombie mafias? "This stuff sounds so interesting," I said, trying another tack. "I'd love to come see how this all works with you making fake brains."

She looked briefly panicked and shook her head in a sharp motion. "No, that's really not possible," she insisted. "So many of the areas are strictly controlled that it's not as if I can bring someone in, even for a tour. And I'm not about to make any sort of waves that could draw attention to myself. The lab director, Dr. Charish, has already been wondering why I've been pulling so many late nights." She visibly gulped. "I'm not *supposed* to be working on fake brains for zombies, for reasons I'm sure you can understand. If anyone ever took a hard look at what I was doing, I could get in a lot of trouble for misuse of resources, even if they didn't know exactly what the goal of my research was."

I frowned, pondering. "What if Zeke wasn't after your research? What if someone else there is doing something similar? Don't you think it would be worthwhile to look around and see if that's the case?"

"Don't even think about it, Angel," Marcus said, a warning tone in his voice.

"What?"

"Sneaking in," he said, giving me a dark glower. "If you were to get caught trespassing it would violate your probation."

Shit. He knew the right buttons to push on me. Going back to jail would suck enough as a regular human, but going in as a zombie would suck a lot harder—especially for anyone in my vicinity when I got really hungry.

"I won't sneak in," I promised.

"Besides," Sofia said, "the security has been tightened up considerably." She frowned and bit her lip. "But Angel has a good point. It's possible that this whole thing had nothing to do with my projects. Under normal circumstances I couldn't imagine that anyone would believe my lab was a target for industrial espionage, *but* there are plenty of other projects going on that would be worth a great deal of money to any of our competitors." She rubbed at her eyes. "I would love to believe that this man was after the work on lipid supplementation or some such thing."

"And you're sure no one else at this lab is doing any sort of zombie research?" I asked her.

She gave a dry laugh. "I suppose anything is possible," she said. "But I think it's highly improbable that there could be two people at this one lab who are separately working on zombie-related research, especially when almost no one knows about zombies in the first place."

"Right," I replied. "Makes sense." Yet there was still a lot about this whole thing that *didn't* make sense. Something was bugging the hell out of me, but I couldn't put my finger on it just yet.

Sofia let out a sigh and stood. "I should be going. I have a lot to do tomorrow."

Marcus moved to her and gave her a hug. "Call me if you need anything or if you see anything suspicious."

She replied with a weak smile and a nod. "Absolutely." Sofia looked to me. "It was lovely seeing you again, Angel."

Lovely? Um, okay. "Likewise," I said.

After she left I flopped back onto the couch. Marcus settled in beside me and let out a low sigh. "The drama never seems to end, does it?"

"Something weird is going on, Marcus," I said. "That dude's head was chopped off. Can a zombie survive that?"

He rubbed a hand over his face. "I never would have thought so, but . . ." He grimaced, shook his head. "I don't know. And I'm too tired to think about it right now." He leaned over and nuzzled my neck. "But not too tired for other things."

I grinned despite my stress. "I guess that means you have a fresh batch of pudding?"

He laughed. "You know me so well." He stood and headed to the kitchen. I turned and watched him go. He was damn good-looking for a zombie. Hell, for a normal human, too. His jeans hugged his ass without being tight, and his shirts were tailored to show the nice v-taper of his lats . . .

I blinked. "His uniform didn't fit," I murmured.

Marcus turned and gave me a questioning look. "Did you say something?"

I stood up. "Marcus, if you were going to go to the trouble of infiltrating a research lab that had fairly decent security, wouldn't you at least make sure you had a uniform that fit properly?"

He returned and set the bowl of pudding on the coffee table. "I suppose, but—"

"Don't you see?" I said, suddenly excited. "He wasn't trying to break in. He was trying to escape! They're doing something at that lab with zombies! Maybe that's how he grew a new body!"

Of all the possible reactions I expected—interest, doubt, delight—I sure as hell didn't expect annoyance.

"Angel, this is getting ridiculous," he said, scowling. I stared at him in surprise as he continued, "You've got it into your head that this lab is the center of some great zombie conspiracy, and it just doesn't make any sense! Is this about Sofia? Are you jealous of her?"

I actually spluttered for several seconds. "Wait. What? Is that what you think this is? Why the hell would I be jealous of her?" Then I narrowed my eyes. "No, really, tell me why I should be jealous of her. Is something going on?"

"No, damn it! Nothing's going on. But you seem really intent on painting her as some sort of bad guy or evil genius."

"That's not what I said!" I stared at him, hurt. "I said something weird was going on at the lab. I never said it was *her*. And why the hell won't you believe me? Why the hell won't you trust me or believe me about *anything*?" I may have been shouting by that last word.

"I believe you about stuff that's believable, Angel! Stop being such a child!"

"A . . . a child?" I stared at him. "You didn't believe me about the dead guy being a zombie. You didn't believe me about the holdup—and I think maybe you still don't." I stood and grabbed my bag. "Fuck you, Marcus," I said as I headed toward the door. "I hope you and your mobster uncle live happily ever after together. After all, you believe everything *he* tells you, and you sure as hell *do* everything he tells you to do!"

I slammed the door behind me. I had no idea if he was trying to follow me, but I didn't look back to see. I climbed into my car and sped away, surprised to find that even though I was upset I didn't feel any desire to cry. *Is that my parasite protecting me?* I wondered. *Or am I simply becoming less and less human?*

Chapter 12

I might not have felt like crying, but I sure wasn't a happy, cheerful camper either. Plus I wanted chocolate, which told me that at least one part of my human side was still working perfectly fine.

Back before my zombification I'd have most likely headed to any one of the many bars that I frequented, downed a painkiller or three, and chased it with some sort of alcohol with maybe a joint as dessert. But apparently my little parasite got unhappy when I did shit like that and made it use up prions or whatever to clean all that junk out of my system. Even though I was only just now learning the why of it, it hadn't taken me long after becoming a zombie to figure out that when I did stuff that was bad for me, I rotted a lot faster.

So instead I headed to Double D's Diner, where I ordered a bacon cheeseburger, fries, a chocolate milkshake, and a chocolate mousse pie for dessert.

The waitress grinned as she jotted down the order. "Now that's an *I don't give a crap* meal if I've ever seen one!"

I managed a smile. "Yeah, that pretty much nails it."

The woman cocked her head and gave me an appraising look. "Lemme guess, you just dumped your boyfriend?"

I let out a short laugh of astonishment. "How on earth . . . ?"

She winked. "Easy. You looked too bummed to be celebrating something. So this is a comfort food thing. Best guess was a boyfriend."

I smiled. "And how'd you know that I did the dumping?"

She gathered up my menu. "Because usually, when the guy does the dumping, I see the girls eating tiny salads—either because they hope to get him back, or hope to snag another guy to make the first one jealous." She rolled her eyes. "Screw that. Life's too short to be with someone for the wrong reasons."

After she headed off to get my drink, I considered what she'd said. Life was too short for most people, but for me it was potentially too long.

I pulled my GED study guide out of my bag but then just stared at the cover. I'd never *ever* considered going to college. That was so far out of the realm of possibility that for pretty much my entire life even the thought of it had been laughable. But now . . . why the hell not? In fact, if I was likely going to be living an absurdly long time, it seemed even more important that I should find a way to make my life a lot more comfortable. I sure as hell didn't want to be delivering pizzas when I was seventy.

Screw it. Even if it took me twelve tries to pass the damn GED, I was going to do it. Not because I needed it for a decent job—okay, yeah, that was a big reason. But I sure as hell wasn't going to put up with intellectual snobs looking down on me forever.

My food came, and I worked my way through a practice test while I plowed my way through my comfort-food extravaganza.

"Well, goddamn," I heard a too-familiar voice say. "Look who's trying to brush some of the loser off her."

Gritting my teeth, I glanced up to see Clive standing by my booth. Clive was my ex-boyfriend Randy's "best bud." Randy was a total package piece of shit, i.e., a cheating, drugged out asshole who'd convinced me that buying a stolen car from another of his "best buds" was a great idea. But Clive was on a whole 'nother level. He and I were about the same height, but he was probably double my weight, and it wasn't fat, either. It was all muscle—and far too much muscle for his size. Clive was also the friendly neighborhood dealer when it came to pills and steroids. And yes, much to my regret, I used to get most of my pills from him, even knowing how much of a skeevy jackass he was. Then, after the zombieism took care of that addiction, he and Randy had tried to get me to steal the pills the coroner's office confiscated so that he could turn around and sell them. Considering that my answer had been "fuck off," I probably wasn't his favorite person right now.

A quick glance around confirmed that Randy wasn't with him, which was a damn good thing because Clive was more than enough asshole for me to be willing to tolerate right now.

"Hi, Clive. Now go away." I bent my head back to my book, then cursed as he snatched it off the table and started paging through it.

"Oh yeah," he said with a sneer. "I forgot that you're a dropout." He dropped the book back on the table, narrowly missing my plate. "Oh wait, no, I read about you in the paper this morning. Talked a lot about you—you being an ignorant felon and all. You lost a body, right?" He laughed. "How the fuck do you lose a body?"

I knew people were staring, but I suddenly realized what was happening. He was baiting me, most likely because I'd dumped his best buddy, and also because I'd refused to steal drugs from the coroner's office for him to sell.

Thankfully the manager chose that moment to walk up to my table. A burly man who'd supposedly worked as a pro wrestler for a while, he clearly wasn't cowed one bit by Clive's steroid driven bulk. "'Scuse me, ma'am," he said to me in a soft rumble while his eyes never left Clive. "This gentleman bothering you?"

I exhaled in relief. "Yeah. Actually he is."

A thin smile creased the manager's mouth. "Sir, I think it's time for you to get the fuck out of this establishment and never come back."

Clive's sneer deepened, but his eyes flicked over the manager's bulk as he clearly came to the realization that this was a battle he'd be hard pressed to come out of unbloodied. "This place fucking sucks anyway." He snorted, then turned to me. "We're not finished. You fucking owe me."

"Get over yourself, Clive," I said. "I don't owe you shit."

He probably would have said something else but the manager took a step toward him. Clive turned and stalked out, and as soon as the door closed behind him I was surprised by a scattering of applause from the rest of the diners.

The manager grinned and gave a slight bow, then turned to me, expression more serious. "That guy's trouble," he said in a quiet and surprisingly gentle voice. "I'll walk you out to your car when you finish eating." It wasn't a request.

"Thanks," I said fervently. I might be a badass zombie, but having an ex-wrestler bodyguard, even for a few minutes, was even better.

He smiled and gave me a rough pat on the shoulder before walking off. I dug into my pie and discovered that I didn't really need comforting anymore at all.

My dad was asleep in the recliner when I got back home. Head tipped back and snoring softly, cigarette ash dotted the front of his shirt and a butt smoldered in the ashtray on the end table. I sighed and stubbed it out. I thought about getting a blanket and covering him up, but I knew that his back would be killing him if he slept all night in the chair.

"Dad." I gave his shoulder a mild shake. "Hey, Dad, you should go on to bed."

He blinked his eyes open, focused on me with an uncertain frown. "Angelkins . . . what you doin' here?"

"I live here, last I checked."

He snorted with a touch of derision, and I couldn't blame him. Last week I'd spent four nights over at Marcus's place, and the only reason it hadn't been seven was because he worked the other three nights, and I didn't feel right staying there by myself.

"C'mon," I said. "You should go on to bed or your back will hurt you in the morning." I took his hand and started to help him out, but he pulled it away.

"I'm not an old man," he said with a scowl. "I don't need help getting out of a damn chair."

"Fine, whatever. I just don't want you to hurt 'cause you'll be a cranky asshole in the morning."

He levered himself up out of the chair. "Bullshit. I'm a cranky asshole all the time. Don't make no difference if I hurt."

"You won't hear me arguing," I shot back.

He snorted, then gave a grimace as he stretched his back out. "Fuck this getting old shit. Don't ever do it."

An odd wave of sadness swept through me. There was a very good chance I wouldn't grow old—at least not the way he was. As far as I knew, I would never have to deal with the usual shit like arthritis and wrinkles. Look at Kang. He'd been in his seventies and looked like he was in his early twenties. "You're not old, Dad. You're just beat up. You got a couple of decades to annoy me still."

"Yeah, I gotta do what I'm good at, right?" He shuffled toward the kitchen. "Don't suppose you brought home any food?"

I winced. I hadn't even thought about stopping by the store. "No. But I can order a pizza if you want."

He waved a hand. "Nah. Take too long. I think we got some mac and cheese."

"Sit down. I'll make it," I told him.

"Jesus Christ, Angel," he said with a scowl. "I'm not a

fucking cripple. I just got a sore back. I can make my own goddamn mac and cheese."

"Fine, then make your own goddamn mac and cheese," I said as I plopped down on a stool at the kitchen counter. "Just try not to whine too much."

"When the hell did you get so fucking ornery?" he asked with a glare, but I thought that maybe there was a tiny touch of pride in the look. Or maybe I was just seeing what I wanted to see.

"This new job. Y'know what's cool about working with corpses? They don't fucking talk back."

He surprised me by giving a bark of laughter. "I still don't see how you can do that shit. It would creep me the hell out, always thinking that a body would start moving and come after me." He pulled the box out of the pantry and dumped the dry macaroni into a bowl. "You used to be so damn squeamish too. How'd you get over all that?"

I shrugged, keeping as straight a face as I could. "I guess I just got used to it. Y'do what ya gotta do, right?"

He poured water into the bowl then stuck the whole thing into the microwave. "Well, at least it's safer than you working those damn convenience store jobs. Always worried about you getting held up and shot some night."

That took me by surprise. It would've never occurred to me in a million years that he could be worried about my safety. Of course it had only been in the past couple of weeks or so that I'd realized he actually did care about me and did not, in fact, simply see me as the cause of all the troubles in his life. It would take both of us a while to get over the habits of reaction that we'd known for so long.

But his comment about being held up reminded me

of what had happened to me the other night. I didn't want to tell him, but I knew without a shadow of a doubt that he'd find out. This was a small town, and gossip flew fast. Hell, I was shocked that he didn't already know, what with it being all over the front page of the paper. Good thing we didn't subscribe.

"Well, um, it's not always safe," I said. I quickly gave him the bare bones description, though I adjusted the story a bit and made it sound as if the gun hadn't actually been pointed at me. In my version the bad guy simply showed the gun and I'd cooperated.

My dad took the bowl of listless macaroni out of the microwave and listened in stony silence as he stirred in the orange cheese powder.

"Guess there's no such thing as a safe job, huh?" he finally said. He didn't look up, but I could see the lines of his face seem to deepen in sadness and worry. "I kinda want to tell you to quit, but . . . this job's been real good for you." He lifted his gaze to me. "This shit ain't normal, right? You won't have people trying to steal bodies from you on a regular basis?"

"No, Dad, I'm pretty sure this is a one time thing," I said, ruthlessly pushing aside the memory of the time I'd been attacked by a zombie for the body in my van. That was a different situation entirely. Really.

"Just keep yourself out of trouble, 'kay?" he said, frowning at me. Used to be that those frowns meant that he knew I was going to get into trouble and he didn't want to be bothered by it. Lately I was starting to believe that he actually gave a shit.

He remained silent for a couple of minutes while he ate, emotions playing over his face. "I'll worry about you no matter what. But I'm real proud of you for fixing your-self up so good." He set the fork down. "I'm trying real hard to make you proud of me, baby." I could see the faint tremble in his hands. He wanted a drink. Wanted it bad.

I didn't even think about it, just got up and came around the counter and put my arms around him from behind. He gave a brief start of surprise, then let out a soft sigh and relaxed while I leaned my head against his back. He felt so fragile, bone and skin held together by sheer will and meanness. I'd known him as a bastard for so long, it almost felt like if he lost that there'd be nothing left of him, nothing to hold him together and keep him real.

God, I hoped I was wrong.

"I am proud of you, Dad." He shivered, and I realized with a shock that he was crying. I gave him a light squeeze, then turned away and headed toward the front door. I knew he didn't want me to see him cry.

Or maybe I just didn't want to see it. I stepped out onto the porch and gently closed the door behind me. Yeah, that was the hard truth. I was the weak one right now. I couldn't be in there with him, watching him fight the need for a drink every second. I'd never fought it the way he was now. I had it easy. Become a zombie and presto, all your old addictions are swept away by one big new one.

I shivered as I walked down to the driveway, wishing I could shake off the worry and doubt and fear as easily. And also wishing that I'd grabbed a jacket on my way out. Yeah, we were in the deep South, but it was early December, and it could still get damn nippy down here.

But an entirely different sort of cold grabbed me as Ed Quinn stepped out from behind my dad's truck.

Chapter 13

My heart slammed at the sight of the gun leveled at me. I'd learned a bit about guns in the past couple of months and a few dozen crime scenes. This one was an automatic, possibly a Glock. No idea what the caliber was, except that it wasn't something tiny like a .22. Either way it was going to suck ass when he shot me. *I'm screwed,* I thought in near panic. I didn't have a stash of brains on me like the last time. As soon as he slowed me down, he'd be able to take my head off at his leisure. And I wasn't tanked up. There was no way I'd be able to reach him before he could pull the trigger.

I clamped down on the urge to shriek or yell for help. The last thing I wanted was for my dad to come out here and be in danger as well. But, oh god, was Ed going to shoot me right here? Would my dad come out at the sound of gunshots? Or come out to find my body?

Except . . . Ed didn't shoot me. I swallowed hard, still

braced for the feel of lead tearing through me, but he remained frozen, gun on me. I managed to pull my eyes away from the gun and actually look at his face. I was expecting him to look angry, or crazy or maybe even agonized. But instead he looked . . . puzzled?

And goth, I suddenly realized. Or maybe it was emo. I never could keep those straight. He'd died his hair black and spiked it except for one longer lock that hung down over his forehead. He had on black jeans that were about a size too big for him, a faded Led Zeppelin t-shirt, and a dark grey hoodie patterned with black skulls and lightning bolts. He also had several piercings—eyebrow, lip, and ears—and I had no idea if they were real or not. I had to admit, as a change of appearance, it certainly worked.

I licked my lips uncertainly. "Hey, Ed. Long time no see." What the hell. If he was going to kill me, I might as well be a smart ass about it.

"Hey, Angel," he said, his voice so close to normal it made the hair on the back of my neck stand on end. "Angel . . ." I could see his throat bob as he swallowed. "Why didn't you kill me?"

I blinked, then frowned. "Huh? Why? Did you want me to?"

He scowled. "No. Of course not." Then he grimaced, swiped at his forehead with his free hand. "Fuck. These past few weeks have been . . . I dunno. Everything's so fucked up." He shifted and leaned against the cab of the truck, but the gun never wavered from pointing at me. I glanced toward the house. Ed was angled so that if my dad were to look outside he wouldn't see Ed and certainly wouldn't see that I was being held at gunpoint.

"Why didn't you kill me?" he repeated. "It doesn't make sense."

"Are you kidding me?" I replied with a flare of annoyance. "How does it not make sense? You've seen me and Marcus walking around all the time and not beating people over the head and killing them. I mean, how can you seriously think that?" I had to fight to keep my voice down. The last thing I wanted was for my dad to hear and come outside. "How the fuck did you get it into your head that we were monsters? Ed, I didn't kill you because I've never killed anyone in my entire life, and I'm sure as hell not going to start with someone who I thought was my friend, even if he did shoot me and his best friend!"

"You said you'd kill me if you ever saw me again. You said—"

"Oh for fuck's sake, Ed. I say a lot of things." I scowled. "Now would you please stop pointing that damn gun at me? It's kinda freaking me out."

He slowly lowered it and held it alongside his thigh. Technically, it wasn't still pointed *at* me, but it would only take a twitch of his hands to do so. "Nothing makes sense, Angel," he said, looking off at nothing. "Everything's so messed up. I didn't kill Marianne. I swear to god. But the others . . . I thought I was doing a great thing. I mean, my parents . . . but then you two . . ." He shuddered and passed a hand over his face. "I screwed up bad."

"What do you want from me, Ed?" I said, probably a lot more bluntly than I should have. Okay, I could probably cross "hostage negotiator" off my career plans.

"Answers . . . ?" he said with a sigh.

I couldn't help it. I laughed. "From me? Ed, I'm a clueless moron."

He shook his head and began to speak, but then we both heard the creak of the front door. A frisson of terror shot through me as Ed lifted the gun again. Maybe he truly was completely off the deep end, and this brief semi-normal was just a lull in his psychosis.

"Don't hurt my dad," I blurted. "And . . . and if you're going to kill me please don't do it where he'll find my body. Please."

Ed gave me a confused look, then his eyes dropped down to the gun in his hand. He swallowed hard.

"I'll find you later," he said, voice hoarse, and then he took off at a run down the road. Within a few seconds I lost sight of him in the gloom. *Find me later?* To talk to me? Or kill me?

"Angel?" my dad said as he came down the steps. "Who was that?" He had a jacket in his hand. My jacket. He was worried I'd be cold. Or maybe it was an excuse to come after me. Either way it damn near made me cry from the fierce joy of it.

"Neighbor from up the road," I told him as I walked back up to the house. "Looking for his dog. Nothing to worry about."

Chapter 14

Not surprisingly, I slept like absolute shit. Hell, it's possible I didn't sleep at all. I finally gave up long before dawn and grabbed a shower. I didn't have to work, but—also, not surprisingly—I suddenly had a zillion questions about Ed and his appearance last night.

Add those to the zillion questions I had about Sofia and the shit at the lab, and I had a full day of detective work planned. Instead of simply throwing on the first piece of clean clothing I could find, I dressed with care—simple black shirt, khaki pants, and low black boots. I brushed my hair back into as neat a ponytail as I could manage, dousing it with plenty of hairspray to try to control the rampant frizz, and spent nearly fifteen minutes on my makeup, doing my best to be conservative yet "fresh!" as the magazine covers would say.

For the final touch, I downed some brains to make absolutely sure I didn't smell.

Since it was still far too early in the day to do anything related to the lab, I chose instead to go to the morgue and do what research I could there. I brought my study guide with me in case anyone wondered why I was coming in to the office on my day off. It was easy enough to say that I needed a quiet place to study. Most people there knew that my home life was less than ideal, so it'd be a believable excuse.

As expected, it was nicely deserted, though the ever-present aroma of formalin greeted me upon entering. After logging on to the computer in the morgue, I pulled up a web browser and checked to see what was publicly available as far as information about Ed's parents. It would have been a thousand times easier to simply look them up on Lexis Nexis, but unfortunately I hadn't yet been trusted with the username and password for that. Damn it.

I had to wade through several pages of search results having to do with Ed as a suspect in the beheadings, but finally managed to reach a page—probably intended for genealogy searches—that gave me his parents' full names, along with dates of birth and death.

Sam and Dawn Quinn. They had the same date of death, slightly over ten years ago, but no other information. A search for online obituaries yielded a little more information, but only useless stuff like where they went to school and shit like that.

I ended up scouring online information for close to an hour before I finally found an article that gave me some info that was worth a shit.

Fiery boat accident claims two lives

Two people were killed late Saturday night when

*their boat apparently lost control on the Tchefuncte
River and struck a concrete pier, catching fire upon
impact. Investigators believe that the boat was trav-
eling at a high rate of speed, possibly due to a mal-
functioning throttle, although full reports are still
pending. Divers recovered the remains of two bodies from the wreckage and, using dental records, the
St. Tammany coroner's office was able to identify
them as husband and wife, Sam and Dawn Quinn,
of Covington, LA.*

I finished the article, leaned back in the chair and
blew out my breath. Now *that* was damn interesting.
Marianne had once told me that Ed's dad died in a boating accident and that his mother later committed suicide.
Had Ed lied to her? Was this fire some sort of cover-up?
And if so, who did it? Ed? Ed was twenty-seven now,
which meant he was seventeen when it happened. Not
completely impossible to imagine, but still fairly hard to
believe. And why would he have done it?

Puzzled, I returned to the page of search results to see
if there were any articles that had more details. There
were some older results from various society functions,
but I skimmed through those quickly, not terribly interested in the fact that they'd attended a fundraiser for the
preservation of wetlands. I clicked on the next search
result, then abruptly paused and returned to the previous page.

Frowning, I took a closer look at the pictures alongside the article. Halfway down was a picture of the two—
at least if the caption was to be believed. Drs. Sam and
Dawn Quinn. Good-looking couple. Both of them tall,

lean, and blond. Interesting that his parents were both doctors. Was that why he decided to become a paramedic?

I scrolled down to see if there were any other pictures of them. There was one more, with a third person as well.

A Mr. Pietro Ivanov.

I frowned. I wanted for that to be some sort of big reveal, some sort of "Aha!" moment, but the more I thought about it the more I had to accept it really wasn't that much of a surprise. Marcus and Ed had known each other since they were kids, and Pietro had taken them on hunting trips every year, so it would make perfect sense that he was friends with Ed's parents.

Skimming through the rest of the articles, I found a few more pages with pictures of them at various fundraisers or other functions. These people sure did love their society page shit. A few more pics of them with Pietro, but there were also some of them with another, shorter, woman who looked vaguely familiar, but the name in the caption, Dr. Kristi Burke, didn't ring any bells. *Probably just someone she worked with.* If she was a doctor it was possible she worked at a hospital around here now, and perhaps I'd seen her in passing one of the many times I picked up a body there. Still, I went ahead and stuck the name Kristi Burke into another internet search, disappointed when nothing came up but the same old society page shit.

Disgruntled over my lack of any sort of real information, I continued to pore through search results, eventually giving up when the results were nothing but odd combinations of names that had zero relation to the actual people. What I needed now was to see the actual accident report of the Quinns' deaths. *Or the death investigation report?* I perked up, then just as quickly wilted. The supposed boating accident had been in St. Tammany parish, not here. I'd have to find time to drive over there and get the reports myself—if they were even public record.

Scowling, I cleared the browser history—a trick Nick had inadvertently taught me quite some time ago— logged off and pushed away from the computer. Derrel or another death investigator would no doubt be able to get copies of the reports, but then I'd surely have to answer a number of questions as to why on earth I was interested in this. And what the heck was I supposed to say? "I think they were killed by a zombie, and the fire was set to cover that up." Yeah, that would go over really well.

As usual, I hadn't managed to find answers to any of my questions, and had only managed to raise more.

I glanced at the time. Seven thirty a.m. I still wanted to see what I could find out at NuQuesCor, but my slightly brilliant plan to infiltrate required that I wait until normal business hours.

With more than a little reluctance, I pulled out the GED study guide and started paging through it. By the time I'd leafed through the Language Arts section, I was uncomfortably aware that simply buying a study guide probably wasn't going to cut it. I needed to enroll in a proper study program with actual teachers and shit. All the faith-in-myself in the world wouldn't help me teach myself this crap, even with a big, fancy study guide.

Still, I stubbornly made myself read through the guide, though I skipped ahead to the math section.

I was still struggling over the section on fractions when Nick came in.

"Cripes, Angel," he said with a frown. "Do you fucking sleep here?"

"Yep," I responded. "Top shelf of the cooler. It's soooo comfy!"

He *hmmfed*, possibly not completely sure if I was joking, then tilted his head. "You look nice," he stated with a frown, in the same way someone might say, "My cat has worms."

"Um. Thanks . . . ?"

He came to peer over my shoulder. "Dividing fractions, huh?"

"Yeah, and it fucking sucks ass," I snarled.

" *'Ours is not to reason why, just invert and multiply,'* " he intoned. I stared at him blankly. He seized a sheet of paper from the printer, snagged a pencil from the cup by the computer, and proceeded to scrawl numbers. "My dad was a math whiz, taught me all sorts of tricks. See, it's the same as multiplying, but you have to flip it." His pencil flew across the paper as I stared. "So, dividing nine by one third is the same as multiplying it by three. See?"

I peered down at the numbers, and suddenly something miraculous occurred.

I understood it.

"Holy shit, Nick. That's easy!"

He grinned. "You just have to know how to look at it."

"Yeah, well that's my problem," I said, grimacing. "I usually don't even know where to start looking."

He plopped into the seat beside me. "I'll tutor you if you want."

I gave him a doubtful look. "I can't really afford to pay—"

He waved a hand. "Nah, I'll do it gratis."

I started to ask him why, but stopped myself. Hell, if he was willing to tutor me for free, I wasn't about to argue. Nick the Prick was getting less and less prickish the longer I knew him.

Then again, I knew that there'd be some sort of catch. After all, this was Nick. Okay, so the number one catch would be that I'd have to spend lots of time with Nick. But for now, I could live with it. I hoped. 'Cause I needed all the help I could get.

Chapter 15

There was a time when I'd liked math and even thought I was pretty good at it. But somewhere around fourth grade someone noticed that my reading speed sucked shit, and I was put into the "remedial" track. It was supposed to be a program where kids like me could actually learn at their own speed, where maybe the teacher could figure out why the hell I read at a snail's pace. Instead it ended up being a place to dump any kid who wasn't a well-behaved model student. This meant that the teachers actually spent most of the class time dealing with disruptive little shits and, since at that time I was pretty damn docile, I was left alone. Which might not have been so bad except that they put me in remedial classes for *all* subjects, including math which I'd been fairly decent in. By the end of that year I was so goddamn bored with being taught math concepts I'd learned two years before, that I stopped paying attention to anything.

Nick could be a pompous ass, but he was a pretty good teacher, with a knack for explaining the math concepts in a way that actually made sense. He was even darn good at the grammar end of things too, and with his help I finally understood the difference between "your" and "you're" as well as "lose" and "loose," and "its" and "it's."

That being said, I damn near cheered when, after an hour of tutoring, Nick got a call to go pick up a body. Even Nick on his best behavior was a lot to take.

I packed up my stuff—including the study guide, the pages and pages of problems I'd worked under Nick's watchful eye, and the "homework" he'd assigned me—and headed to NuQuesCor.

As angry as I was at Marcus, I wasn't stupid enough to ignore what he'd said about violating my probation. I knew something weird was going on at that lab, but any attempt to sneak in would definitely rank up there with some of the stupider things I'd done in my life—and I'd done some hugely stupid shit, trust me.

Therefore I wasn't going to do any sneaking at all. Well, maybe a teensy bit. But I wasn't going to break any laws. Or at least I wasn't *planning* to break any laws. With my history, it was probably best not to make sweeping statements like, *This will be totally legal!*

The broad atrium at the entrance to NuQuesCor looked a hell of a lot different during the day when there were people there, all seeming to be walking with great purpose, or clumped together having Very Important conversations, or waiting not terribly patiently in line at the coffee stand.

Panic shimmered through me briefly, but I managed to choke it down and force myself to move forward to the broad desk that dominated the center of the area.

The security guard looked up as I approached. He gave me a quick once-over assessment and apparently decided that I didn't immediately warrant expulsion since he then gave me a thin, professional smile. "Can I help you?"

Ha! It should be 'May I help you?' I mentally jeered, though I knew this wasn't the time or place to display my newfound knowledge of grammar, courtesy of Nick. Instead I simply echoed his professional-level smile. "I hope so," I said. "I'd like to apply for a job."

His smile shifted immediately to a slight frown, and I received yet another raking glance. "I see. Do you know what position or department you wish to apply to?"

Oh my god, I really was becoming sensitive to grammar. What the hell was happening to me? "Um, custodial . . . ?" That was probably the only department I could hope to qualify for.

A smirk danced across his mouth, and he nodded. "Of course. We happen to have a recent opening in the custodial department." He reached into a drawer and pulled out a single sheet of paper, but paused before handing it to me. "I'm assuming you don't have a resume or a CV?"

I had no idea what a CV was, but I figured I didn't have one. "No, sorry."

The smirk increased by a few millimeters. "Then you'll need to fill this out," he said, passing the sheet over to me. A quick glance confirmed that it was a basic employment form. I'd filled a few million of these out in my years of skipping from shitty job to shittier job.

"You can fill it out right over there if you want," he said, gesturing toward a grouping of tables in the corner by the coffee stand.

"Thanks," I said.

"Oh, wait," he said as I began to turn away. He let out a low chuckle. "Almost forgot to give you the other part." The smirk was at full power now as he set a sheaf of paper that had to be at least ten pages thick in front of me. "This is a secure facility, you understand. We need this information for the background checks we do."

I plastered on a smile and picked up the stack of paper. "Even for the janitors?" I asked gamely, though I knew what the answer would be.

"Absolutely," he replied. "After all, they go pretty much everywhere."

"Right." I tried to see his name on his security badge but it was cocked around, and I couldn't read it. "You've really been a lot of help," I said, gushing just a little. "What's your name?"

"Lombardo," he replied.

"Lombardo . . . ?" I gave a titter that sounded stupid and obnoxious even to me. "That's your first name?"

His eyes narrowed with a touch of disgust. "No. First name is Steve."

"Gotcha!" I chirped. "Thanks a million, Steve. I'll just go and fill these out. Can you answer one more question for me?"

He was really ready to get rid of me, but he sighed and said, "Sure. What is it?"

"Is there any way I can get an interview today? Or maybe just a tour?" I put on my best bubbly attitude. "See, I'm just starting college, and I want to major in biology, and I would *so* love to do research and stuff and would love to see more of what y'all do here!" Damn, I wished I was cuter. Or bustier. Or both.

His expression didn't waver one bit as he pulled out yet another paper and practically slapped it onto the desk. "Tours are only given in groups of four or more and have to be scheduled in advance and on the dates indicated on this sheet." He said it all in a monotone that told me he'd said it about a billion times before. I noticed he didn't answer the part about the interview.

I looked down at the sheet to see a calendar with a smattering of dates marked out in green, and below that a list of rules and guidelines for tours that included things like "Government-issued ID required for all tour members" and "No cameras or recording equipment of any kind allowed" and "All tour members consent to a search of their property and person."

"All righty then," I said, then gathered up the various papers and headed on over to the tables in the corner.

Scowling down at the papers, I settled in to work. So far I was batting zero in my Quest To Break In Without Breaking Laws. I saw Lombardo eyeing me from the desk, so I made sure to pull out a pen and look like I was actually filling the shit out. I figured I'd give it a few more minutes to give the appearance that I was at least making an honest effort, and hopefully some sort of miracle would occur that would allow me to get beyond those security doors. Like, maybe an asteroid hitting the security desk in the lobby. I sighed. At this point that was probably the most likely scenario for me to get past him.

I had a bit of fun making up a name for myself along with all sorts of improbable educational background.

Honors programs? Sure! Summers abroad? Hell, yeah!
The stack of papers for the background check wanted
me to list every job I'd ever worked at, everywhere I'd
ever lived, and provide an insane number of references.
Needless to say, I lied about every single one of those.
Mostly because there was no way in hell I'd be able to
remember all the jobs I'd had.

After about half an hour I'd plowed through the
whole stack of paper. And, sadly, no asteroid had yet
landed on Mr. Steve Lombardo. Gathering up the papers, I made ready to return to the desk and once more
try to bluff my way into an interview, when the man I
recognized as the head of security walked past me and
to the coffee stand. Hard to miss with that square jaw,
military-grade haircut, and Secret Service-type suit.

"Morning, Sandra," he said to the barista. "Medium
Americano, please." He paid then casually scanned the
area while he waited for his order. His eyes rested briefly
on me, and he gave me a polite nod with no hint of rec-
ognition in his eyes. I returned the polite nod with a chin
lift of my own, though I had to do everything in my
power to keep my face as neutral as possible.

Because, after hearing his voice, I knew without a
shadow of a doubt that this was the man who'd held me
up at gunpoint and stolen the body of Zeke Lyons.

Chapter 16

I gave the stack of fiction-heavy employment paperwork to Mr. Lombardo, and got the hell out of there, doing my best to not draw any more attention to myself than possible. Head Security Guy hadn't seemed to recognize me as the chick he'd held up, but I wasn't going to give him any more opportunity for that little fact to click in.

Besides, I'd already confirmed what I'd suspected: someone in that lab was up to something completely fucked up. And Sofia was either involved or in a shitload of trouble.

I headed straight for the sheriff's office and the entry marked "Investigations." I didn't take any chances and identified myself to the receptionist as "Angel Crawford with the coroner's office" before asking to see Detective Ben Roth. However, I was told that Detective Roth was out observing an exhumation.

Ding! "Of Zeke Lyons?"

"That's the one," she replied.

I thanked her and left. I knew exactly where Zeke was buried. Since no one had come forward to claim his body, he'd been given a pauper's burial at Riverwood Funeral Home.

Ten minutes later I pulled up at the cemetery. The area set off for the pauper burials was distinct mostly because it lacked any headstones. Riverwood had a contract with the parish to bury any body that remained unclaimed. However, since they didn't want everyone to get the idea that this would be a great way to get around the cost of having a proper funeral and burial for their loved one, the graves weren't marked, which meant that if the families wanted a grave they could actually visit, they'd have to pay for a plot. Riverwood kept track of who was buried where using markers and GPS coordinates, which was how they now knew where to dig.

I'd stupidly expected there to be men with shovels, but instead a backhoe was busily excavating earth—which really did make a lot more sense. Standing on the other side of the backhoe was Allen Prejean, looking as sour as ever. He was facing away and didn't see me, which suited me just fine.

Detective Roth was on this side of the grave, saving me from having to pass by Allen. Ben looked like he hadn't changed clothes since I'd last seen him—and had probably slept in them as well, to judge by the impressive array of wrinkles that patterned his shirt. As I approached he jerked his head up in a way that made me suspect he'd been dozing standing up, or at least close to it.

It took him a couple of seconds to focus on me. "Oh, god, not you again," he moaned. "Haven't you done enough?"

Stunned, I groped for something to say, finally coming up with, "What the fuck, dude?"

He sighed, scrubbed both hands over his face. "Sorry. But you have no idea the shitstorm that's been going on," he said, face falling into mournful folds.

"Um, you mean because the dead guy was someone who was supposed to already be dead?" I ventured, gesturing at the backhoe.

"God. Yes." He let out a groan. "You should hear the various theories being thrown around. People are batshit insane."

"Sorry, Ben," I said. "I was only hoping to help y'all figure out why someone would want to steal the guy's body."

He heaved a sigh. "I know. But on one side I have people insisting that the first victim was identified wrong and couldn't have possibly actually been Lyons, though the prints that were taken from that body have been checked three different times now and still come up the same as the ones taken from the watch. So now I also have people trying to figure out how the dead guy from the lab could have the headless dead guy's watch—without getting any of his own fingerprints on it."

"And the scar . . ." I said.

"Yeah. That's the part that's freaking everyone the hell out. I've lost count of the number of times I've looked at those crime scene pics and compared them to the Driver's License pics I have of Lyons." Ben spread his hands helplessly. "It looks exactly like the same guy.

So, what? A father and son who happen to have the same scar?"

"They wouldn't have the same fingerprints," I said.

He smiled grimly. "Yeah. Well, I also have the people who say that the older guy's from an alternate dimension, or that the killer who took the head somehow managed to regrow the guy's body." He rolled his eyes. "I'm telling you, the crazy theories are all over the place. But the 'real' Norman Kearny hasn't been back to his apartment since the night his imposter died, according to his neighbors. They also confirmed that he worked at Nu-QuesCor."

I had no doubt that the real Norman Kearny was dead. *But did Zeke kill him to take his place, or did someone at the lab kill him to help cover up an escape attempt of a captive zombie?* Either way, I doubted we'd ever find a body.

"Wow," I said. "Well, I don't know if it'll help you figure out what the deal is with Zeke Lyons, but I'm pretty sure I know who held me up."

He perked up at that. "Seriously? And how do you know that?"

Shit. I couldn't tell him that I had a grand plan of somehow sneaking in, albeit as legally as possible, under the guise of applying for a job there under a fictitious name. "I, uh, was over at NuQuesCor to see a friend of Marcus's." That wasn't a complete lie. Sofia was a friend of Marcus's. And I might have been interested in seeing her. "I overheard the head of security," I told him. "And I swear to god it's the guy. I'd know that voice anywhere."

"His name is Walter McKinney," he said absently. I wondered briefly how he'd know this, then realized he

probably got the guy's name and info on a witness statement. Ben pursed his lips while he considered what I'd
told him. Hope flared in me as it seemed that he wasn't
rejecting it outright. But the hope sputtered as he grimaced. "I don't know if I can get a warrant just on the
basis of recognizing his voice, Angel. The brass is going
to want a lot more to go on before they risk making
waves with NuQuesCor and their backers. Besides, why
would this guy want to steal a body?"

I knew why. *Because he knew that the body would be
ID'ed during the autopsy, and it would come back to
someone already dead.* And it totally would have worked
if I hadn't put the watch into property storage.

I gestured toward the grave. "Look, we already know
something completely screwed up and weird is going on,
right? I mean, we have a guy who somehow died twice."
I knew what they'd find when they opened the casket up.
A body with fingerprints to match Zeke Lyons and the
ones on the watch.

"Supposedly," Ben stated. "Until the coffin is opened
up, I'm reserving judgment." He shook his head. "But
even so . . . I'll admit there's some precedent for a voice
lineup, but with everything else going on with this case,
and . . ." He trailed off, and I knew without a doubt he
was holding back from saying that, with my history, I
wasn't exactly a reliable witness. "With all the weird
stuff," he said instead, "it's just too, well, *X-Files*. No
judge in the world would take this seriously enough to
grant a search warrant."

I could feel a knot building up in my throat, made
worse by the look of pity that Ben gave me. He was being nice, damn it, and it fucking sucked. I was trying so

damn hard to change my life and yet my past still kept biting me in the ass. "It's cool," I said as calmly and evenly as I could manage. I even forced out a smile that hopefully didn't look too sickly.

"I'm sorry, Angel," he said. "I just need more."

I nodded. "It's cool," I repeated. "Lemme know what you find in the coffin," I said, then turned and left without waiting for a response. I knew if I stayed there another second I'd either start crying or punch someone in the throat—though I liked to think it would've been Allen Prejean instead of Ben.

And, damn it, I still had a little pride left, even if my self-control was hanging by a thread.

Chapter 17

I went home, stripped off my clothes, and crawled under the covers in an effort to grab something resembling a nap. I was tired enough to fall right asleep, until a loud banging on my bedroom door yanked me awake.

"Angel!" my dad yelled from the hall. "Wake the fuck up and open this goddamn door now!"

I groaned and sat up. "I'm awake!" I croaked. "What the hell's wrong?" I looked blearily at the clock on my nightstand. Wow, I'd managed to get a whole hour of sleep. Go me.

"Get the fuck out here! I need to talk to you!"

It didn't sound like a *I need to talk to you about what color we should paint the house* either. More like *You're a fuckup and I want to yell at you because it will make me feel better.* Trust me, I knew the difference.

"Gimme a sec," I shouted.

"I mean it!" More pounding, as if he wasn't sure if I was awake. "I'll break this damn door down!"

"Gimme a fucking second, Dad! I'm putting on some fucking clothes so, unless the goddamn house is on fire, chill your ass out!"

I heard him muttering under his breath, but the pounding and yelling both stopped. Maybe he remembered the last time we had a confrontation—the one that had ended with me using only one hand to hold him pinned against the wall a foot off the floor.

I yanked on a pair of sweatpants and a hoodie, quickly spun open the combination lock that I'd installed on my mini-fridge, and downed about half a bottle of brain-shake. Things had been decent and non-violent between my dad and me for the past several weeks, but that didn't mean I trusted it to stay that way. Besides, I felt like shit and needed the push of awesome that being full on brains gave me. It wasn't a physical thing—mostly a fucked up accumulation of the past few days' emotional knocks. Marianne's death, the holdup, the bullshit with Pietro, and the breakup with Marcus. And Ed. That right there was damn good reason to stay tanked up.

"Dear Universe," I muttered as I tugged slippers on. Damn this house was cold. "I'm ready for things to swing back my way now." Yeah, I was selfish like that.

I stomped out to the living room—or at least, as much stomping as fuzzy slippers would allow. "Okay, what's the deal?"

In answer he thrust a newspaper in my face, so closely that I had to take a step back in order to actually see what it was. Scowling, I took it from his hands and peered at it. It was the front page, with a picture in the middle of a house with crime scene tape strung across the front of it—Marianne's house, I realized.

And then I saw what had my dad so riled up. There in the bottom left were two people sitting on the curb: Marcus, and me with my arms around him.

I lifted my eyes to his, utterly refusing to show any sort of guilt or shame or chagrin or anything else. "Yeah? So? A friend of mine was murdered."

That took him aback, but only for a second. He jabbed a finger at the picture. "Yeah, well why the fuck you bein' all huggy and shit with that cop? Y'know who that is, right? He's the motherfucker who arrested me!"

I set the paper down on the table, crossed my arms over my chest. "Uh huh. He was."

My dad's face reddened. "What the fuck are you thinking? Why'd you betray me like that?"

I probably shouldn't have, but I let out a bark of laughter. "Betray you? Are you serious? Dad, get a fucking grip."

He jabbed his finger at me, though I noticed he was careful not to actually touch me. "That cocksucker put me in handcuffs! I spent three days in that shithole jail because of him!"

"No, Dad," I replied, raising my voice. "It wasn't because of him, and you know it! You got arrested 'cause you were beating the shit out of me. Remember that? Huh? So don't go fucking blaming him, and don't you dare tell me who I can and can't talk to or date or anything else like that!"

Pain and guilt spasmed across his face, and I instantly felt guilty for bringing up that time. Though in the next instant I reminded myself that he was the one who'd actually brought it up.

"Look, Dad," I said, lowering my voice and uncrossing my arms. "The thing is, you and me, we're a couple of fuckups, but at least right now we're trying to not fuck up quite so often." I shrugged. "Besides, if it makes you feel better, he was also the cop who arrested me for having that stolen car."

He grumbled, but some of the anger left his face. "It just don't feel right cozying up like that to a cop."

"Dad, Marcus is the one who helped me get off drugs and got me the job I have."

He gave me a look of surprise. "Why the hell would he do that?" Then his eyes narrowed. "Probably trying to get into your pants."

Hmm, so maybe now wasn't the time to tell my dad that Marcus and I had dated. Hell, we were broken up now anyway, so maybe it didn't make any difference now. "No, he just thought I had potential and had gotten a raw deal." I looked back down at the paper. "We're friends now," I said, while hoping it was still true. "And I was giving him a hug because a friend of ours had just been killed." I looked up and met my dad's eyes. "Can't you understand that?"

"I'm not a fuckin' monster, Angel," he replied, voice gruff. "I've dealt with my own share of grief, y'know."

Sighing, I nodded. I knew he was talking about Mom. She'd been the love of his life, and he would have done absolutely anything for her. But she'd also been mentally ill and terribly abusive and neglectful of me, and when my dad had been forced to make a choice between the two of us, he chose me.

My dad blew out his breath and sank down onto the couch. "Look, I'm the kinda guy who holds a grudge. Go and hug on him all you want, but don't expect me to not get pissed."

My calm evaporated. "Dad, that's fucked up. If you want to spend your whole life being angry at people, fine, but some day you're gonna turn around and realize that there's no one left for you to like, because you're determined to be some sort of unforgiving hardass." I shook my head in disgust and stomped back to my room. "Y'know what?" I called back over my shoulder. "I may go see if I can find someone who's pissed me off, just so that I can make nice with them."

So, of course, after being all high and mighty and above reproach with my dad, I felt like a bit of a jackass that I was still mad at Marcus. It didn't seem right that it had only been one day since Marcus and I had our big fight. It also felt odd that I didn't have the automatic assumption that this was just a "thing," and that it would pass, and that we would of course get back together again. That's how most of my relationship with my ex-boyfriend, Randy, had been. We'd dated on and off for years, with a thousand breakups in that time. Yet we'd never split up over the sort of things that needed to be talked out or worked through in order to save a relationship or make it stronger. Our breakups had always ended when one of us had simply grown tired of being alone. Never any fanfare or celebration or deep talks. Simply slipping back into the same old routines—same old ruts, I knew now.

But this thing with Marcus was different. I was different. At least I hoped so. If I was going to be with Marcus—and, to be honest, I wasn't certain if that was what I wanted—I wanted it to be a real relationship. A partnership. Yeah, two people growing up and growing old together. That sort of thing. I *thought* it was possible with Marcus but certainly not the way we were now.

Did that mean it was a good sign that I was suddenly itching to call him and talk things out? I didn't want to write him out of my life. *I do want this to work.*

Or maybe I was a stubborn deluded twit who didn't know how to let bad things go. My history could certainly prove that true.

On the other hand, I did have stuff that I wanted to tell him—stuff I thought he really did need to know. I finally settled for sending him a text, still somehow feeling as if I was breaking some unspoken rule by being the first to cave.

Need to talk to you re headhunter pls. Also stuff re body theft. Important.

I hit send and sighed. Would he read this as me apologizing? Because, honestly, I wasn't ready to apologize for anything. I didn't think I needed to. Again, was I being a stubborn twit?

I watched my phone like a hawk for nearly ten minutes, and right when I'd decided he was going to blow me off it dinged with an incoming text.

But it was from Ben, not Marcus.

Body in coffin. No head. Prints match Zeke Lyons. Fuck my life.

I couldn't help but smile. Poor Ben. I had no idea how the authorities would end up explaining this. However they did it, I had a feeling it would involve lots of lying.

It was another five minutes before my phone dinged again, this time with a response from Marcus.

Sorry, was on a call. Meet at Fowler street boat launch after I get off shift at 8?

Relief began to unknot the tension in my back. *Sure thing.*

The boat launch was deserted at this time of night, but sodium vapor lights had been installed a few years back that kept the large gravel lot from being too creepy. Still, I parked well away from the water's edge and stayed in my car with the doors locked. The mere fact that no one had ever seen gators or giant squid or other nasty beasts in the Kreeger River didn't mean there wasn't something lurking in that dark water, waiting for someone to get too close.

Yes, this zombie was a bit of a scaredy cat.

I brought the GED study guide to pass the time and was struggling through the section on gerunds when Marcus's cruiser pulled into the gravel lot. I quickly marked my place and stuffed the book under a jacket, climbing out of my car just as he got out of his. He was still in uniform. Damn, he sure did rock it.

We both stood awkwardly for a few seconds before I finally blurted, "Thanks for coming to talk to me."

He nodded stiffly. "I've been worried about you." I opened my mouth to speak but he lifted a hand. "And not because I think you can't take care of yourself, because I know you can. There's just a lot of weird shit going on . . ." He paused, took a breath. "And I do care about you."

"Thanks," I said, voice a little rough. "I care about you too." The awkward silence threatened to descend again, and I hurried on. "I saw Ed yesterday."

Marcus stiffened visibly, eyes narrowing. "Where? Did you call it in?"

"At my house," I said. "And no, I didn't call it in. Because I didn't know how to explain why he'd be coming to my house, or why I might have more reason than most other people to feel threatened by him."

His jaw tightened in a grimace. "Okay. I can understand that. But still, if you saw him near your house—"

"No, you don't understand," I said. "He confronted me." I exhaled and ran a hand through my hair. "Marcus, it was really. . . . odd." I quickly related what had happened, complete with him holding me at gunpoint, his insistence that he didn't kill Marianne, and his question about why I didn't kill him.

Marcus scowled blackly when I finished. "I don't like it. He's playing some sort of game."

"But what? He could have shot me so easily," I said. "He didn't. And, I gotta be honest, I never did think he killed Marianne."

His scowl didn't lessen. "You'll excuse me if I don't want to believe he's innocent. He shot me in the head, remember?"

"Yeah yeah yeah, and he shot me twice in the chest," I retorted. "But we're zombies. Marianne isn't."

"I still don't trust him, and you shouldn't either," he shot back.

I threw up my hands. "Who the hell said I was trusting him, Marcus? Would you please give me some goddamn credit? I'm merely saying that maybe we shouldn't have tunnel vision and maybe think about the fucking possibility that someone else killed Marianne! We at least owe her that much!" I realized I was shouting. I took a deep breath to get some control, defiantly crossed my arms over my chest, and leaned back against my car.

Anger pulsed behind his eyes, but to my surprise he gave me a jerky nod. "You're right. It's not fair to her. So what info do you have on your holdup?"

"I went to NuQuesCor yesterday—"

"Angel, for the love of god! I told you—"

"Would you shut up and let me talk?!" My hands had curled into fists, and I was breathing hard. "Fucking hell, Marcus! You're so convinced I'm a goddamn idiot that needs to be watched over and babysat that you never give me any fucking credit for good judgment!" Suddenly I didn't want to go through this anymore. He wasn't going to take me seriously. He would dismiss my identification of the security guy as surely as Ben did. "Forget it," I said, turning and heading for my car door. "You're just as bad as everyone else. I'm the loser felon chick who can't be trusted and has to be protected from herself."

He must have poured on the zombie speed because all of a sudden he was there, his hand on mine as I reached for the door handle. "Angel, please," he said, voice low. "I'm sorry. I'm trying, I swear I am." He lifted a hand and gently wiped at my face, and I abruptly realized that I was crying.

Well, try harder, I wanted to growl, but I knew that would be petty and useless. Instead I took a deep breath in what I already knew was a doomed effort to keep my voice steady. "I went to the lab and pretended to apply for a job," I told him. "While I was there I heard the head of security, Walter McKinney, and I'm almost positive that's the guy who stole the body."

I looked up into his face, searching for any sign he believed me. But he kept his expression emotionless and I couldn't tell either way. "Okay," he finally said. "I'll look into it."

I shook my head. "I'm not asking you to look into it. I just want you to believe me."

He put his hands on my shoulders. "Can I do both? Look, my uncle and Sofia still think that Zeke Lyons was working for a rival faction that was trying to steal Sofia's research. If that's the case then maybe this McKinney character was working for these rebels."

"Rebels?" My lips twitched. "Seriously? A rebel alliance of zombies?"

Marcus didn't share my amusement. "It's a serious issue, Angel. Whoever has access to an alternate source of brains is going to be practically unstoppable."

That killed my amusement. "Okay, so you're looking at warring factions of zombies fighting for control of the fake brains that can make them superundeadhumans." I narrowed my eyes. "Why can't they just fucking share?"

"Well, my uncle disagrees with the goals and policies of these other zombies. He feels it's important for us to remain on our guard against other zombie hunters and—"

I drew back. "So this is all politics? Are you shitting me?"

"No, it's not all politics," he replied, anger tingeing his voice. "Even an improved supply of brains won't make us invincible. There will still be people who think we're monsters. It's important to maintain a low profile and make sure that the zombie population is controlled, as well as the supply of brains."

I could see that this was about to degenerate into the same argument we'd had before, and I didn't have the energy or will to go there again. "Has Sofia managed to successfully make these replacement brains yet?"

A flicker of a grimace passed over his face. "She says she's had a few hiccups, but she feels confident that she's close." he said. He offered me a smile. "Just think, soon you might not be tied to working in a morgue for the rest of your life."

I didn't bother to point out that I liked working there. Because as much as that was true, I also knew I'd jump on the chance to not *have* to work there. "I still don't understand how Zeke could be alive—or dead, rather— if his head was chopped off."

"That one has me baffled too," he admitted. "But I think that's even more evidence that this other faction of zombies is making strides with their own research." He spread his hands and shrugged. "There's so much we still don't know about how the parasite works." His phone beeped, and he pulled it off his belt to peer at the screen. "I need to run." He looked back up at me. "Please—and I swear this isn't me trying to babysit you—please resist the urge to poke at this. You got caught in the middle completely by accident. I doubt that the guy who stole the body had any idea you were a zombie." He squeezed my shoulders. "I don't want you to become a target."

"You'll ask Sofia about McKinney?"

He looked like he wanted to sigh, but he didn't. "I will. Promise. I'm heading to Lafayette tonight to visit my folks, but I'll get up with her before I go."

"All right then," I said. "I'll stop poking at the lab stuff."

He smiled, and for an instant I thought he was going to kiss me, but instead he simply released me and turned and headed back to his car. I watched as he drove off, then climbed into my own.

Good thing I was a lying, untrustworthy bitch. 'Cause there was no fucking way I was letting this shit go. Not as long as I was the one being slammed in the news. Both the zombie mafia and the rebel zombie alliance could suck my white trash undead ass.

Chapter 18

I slept late enough to feel almost rested, and went on in to work my noon shift. However, when I swiped my card at the back morgue entrance, the card reader stubbornly refused to let me in and instead kept blinking a "fuck you" red light at me. Scowling, I got back in my car—'cause I was lazy like that—and drove around to the front.

The receptionist, Rebecca, gave me a bright smile as I walked in. "Hi, sweetheart. Don't normally see you coming through this way."

"Yeah, there's something wrong with my card," I said. "Can you buzz me through?"

The smile slipped from her face. "Of course." She bit her lip as she looked at something on her desk. "There's a message here for you to see Allen when you come in." Her eyes were shadowed with worry, and I didn't need a high school diploma to put the pieces together. Card not working *and* a note to see my supervisor?

"Have I been fired?" I managed to ask.

Her eyes narrowed. "You'd better not have been!" she announced, but there was a shimmer of doubt in her eyes as she pressed the button to let me in.

The door buzzed, and I went on through, anger and dismay fighting it out in a hard knot within my chest. I began to head down the hallway to Allen's office, but Rebecca reached out and stopped me with a hand on my arm.

"No matter what happens, you'll always have friends here, darlin.'"

I forced out a smile for her. She gave me a little pat, then turned back to her desk. I continued on to Allen's office, deeply grateful when I didn't run into anyone else on the way.

His door was open. I didn't bother knocking on the doorframe or anything polite like that. I simply came in and plopped down in the chair in front of the desk. "Hi, Allen. My card isn't working. And I have a message to see you. Have I been fired?" And hey, I managed to say it without sounding like I was about to burst into tears.

He frowned at the still open door, but I wasn't about to get up and close it so that he could say the bullshit he had to say in private.

"You're not fired," he said, returning his gaze to me.

"But?" Because it was obvious there was a gigantic "but" coming.

His mouth tightened into a thin line. "But . . . the coroner feels that it would be best to let all of this . . . messiness blow over."

"You mean until after the election's over?" I said. I stuffed my hands into the pockets of my jacket. I wanted to hide that they were clenched to keep them from shaking. The election was over three months away. If I was super careful I might be able to make my stash of brains last that long. *But then what if he loses?* His opponents were nobodies, and he was heavily favored to win, but stranger things had happened. And why would his replacement possibly want to take a chance on hiring *me*?

Allen leaned back. "You're taking a leave of absence for personal reasons. Once Dr. Duplessis secures the reelection, you'll have the option to return from your leave to your former position." He cleared his throat. "Of course it would be unpaid leave. I'm sorry to say that you haven't been with us long enough to have that much vacation time."

I stared at him while everything he said tumbled over in my head. "Wow," I finally said. "I must admit, I wasn't expecting this."

"Haven't you been reading the papers?" he asked with a snide curl of his lip. "It's been on the front page since the incident."

"Yes, I've been reading the papers," I shot back. "Despite what you think of me, I'm not illiterate. I totally expected that at some point I was going to get fucked. What I didn't expect was to be asked to fuck myself." I stood up, aware that I was beginning to shout, but I had no desire to control myself. "Well, you know what? It's not going to happen. I'm not going to meekly take myself off so that the coroner can avoid a nonexistent scandal. *I was held up at fucking gunpoint!* Why the fuck doesn't he grow a pair of fucking balls and come out and say that? And, y'know what? He can grow a pair of fucking balls and fire me to my goddamn face if he wants me gone!" I was beyond shouting at this point. I was shrieking like an insane bitch. Hey, at least now there was legitimate reason to fire me.

I didn't give him a chance. I spun and stormed out, holding my fury and hurt close to me, and didn't look around even though I knew there were plenty of shocked observers leaning out of office doors. I thought I heard Reb whisper, "Good luck, babe," as I stormed past her and through the security door, but I couldn't be sure. I liked to think she did.

I drove out to my storage locker and numbly counted up my stash even though I had a pretty solid idea of how much I had saved. If I was careful and wasn't too active and didn't get hurt, I could probably last a couple of months. And what then?

And then I'm fucked. Unless Sofia manages to get her fake brain formula right by then.

Why the hell had I gone off on Allen like that? Yeah, sure, the whole "leave without pay" thing was bullshit, but at least it would've most likely been temporary. Life was full of bullshit, and sometimes it was smarter to suck it up and wait for a better opportunity.

With a sense of complete despair paired with a fair amount of self-loathing, I shut and locked the freezer and the storage unit. I stopped at the first store that sold cheap clothing, bought a t-shirt, and changed out of my coroner's office shirt. I briefly considered chucking it into the trash, but then changed my mind and shoved it into the trunk of my car. I really had loved the job, and just because Allen and the coroner were jerks didn't mean I needed to scrub it from my entire life.

Now if I could only find something that would help

take my mind off the complete clusterfuck my life had become.

I couldn't get drunk. Drugs didn't work on me anymore. Even cigarettes did nothing but burn my brains up and make me feel dead. And for that matter, even feeling dead wasn't an escape since it always came with a hunger that wouldn't go away until it was satisfied.

In other words, being bummed and depressed as a zombie sucked complete ass.

I finally stopped driving and pulled into the parking lot of Lou-Ann's Café. That was one thing the morgue job had been good for—after so many months of working odd hours I knew where all the good greasy spoons were. Not to mention which ones had bathrooms that were fairly clean.

Lou-Ann's had decent bathrooms, and more importantly, a really good key lime pie that would have to be my substitute for drugs and alcohol. I sat at the counter and ignored everyone else around me while I focused on enjoying every bite of the damn pie. I was vaguely aware that someone sat next to me and did his best to hit on me, but I ignored him and kept eating and eventually he got the message and slunk off.

The waitress didn't make any attempt to engage me in conversation, which I appreciated more than she could possibly know. I made sure to give her an insanely large tip, and when I headed out I was somewhat calmer. And fuller. And at least I didn't have to worry about diabetes.

I was nearly to my car when I heard an aggravatingly familiar voice from behind me. "Look who it is—the cunt from the newspaper."

Looking back, I saw Clive's sneering face. I was pretty

sure he hadn't been in the café while I was there, so I figured he was on his way in. "Get it right, Clive," I said. "It's 'fucking bitch.'"

He snorted. "I'll just go with fucking loser. It's only a matter of time before you end up back in jail, y'know."

I rolled my eyes and continued to my car. I'd just opened the door when he spoke again.

"Maybe you can share a cell with that fuckup loser of a dad you got."

Goddammit, but I was getting really sick of people shitting on me and my dad. I stopped, turned, made a quick scan of the parking lot then took two steps toward him. "What did you say?"

Clive's mouth spread into a sneering grin. He straightened his shoulders as he closed the distance between us, deliberately flexing and pushing his chest out a bit—which almost made me laugh. I weighed barely a hundred pounds. He was bowing up to me?

"I said your dad's a fucking loser—"

That was all he got out before my fist connected with his face as hard as I could manage. I wasn't full up on brains, but I was pretty damn close, and I was able to hit him hard enough to send him reeling back, clutching at his nose.

"You fucking bitch!" he screeched as blood began to fountain through his fingers. "You broke my fucking nose!"

I grimaced and looked down at my right hand. I'd never really learned how to punch, and it showed. Two of the bones in my hand were clearly bent at angles that weren't supposed to be there, and blood seeped from a wide cut across my knuckles. It hurt like fuck-all but even as I peered at it, the pain began to fade to a dull background ache.

Clive let out a wheezing noise that I suddenly realized was him laughing. "You stupid bitch," he gurgled through his bloody fingers. "I'm calling the cops. I'm pressing charges. And your loser ass will be going back to jail."

I lifted my eyes to his. "Okay. Call them," I said, absolutely loving how calm I sounded. "I'll wait right here."

Clive fumbled his phone out of his pocket. I watched him thumb nine-one-one on the keypad, listened to him tell the dispatcher that he'd been attacked and was holding the perpetrator—me—and needed the cops to come so that I could be properly arrested. While he did this, I casually reached into my car and pulled my bottle of brain smoothie out of the cup holder. I took several long gulps, resisting the urge to grin as I felt the bones pulling back together.

"Don't you fucking try and run from me, bitch," Clive told me after he disconnected. "They said they have a unit right around the corner."

I shrugged and took another pull from the bottle. Might as well finish it off just in case he decided he didn't want to wait for the cops and would rather take his fury out on me in person. I was careful to hold the bottle in my left hand, and deliberately kept my right cradled against me to make it look as if it was still hurt.

He fumbled his car open and snagged a towel out of the backseat, held it to his face. "Then again," he said, "maybe you should run." He let out a nasty laugh. "Y'ever been tasered? I'd fucking pay money to see that."

I set the empty bottle back in the cup holder. A quick

glance told me that there was still a smear of blood on my knuckle, which I left there for now. But when the two sheriff's cars pulled into the parking lot, and Clive took his eyes from me, I took that chance to quickly lick the blood off. Gross, I know, but I didn't want to wipe the blood on my clothes anywhere it might show.

I vaguely recognized the deputies who stepped out, but I doubted that they could do the same with me since I wasn't dressed in my coroner's office gear anymore. I didn't say anything while Clive indignantly told them the story of how I'd hauled off and slugged him. He actually stayed pretty close to the truth, probably because it really didn't need any sort of elaboration. He knew perfectly well that even a misdemeanor battery arrest would violate my probation. And, with the damage to his nose, it could possibly even be considered a felony.

The two deputies listened to his account with the occasional glance toward me, clearly thinking something on the order of, "this tiny thing broke your nose?" But they let him finish before turning to me.

"He made the whole thing up," I said before they could speak. "I was out here making a phone call when he came stumbling around the corner with a bloody nose, then he started babbling about how I'd hit him."

Clive puffed up. "Oh yeah? Check her hand! She broke her fucking hand on my nose!"

I locked eyes with Clive and extended both my hands to the deputies. I didn't say a word while they carefully examined my knuckles, fingers, and the condition of the various bones.

They exchanged a look, then turned back to Clive. "Not a damn thing wrong with her hands, sir," one said.

"There's no possible way she punched you—and certainly not hard enough to break your nose. Why don't you tell us what *really* happened?"

Things really went downhill for Clive after that, though for me it was a truly beautiful thing. I watched in serene glee as he argued, then frothed, then, when they attempted to cite him for disturbing the peace, he fought, which earned him the tasering he'd taunted me about.

And, on top of all that, they found steroids and painkillers in his vehicle—enough to get him charged with possession with intent to distribute.

All in all it was the best high I could have ever asked for.

Chapter 19

As I drove home, distant flashes of lightning were putting on a spectacular show in the clouds to the west. And, at least for the moment, I was in the perfect mood to appreciate the beauty of it. Every time I started to think about how badly I'd screwed the pooch with my job, I summoned up the memory of Clive shrieking like a little bitch as the Taser probes hit him. Yeah, I'd lectured my dad about being forgiving and all that shit, but sometimes forgiveness was overrated.

My phone rang, and I was more than a little surprised to see that it was Sofia. I made a face, regretting my decision to actually put her number into my contacts list. I was in a really good mood right now, and I doubted that she had anything to say to me that would keep that good mood going. And I sure as hell didn't want to get sucked into a "Let's do coffee" date or something equally lame. Therefore, I channeled my pettiness and immaturity and let it go to voicemail. That was a decent compromise, right? I was willing to listen to a recording of her. I simply didn't want to actually talk to her.

I waited for the ding that would tell me I had a new voicemail, but instead my phone rang—Sofia again. I sighed, dialed down my pettiness, and answered.

"Angel, I need your help!" she gasped. "Oh my god, I don't know who else to turn to. I can't reach Marcus, and there's someone outside of my house and—"

"Whoa, wait! Sofia, slow down. Marcus is in Lafayette. What the hell is going on?"

I heard her take a shuddering breath. "I think I'm in danger. I keep hearing sounds outside my house."

"Have you called the cops?" I asked.

"Yes!" she wailed. "I called them, and two cops came and they checked around the house and they said they didn't see anything. But ten minutes after they left I started hearing it again. I ... I think someone is maybe just trying to scare me." She gulped. "And they're succeeding. I know we barely know each other, but is there any way you could ... come over here?"

You have got *to be kidding me*, I thought with unchecked annoyance.

"Please," she said, voice cracking. "I know it's stupid, but I'd feel so much safer if ... if you could come by for a bit. The cops won't stay but ..."

But I'm a zombie and hard to kill and could actually offer a bit of security. I sighed. "Okay." Shit. When did I become so nice? "Where do you live?"

"Oh my god, thank you thank you! I live in Breckenridge Estates. I'll text you the address."

I racked my brain for where the hell that was. Oh

yeah, it was a new subdivision out off Highway 1790. "Okay, I'm probably only about ten minutes away."

"I'll be watching for you. Honk when you pull up, okay?" she said. "I don't even want to peek out the window at this point."

I bit back a frustrated sigh. "Sure. See you soon." And then I disconnected before I could be pulled into more paranoid angst.

But is it really paranoia? I had to wonder. There was definitely some weird shit going on. And if I had to be honest with myself, my dislike of her stemmed mostly from our encounter at Pietro's . . . and, if I really *had* to continue being honest with myself, from my jealousy of her and her friendship with Marcus, even though I didn't believe for a second that the two were anything more than friends. Didn't matter. I envied their closeness, however platonic it was.

I mused on this as I drove—easy enough to do since there wasn't much else to occupy my attention out here. Highway 1790 ran from one end of the parish to the other, with a big stretch in the middle through woods and swamp that I affectionately called Bum-Fuck Nowhere. Back in my don't-give-a-shit days, I used to come out here and get whatever car I was driving to its top speed—which was awesome when I was in a Camaro that Randy had been fixing up, but was pretty damn lame in my Honda.

I didn't stick strictly to the speed limit, but I did my best not to go more than ten miles per hour over. Which was probably a damn good thing when I saw something shimmering in the road ahead of me. Unfortunately I was still almost on top of it before I saw the glint of spikes.

I slammed on the brakes out of pure instinct, but I

was already too close for that to do any good. A second later the road spikes ripped through my front tires with a *bang* that I felt as much as heard, quickly replaced by the shriek of metal on pavement and the thump of rubber slapping the side of my car.

I fought the steering wheel and pulled the car over to the side of the road, gasping raggedly in reaction. *What the fuck?* Why would police spikes be out here with no cop car in sight? *No cop car means it's not cops*, I told myself. I was on a straight and empty stretch of road with at least fifty feet of knee-high grass on either side before it turned into scrub marsh and scattered trees. A perfect ambush spot. I needed to get the hell out of there, and my only option was to run for it and hope to lose whoever was after me in the marsh. *Gators. Giant Squid. Oh, man, this is gonna suck.*

My purse was god-only-knew-where on the floor, along with my phone. I automatically reached for the water bottle of brain smoothie, cursing as I remembered that I'd finished it off after punching Clive and hadn't replaced it. I was still pretty tanked up, but it sure would have been nice to have some extra on hand. 'Cause I had a feeling I was about to burn up a whole lot.

Bolting out of the car, I took off at a sprint for the woods on the other side of the highway. I heard a gunshot and bit back a screech of panic as I increased my speed. But the next gunshot came with a searing pain in my left calf that sent me sprawling into an awkward tumble on the asphalt.

It's Ed. My thoughts whirled frantically as I stumbled back to my feet and started running again. *He's finally come back to finish me off.*

I could hear footsteps behind me, the loping pace of someone who knows that they don't need to run their prey down. Something hard hit me in my lower back, and I fell again, landing heavily on my hands and knees in the gravel of the highway shoulder. Pain flared briefly, but then it faded to a dull sense of pressure even as everything around me shifted to a greyscale monotone. I could still see and hear and smell, but it was as if everything was abruptly dialed back to the absolute basics. This gunshot wound was obviously a lot worse, and my body was abandoning all those extra resources right now. I wanted to scream at it that it needed to put all the energy into my legs, because once my head got chopped off it wouldn't make a difference.

I managed to get to my feet again and resumed my race to the woods in what was now an awkward shambling jog.

"Oh, please don't make me chase you down," my pursuer called out.

That's not Ed, I realized in cold shock, though I didn't slow down. That was McKinney. What the hell?

"I have no intention of killing you," he continued. I risked a glance back. He was a good fifty feet from me, still on the other side of the highway. He'd probably been hiding in the grass. And now I could see a dark car parked a distance away, almost invisible in the gloom. "Right now I'm simply trying to slow you down and weaken you," he said. "If you resist, I'll have to keep shooting you, so I suggest you stop and come along quietly."

Like that was going to happen, I thought grimly, then jerked as something punched me in the back again. I stumbled to my knees, breath coming in a rasping growl. I looked back at him as he stepped onto the highway. Hunger snarled and flailed as what I now knew was my parasite clamored for resources to repair the damage. Could I take him? How many more bullets would he be able to pump into me before I reached him? Too many. *No*, my instinct breathed, *let him come to you*. Then I could put everything into one last attack . . . I could smell his brain. That's what I needed to survive this.

The sudden roar of a car engine and the sound of more gunshots slashed through my grotesque plotting. McKinney jerked and collapsed as time seemed to slow—or maybe it was my perceptions that were completely screwed. It felt like I only had time to blink once as a black Dodge Charger screeched to a stop between McKinney and me. The driver darted out, and I barely had time to grunt in surprise before he scooped me up, threw me over his shoulders in a fireman's carry, then dumped me into the backseat of his car. In the next instant he was back in the driver's seat and flooring the gas pedal. I thought I could hear some more gunshots, but at the speed my unexpected savior was going, I knew we wouldn't be in range for long.

I curled up on the back seat to stay out of the line of fire, but also to give me a few seconds to fight back the hunger. I could smell my rescuer's brain, but there was still enough of Me in control to know I was better off letting him live. As soon as I was fairly sure that I wasn't going to attack the driver, I struggled upright. I looked behind us, but I couldn't even see my car anymore.

"I don't know who you are, but you saved my ass back there," I rasped. God, my voice sounded like hell. I peered at the back of the driver's head. "So, who the hell are you, and how did you know my ass needed saving?"

The driver let out a low sigh. "Hi, Angel. Long time no see."

If I'd been able to feel anything, I'm sure I would have felt as if ice had been poured over me. The man who'd just saved me from whatever fate McKinney had in store for me was Ed.

Great. If this isn't out of the frying pan and into the fire, I don't know what is.

I was pretty sure I could survive jumping out of a car going at—I glanced at the speedometer—ninety-three miles an hour. It would suck giant donkey balls, but with enough brains I'd recover. *But I'm already in bad shape.*

"Please don't jump out of the car, Angel," Ed said, obviously knowing what my reaction to seeing him would be. "I'm not going to kill you, I swear."

I paused in my reach for the handle. "Why the hell should I believe you?" *Or better yet, why shouldn't I let the hunger have its way?*

He slowed to make a turn, then sped up again, carefully checking his rearview mirror. "I need to talk to you."

"About what?" I asked, distrust thick in my voice.

He licked his lips. "About . . . you, and Marcus . . . and Marianne." He looked at me in the mirror. "I didn't kill her, Angel. I swear I didn't."

"I know," I said without thinking. "I mean . . . I had a hard time believing you did. It didn't make sense for you to kill her." I ran a hand over my torso. There were two wounds on my stomach where the bullets had exited, but I wasn't bleeding anymore. That wasn't necessarily a good thing. Especially since I was extremely aware that there was a nice healthy brain in the car with me. "Ed, you need to let me go. I've been shot."

"I need to talk to you," he repeated. "I'm taking you someplace safe."

I tried to swallow, but it was getting difficult. "You don't understand. It won't be safe for you. I need to eat."

His hands tightened on the steering wheel briefly. "Ah. You mean brains."

"Yeah. I have a stash. I just need to get to them—"

"I'll get them for you," he said. "But I need to get you someplace safe first."

"Why should I trust you?" I demanded. The rasp of my voice was getting harsher and my tongue didn't want to work properly. "You tried to kill me and Marcus not long ago."

He took another turn, then another. At this point I had absolutely no idea where we were. "I know. But . . . please. I swear I'm not going to kill you. I *have* to talk to you."

Fuck. At this point I probably didn't have much choice. If I tried to escape now I'd be so mindless from hunger I'd end up attacking the first live person I came across. A shudder ran through me. *No. Not going there.*

A few minutes later he pulled into a long winding driveway that led to a small single-story brick house with no lights on. He drove around to the back, got out, then opened the car door for me. "Do you need help?"

I shook my head stiffly. "You need to stay back," I managed, as the hunger tightened my stomach. "I need brains."

"Tell me where."

I climbed out of the back seat, gritting my teeth against the urge to leap on him. If I told him where the freezer was and this was all part of some wild ruse, he'd be able to destroy my entire stash. I'd definitely be fucked then.

You're already fucked, Angel, I silently snarled. "Stor-This on Highway 1291. Unit five three four." I quickly gave him the combinations to the gate and the unit.

He gave a terse nod. "That's not far. Get inside. Keep it dark. I'll be back as soon as I can."

I headed to the house, but instead of getting back into the car, he threw a blue tarp over it and headed for the garage. "I'm switching cars," he called back over his shoulder. "That asshole will be looking for that one. Now get the hell inside, please?" He pulled the wide garage doors open, and less than a minute later rumbled off in an old Chevy truck that looked almost as bad as my dad's, if that was even possible.

I turned and shambled into the house, praying that I hadn't made a colossal mistake.

Chapter 20

It wasn't a big house. Not much bigger than my own, though certainly newer and in better condition. My senses were pretty dulled, but the occasional flash of lightning through the gaps in the heavy curtains showed me that the house was almost completely empty of furniture except for a ragged sofa and a folding chair in what appeared to be the living room.

The thunderstorm had finally made it here, and rain was coming down in driving gusts, but my stomach didn't give a crap. Hunger gnawed at me, yowling at me to go, hunt, find someone with a brain for me to eat. I felt a tickle on my cheek and rubbed my hand across it only to come away with a three-inch long patch of flesh. Numb horror burrowed through me as I flung it away. *My face. That was part of my face!* I sat in the middle of the floor and wrapped my arms around my legs, suddenly glad that I was wearing long sleeves because it kept me from having to see skin sliding off my bones. How long would it take for Ed to get back? Would I be so far gone into the hunger that I'd attack him?

I jerked in surprise as the back door cracked open. I caught a quick glimpse of Ed as he tossed a plastic bag inside and quickly slammed the door closed again.

A guttural snarl came from my throat at the smell of him, but before I could lunge for the door, I caught sight—and scent—of the packages in the bag. Shuddering in relief, I tore open the box and into the brain-covered pizza, scraping the toppings off to shove into my mouth. I didn't need the crust right now. That would only get in the way.

Sensation began to return, and the hunger settled into something manageable. I reached for the curry chicken next since I knew there wasn't any chicken in it. A tingle in my cheek told me that my face was putting itself back together. I knew that Ed knew I was a zombie, but that didn't mean I wanted him to see me rotting and falling apart.

I waited until the hole in my face was completely closed up before I called out, "It's okay now. It's safe."

He eased the door open, eyeing me cautiously. I peered at him in the gloom. "I take it there's no electricity?" I asked.

"Nope. This is a foreclosure," he told me. "Been empty for close to a year. And best not to have any lights until we can seal around the windows." He held up a large plastic bag. "I have a lantern and duct tape. We should tape the curtains down around the windows before we turn on any light. This place is pretty secluded, but no sense taking any chances."

Well, now I knew where he'd been staying the past

couple of weeks. I gave a nod toward the gun in his other hand. "You planning on shooting me again?"

"Only if you come after me," he replied.

I nodded and kept eating. "Understandable. Did you happen to grab any of the plastic containers? Those have more brains in them."

Disgust flickered across his face, but he didn't voice it. He continued in and shut the door behind him. "I picked up a cooler. I brought as many containers as I could fit into it. What's the stuff that looks like spare ribs?"

"Spare ribs," I said. "I didn't have room in my freezer at home."

"That's disgusting," he breathed.

"Really?" I said through a mouthful of brain and cheese. "I'm pretty fond of spare ribs, myself."

He winced. "No, I mean that you have it in the same freezer as all the . . ." He gestured toward my little picnic. "Remind me to never eat at your house."

I grinned. "It's all wrapped or sealed up. I doubt that any brain bits could possibly get on anything else."

"It's still freaky," he muttered.

I wiped my mouth, did a careful physical assessment. My various wounds seemed to be healed up, and my senses were back to normal. Perhaps a little higher than normal. I was well and truly tanked up right now, which I figured was a smart move considering whose company I was in.

"No," I said calmly, "what's freaky is that you're having this polite and friendly conversation with me, and just a few weeks ago you called me a monster and shot me. Twice." I gave him a hard look. He had his gun, but I knew how fast I could move right now if I wanted to.

Apparently, so did Ed. He set the gun and bag on the folding chair before he sat heavily on the floor. "Yeah," he said in a low voice as he leaned back against the couch. "I did."

I stood, brushed myself off. He watched me warily as I moved to the folding chair, visibly relaxed when I pulled the duct tape out of the bag instead of going for the gun.

"Okay, help me try to figure something out here," I said as I moved to a window and started taping. "What happened to your parents?"

Grief and horror skimmed across his face. "The official report said it was a boating accident. But that's not what it was. I saw it."

"Saw what?" I prompted.

His eyes lifted to mine. "I saw a zombie eating my dad's brain."

I kept my face immobile though I wanted to wince. I knew zombies sometimes killed people for brains, especially when they were hungry enough. I'd been that hungry once—okay, twice, including tonight—and had barely held on to my humanity until I could find brains. "Your mom too? It killed them both?"

"My mom was shot," he said in a flat voice. "In the chest. Twice. I could see the . . . the wounds. The gun was lying on the deck. Then I saw my dad . . . his head was bashed in. The boat anchor was all bloody and . . ." He took a shaking breath. "I figure it shot her, then my dad tried to save her, and it turned on him . . ." He trailed off and squeezed his eyes closed.

I continued to tape down the edges of the curtain as I turned over what he'd said. "Wait. I'm confused. Were you *all* on a boat? Where did the zombie come from? How did you make it out alive?"

"No, no," he said. "They were out on the dock behind our house. We lived on the Tchefuncte River, and my folks had a pontoon boat that they liked to take out in the evenings. I heard a gunshot, then some yelling and ran out and saw . . . saw the zombie." He swallowed. "I didn't know it was a zombie. I just thought it was some psycho."

"Uh huh. And how did the story become a 'boating accident'?"

He closed his eyes for a moment. "I ran back to the house and called the cops. Shit, I was seventeen, and I knew no one would believe me if I said a monster was eating my dad. I just told them my parents were dead, that something awful had happened." A shudder ran through him. "I was hysterical, but still, I knew I couldn't tell them the truth." He stood suddenly, though to my relief he left the gun on the chair. "I ran back out with a baseball bat, and . . ." His hands clenched into fists. "I came out just in time to see the boat going full speed toward a pier on the other side of the river. Saw it crash and burst into flame . . ."

"And your parents' bodies were recovered on the boat?"

He nodded.

I scratched my head. "Look, it's real possible that the zombie did kill your parents, but just on first sniff, I'm seeing some weird stuff about all this."

"Of course it's weird," he began, but I waved him silent.

"No, wait, hear me out. First off, why would it shoot your mom but not your dad?"

His forehead creased. "Maybe it was out of ammo."

I shrugged. "Maybe. But the next thing is bigger: I don't see how it could have put them on the boat and sent it crashing into the bridge."

Ed leveled a frown at me. "What do you mean? That wouldn't have been hard at all. Drag them on board, set a fire, jam the throttle, jump off."

"No, I get that part. But here's something you don't understand about zombies." I smiled thinly. "I guess I'm sort of an expert witness about this shit now."

He crossed his arms over his chest. "Go on."

"Any zombie that was hungry enough to kill someone wouldn't have had enough . . . mind to be able to figure out all of that—the getting rid of the evidence stuff." I moved to the other window and began taping those curtains down as well. "So either someone else did the stuff with the boat, or a rogue zombie was killing people before he was crazy hungry—which I admit is possible, but it seems like he would have done a better job picking his victims. Or, there wasn't a zombie at all." I watched him as I said this last one. "Ed, how on earth did you know about zombies back then? What made you seriously consider that as a possibility?"

"I didn't. Not really," he admitted. "After the accident and the investigation, I managed to convince myself I'd imagined it. Shock, hysteria. That sort of thing. After a while I simply accepted that it had been a horrible accident."

"What changed?" I asked, frowning.

Ed grimaced, rubbed at his eyes. "About six months ago I got a package in the mail. It was a notebook—a personal journal of my dad's."

I pressed the tape down on the bottom of the curtain, then got the lantern out of the bag and flicked it on. It wasn't a lot of light, but it was better than pitch darkness, and enough for me to see what Ed was wearing—black and grey striped pants tucked into studded boots, black shirt with dark red skulls. It also looked like he'd picked up a few more piercings somehow. He definitely didn't look anything like the Ed I'd known before. "Okay," I said, "and something in that journal convinced you that zombies exist?"

"It was only a few dozen pages. Most of the rest had been ripped out. But my dad wrote about how the zombies were real and that the person they used to be was dead and gone and all that was left was a monster." Even in the dim light I could see the guilty flush crawl across his face. "And, he, uh, wrote about how it was spreading like a plague, and he had theories about how to kill them." He gave an uncomfortable shrug, not looking at me. "The basic gist was: slow them down then cut their heads off."

"And . . . that's when you decided to become a zombie hunter?" I asked, my voice thick with disbelief.

He narrowed his eyes, scowled. "No. No, of course not. I mean, I didn't know what was going on, and I'd made myself forget what happened on the boat, so I figured this was just some sort of novel or story that my dad had decided to write. I mean, really, who the hell could believe that?" He paused, looked down at his hands. "Then, about a week later, I got another package. This time it was some of my mother's correspondence."

"Wait," I said with a slight frown. "What kind of doctor was your mother?"

"Neurologist. She had a practice, but she enjoyed the

research end of things more," he explained. "Anyway, this was printouts of several emails. The recipient was blacked out, so I have no idea who it was intended for, but it was a series of conversations with her going through a number of theories she had on how zombies actually functioned and why they needed brains—"

"Prions," I interrupted, perhaps a bit smugly. "The parasite needs prions as building blocks."

A grimace flickered across his face. "Um, right. And after reading all that I . . . I started to realize that I really had seen what I thought I'd seen."

I opened my mouth to speak but he held up his hand. "And, no, I *still* didn't immediately go out and start slaying zombies."

"Then why?" I asked in exasperation.

He sighed heavily. "It was almost a month afterwards that I got another letter directing me to a secure website. All sorts of passwords and ID verification stuff, and there was a message for me there that told me my parents had been zombie hunters—part of a secret society that had been trying to wipe out the, um," his eyes flicked briefly to me, "zombie menace before it turned into an unstoppable plague." He groaned and dropped his head back, covering his eyes with his forearm. "Fuck, Angel, by that time I was so tied up in knots, and so much of it made sense along with the stuff from my parents . . . I bought it, hook, line and sinker, and told them I was in."

I thought about this for a moment. Could it be true? Were his parents also zombie hunters? Pietro had certainly made it sound as if there was an organized cabal-type thing. "And you used Marianne's dog to let you know who the zombies were," I said.

"Right." He sighed. "Kudzu is a cadaver dog. If some-one smelled like a dead person, that gave me a reason to look into them. Then I'd watch them for a bit, see if they ever started smelling or rotting. I'd sometimes check them out on Lexis Nexis to see if there were any hiccups in their info that would be there if they were older than they looked. That sort of thing." He stood and moved to one of the windows, peeled a small section of tape back and peered cautiously out through a thin gap.

"Zeke Lyons was one of your victims, right?" I asked. He nodded without looking back at me. "Did you know that somehow he regrew his body?"

Ed whipped his head around to stare at me. "Regrew? What do you mean? Like a lizard regrows a tail?"

"Yeah, except that it was the *whole* body, with the right fingerprints and everything." I had a sudden bizarre image of a full-sized head on a teeny-tiny body as it grew back, like a bobble-head doll. "Same head, though. Had a scar on his chin, same as on his driver's license. And his body was still in its coffin at Riverwood." I paused. "So, what did you do with the heads?"

He pressed the tape back down. "I don't know how he regrew a body, but I had to deliver the heads to a drop point." He flushed. "I, uh, got points for verified kills." He groaned and raked a hand through his hair. "I don't know why I didn't even think to question it. I actually burned the head of the first one I killed, but they insisted that wasn't good enough, and I had to deliver the heads in order to ensure proper destruction."

I could feel my eyebrows climbing to my hairline. "And who the hell is 'they'?"

Ed shook his head. "No clue. My only contact was

through that website. God damn it, I thought I was doing this great and awesome thing, ridding the world of a terrible threat." He looked over at me, eyes full of guilt and agony. "But then you didn't kill me when you had the chance. And then you even saved Marcus. That's not something a monster would do." He stooped, dimmed the lantern slightly. "I'd gone so far off the deep end, it took me awhile to figure out that whoever these other zombie hunters were, they didn't have the whole story. And then I started, finally, to wonder about the heads." He scowled at himself. "And that's when things really went to shit."

"How so?"

"I used that secret website. Told them I'd been busted but also told them I thought we were wrong about zombies being monsters. And I also asked about the heads." He gave a dry laugh that turned into a sob. "I snuck into Marianne's house while she was gone. Used her computer."

"Oh, no," I breathed.

He nodded, a stiff jerky motion. "She came home just a few minutes later. I stayed, had to talk to her. God, I missed her so much." He paused. "I was going to marry her. We'd already talked about it, knew it was what we both wanted. But I knew I had to leave, for her sake." He let out a shuddering breath. "I told her what I'd done, told her I loved her. Told her I was sorry. I was on my way out the back, when I heard her answer the door." He scrubbed a hand over his face. "Then I heard the shot. I ran back . . . but it was too late. He didn't see me, but I saw him." His expression turned grim. "Same guy who shot you tonight."

I stood. "His name is Walter McKinney. He's the head of security at NuQuesCor. But ... why did he kill Marianne?" I asked, baffled.

Ed's throat bobbed as he swallowed. "Maybe they thought I'd talked to her and told her what was going on. Or maybe they wanted to be sure the heat stayed on me to keep me out of their way." He shook his head. "Or maybe they simply wanted to fuck with me as much as possible."

"Those fuckers." I fell silent, thinking. Pieces of the puzzle were finally starting to settle into place. "Dude. You were used. You gave them the heads, right?"

He stared at me for several seconds, then a grim look settled over his face. "They didn't destroy them, did they?"

"They're doing zombie research at that lab, and they needed zombie brains!" I paced in the small living room. Did that mean Sofia was behind all of this? But surely Pietro wouldn't have approved of the murder of zombies, even ones that weren't part of his group. "You chopped off Zeke's head, gave it to them, and they somehow regrew him a body." And how would that work? Just give the parasite enough brains to fix things up? *I guess if it could repair a bullet hole in Marcus's head ...* Wow, those were some industrious little fuckers. "But something went wrong," I continued. "The body we picked up at NuQuesCor was Zeke Lyons, and he was old—at least twenty years older than he should've been. And when he fell off those stairs, he died." I sat, jiggling my legs in excitement. "Oh my god, fake brains! Sofia's fake brains! She used them to grow a new body for this dude." Then I grimaced. "But she said the research wasn't finished. Why would she use fake brains that she knew wouldn't work right? That part doesn't make any sense."

"Sofia Baldwin?" Ed asked.

I nodded. "You know her?"

"Yeah, we all went to high school together," he said. "She's fucking brilliant. How the hell does she know about zombies?"

"I guess Marcus told her," I said, shrugging. "She's known since right after he was turned, apparently."

"Oh." He nodded slowly. "So . . . he told her, and not me."

I grimaced in sympathy. *And how different would everything be now if he* had *confided in Ed?* I thought. Would McKinney and Sofia or whoever have found someone else to collect zombie heads for them?

Ed took a deep breath and straightened. "You just said the guy was old and died," Ed pointed out. "Maybe that's how she knew the research wasn't finished. Maybe Zeke was the test subject."

"I guess that fits," I said slowly. I had the feeling I was missing something, and it was driving me nuts. I didn't like Pietro, but this didn't seem like something he would tolerate one little bit. Maybe some other zombie faction was involved? And had Zeke been trying to escape, or was he trying to break in to get more of Sofia's fake brains?

"But why did they have me kill the zombies and deliver only the heads?" he asked. "Why not just have me locate them, and then capture them—the way they were trying to do to you?"

"Probably because kidnapping a live zombie is a lot more complicated than simply killing one."

"Or maybe the whole point was to see if they could regrow zombies?" he suggested.

I made a face. "Seems like it would be just as effective to cut off some other body part to test these alternate brains. But whatever the reason, it does seem like they want a real live zombie now." I paused, narrowed my eyes. "Which also means that call from Sofia was bullshit." I quickly explained to him about the panicked phone call from her and was pleased to see his expression darken. "That bitch set me up," I continued. "How else would McKinney have known to set up his ambush for me on that highway?" I growled under my breath.

"GPS tracker," Ed stated.

"Hunh?"

His shoulders lifted in a shrug. "I mean, yeah, he clearly knew you were going out to her house and it does sound like she's behind this, but he wouldn't have known when and where exactly to set the spikes out unless he knew exactly where you were." He paused while I attempted to digest this. "It's how I found you," he added, doubling my shock. "I put one on your car when I was by your house."

I stared at him. "Are you serious?"

"Yup. I've been following you for the last couple of days," he said with no trace of apology in his voice. "Kind of funny to think that you probably had two tracking devices on your car."

"Yeah," I scowled. "Real funny. Okay, so Sofia lured me out there and . . ." I straightened as fear spasmed through me. "Marcus. I need to warn Marcus." I'd told Sofia he was out of town, but if she got hold of him and told him she was in trouble, I had no doubt he'd come running into whatever trap she and McKinney had ready for him.

I automatically looked around for my purse, then realized that everything was still in my car out on the highway. "Shit! I don't have my phone. Do you have one?"

"I stopped carrying one. Too easy to trace back." He swallowed harshly. "I've grown a little paranoid, y'know."

"Well we need to go find a phone," I said, throwing the brain-food I hadn't eaten back into the plastic bag.

"There's a pay phone at the XpressMart on Highway eighty-eight," Ed said.

I stood, hefting the bag. "And once we've done that we need to pay Sofia a visit."

A whisper of a smile twitched at his mouth. "Perhaps you should clean up first?"

I blinked, looked down at myself. "Oh. Yeah. Blood everywhere. Good point."

"There's bottled water and a change of clothing out in the car."

I raked a gaze over his own apparel. "Please tell me it's not goth chick stuff to match yours."

He gave a dry chuckle. "I would never do that to you. It's cargo pants and a midriff sweatshirt that says 'Redneck Princess.'"

"Thank god," I breathed. "I have a signature look, you know."

"You're a style icon, to be sure."

Chapter 21

My nerves were shot by the time we pulled into the parking lot of the XpressMart. It certainly wasn't a shining example of the XpressMart franchise. The "pr" and "M" in the sign were burned out, and one of the front windows had been replaced with a large sheet of plywood, on which someone had spray-painted a giant picture of a penis. But the pay phone still worked, and I had a fistful of quarters that I'd fished out of the console of Ed's truck, though I actually had no clue how much it cost to make a call. I couldn't remember the last time I'd used a pay phone, if ever.

"I'll keep an eye out," Ed said as I dumped coins into the phone. I sure as hell hoped he didn't turn evil again. I was going to get whiplash with the insane loyalty switching here.

I paused with my finger hovering over the buttons. "Um, do you know Marcus's number?" I asked Ed with a sheepish grin. "I have him in my contacts. I never have to actually dial it, y'know?"

Ed rolled his eyes and rattled off the digits. I dialed, shifting from foot to foot while I waited for Marcus to pick up. When it went to voicemail I groaned, then mentally fumbled for what to say during the brief outgoing message.

"Marcus, it's Angel. There's some weird shit going on, and you need to watch your back. The security guy from the lab shot me and tried to kidnap me, but Ed saved me, and, oh yeah, Ed's cool now, but I can't explain that now. But there's some kind of conspiracy to get zombie heads, and it has to do with Sofia's research and the zombie factions. Oh! I was totally right about Zeke Lyons. Ed said he gave the heads to someone, and we think they grew zombies back from them. Oh, and Sofia's a bad guy. Don't trust her! And anyway, I don't have my cell phone, I'm on a pay phone, but I'll try and call you again soon. Just, please be careful."

I hung up, turned to Ed. "That was total incoherent babble, wasn't it?"

He looked as if he was biting his lip to keep from laughing. "Well . . . you'll definitely get his attention with that message."

"Ugh. Whatever. I'll try him again in a bit." I could feel my expression settling into a scowl. "Lets go find Sofia."

I had her address in my text messages, but I realized it was more than possible that it wasn't actually her address and had been given to me to lead me into McKinney's ambush. Therefore, Ed and I agreed that we should find out for sure. Looking her up in a phone book seemed like the logical first step, but finding a phone book was more of a challenge than we expected. There wasn't one by the pay phone, and the clerk in the XpressMart simply gave me a vacant look when I asked if she had one. Ed then came up with the idea of finding a computer with internet to look her up, but I reminded him that the library was closed and the only way we would get to a computer at this point would be to break into someone's house.

After several minutes of argument and increasingly pointless debate, we finally agreed that we should at least go and make sure that the address she gave me *was* bullshit before we took the step of breaking into someone's house for the sole purpose of surfing the web. Yeah, we were some serious tactical geniuses, for sure.

Breckenridge Estates was still mostly under construction, and only every fourth lot or so had a finished house on it. It wasn't very large, either, and pretty much consisted of two long roads that curved off from either side of the entrance, each ending in a *cul du sac*—which, in a satellite photo, looked like a pair of ovaries. In between the "ovaries" was a swath of woods—green space that was probably used for drainage—which, in a satellite photo looked like, well, bush.

And the only reason I knew this was because Nick had somehow discovered it and made sure everyone else in the office saw it as well. To his credit, this was totally my level of humor, and I'd thought it was hysterically funny. But, hey, if not for that I wouldn't have known where Breckenridge was and how it was laid out.

I shared my wisdom with Ed as he drove, deeply disappointed when he failed to see the extreme hilarity in the layout. Oh well, maybe it was something that had to be seen to be appreciated.

As we entered the subdivision Ed put his hand on his gun, and I slouched down in the front seat of the truck.

"There's the address she gave me," I said, peering up over the dash at the very ordinary brick ranch-style house. I frowned at the blue Mazda in the driveway. "And that's her car." Guess it wasn't a bullshit address after all.

I started to tell Ed not to pull into the driveway, but he obviously had a healthy dose of common sense and simply drove on past the house. I didn't see any movement behind the curtains as we drove by, but there were other ways for her to be watching out for us. Surely by now McKinney would've let her know I'd escaped. But would either of them be expecting me to come here?

"This could be another ambush," I told Ed as we rounded the curve.

He gave a terse nod. "That occurred to me as well. There's a bag behind the seat. Has night vision goggles in it. I'm going to park on the other side of that green space, and we can approach through the trees."

I leaned over the back seat and saw a black nylon tactical bag. It was a lot heavier than I expected, and when I got a look at the contents I saw why.

"Holy shit, dude." Not just night vision goggles, but also a variety of handguns, ammunition, road flares, and what looked like a stun gun. "Can I just say how glad I am that you're doing the good guy thing right now?"

Ed smiled tightly, but shame flashed through his eyes. He parked the truck in an empty driveway in the left "ovary," grabbed the bag and got out. I scrambled out after him, then had to struggle to keep up as he took off at a lope toward the trees. About a dozen feet into the woods he stopped and crouched, fished out a pair of the goggles and handed them to me. I took them gratefully since I could barely see my hand in front of my face.

The world leapt into green and black focus, *just* like in the movies. "These are so cool," I breathed.

"Can you shoot a gun?" he asked.

"I'm not a great shot or anything, but I know which end to point at the bad guys," I replied.

"Good enough." He pressed the butt of a pistol into my hand. I couldn't see details with the goggles on, but it wasn't a very large gun. Some kind of automatic. Bigger than a .22 but smaller than a .45. And that was about the extent of my gun knowledge.

He began moving through the trees, and I followed, doing my best to be quiet but certain that we sounded like a pair of rampaging elephants. It probably took us close to fifteen minutes to get through the stretch of woods, part of which was a swampy section that we had to wade through, soaking us to our knees. I kept scanning but didn't see anyone lurking in the woods lying in wait.

We dropped to the ground a few feet from the other edge of the woods and watched the house for several minutes. Finally Ed turned to me and pulled his goggles off. "Too much light around the house for night-vision now," he said in a barely audible voice. I quickly tugged mine off, then had to blink a few times to get used to normal vision again.

"I don't see anyone," I said, doing my best to match his low volume.

"Me neither."

I took a deep breath. "I don't smell anyone either."

He shot me an uncertain look. I shrugged and smiled sweetly.

"Uh, okay," he muttered. "Well, I think we should go for it."

We shifted into crouches, then moved quickly through the back yard and pressed ourselves up against the house. I edged to the door and started to reach for the handle, but Ed grabbed my arm before I could touch it.

"No gloves," he hissed, giving my hand a pointed look. I winced. Oh, yeah. Probably best not to leave fingerprints.

But he didn't release my arm. "Look at the door frame," he said.

I followed his gaze, cold settling into my gut at the scrape marks around the lock.

"Lock is broken," he whispered, grim expression coming over his face. He gave the backyard another quick scan, then—since he did have gloves on—gently tugged the back door open.

"Stay here while I check it out," he murmured.

"The fuck I will," I shot back.

He gave me a sharp look. "You're a big tough zombie," he whispered. "How can you be afraid to be left out here alone?"

" 'Cause I'm also a neurotic chick who's already been attacked once today," I whispered back with a scowl.

He processed that, then nodded. "Fair enough. Follow me, and try not to shoot me in the back."

"No promises," I muttered.

He snorted in response and slipped inside. I followed

and quietly pulled the door closed behind me. The house was utterly silent except for the hum of the refrigerator. The cold feeling in my gut began to increase as we moved through the kitchen and into the living room.

Yet even with the sense that something was really fucked up, it still shocked the hell out of me when I saw Sofia lying in a pool of blood in the middle of the floor.

I stopped where I was as I took it all in. She was on her back with one leg bent up under the other and her right arm flung out to her side. Her eyes were open, and blood tracked across her forehead from where she'd been shot in the head. I couldn't tell if that was the only wound, but either way she was clearly dead. I'd seen hundreds of bodies before, of course, but I'd always been prepared for it. This time, though, I'd been coming here to lay into her and hopefully find out what the hell was going on. I'd never honestly believed that she'd ever really been in danger.

I let out a shaking breath as I scanned the room. No sign of struggle—just like Marianne's house—except for a knocked-over can of Coke that had made a large brown stain in the pale carpet. Sofia didn't keep a terribly neat house, though the mess was mostly clutter, not dirt. I moved over to the table. A desk calendar covered much of the surface, surrounded by stacks of books and magazines. The calendar was at least two years old and covered with notes and phone numbers and reminders. *She probably didn't want to get a new calendar because then she'd lose all the information scrawled onto this one.* I could appreciate that mentality. I almost liked her a bit more now that I knew she hadn't been perfect. Almost.

"We need to get out of here *now*," Ed said, grabbing me by the arm.

"Hang on," I said, peering at one phone number that was circled. Above it was scrawled "K@ScottFH." The number looked vaguely familiar, as if it was one that I'd dialed a few times. It wasn't Marcus's, I knew that much. What the hell did K@ScottFH mean? Was it an email address? If so wasn't it supposed to have a "com" or "net" at the end?

I didn't want to risk touching anything so I did my best to memorize it and the number instead of finding a pen and scrap of paper. Ed tugged on my arm again, but this time I didn't resist and allowed him to lead me to the back door. He eased it open and did a quick scan, then seized my hand and took off at a run toward the woods. I had no problem keeping up, and when we reached the woods, I pulled the goggles back on as if I'd worn them a thousand times. I didn't say a word as we returned to the truck, remaining silent until we were well away from the house and the subdivision.

"You okay?" I finally asked.

Ed's hands tightened on the steering wheel. "Not really," he said. "I've known Sofia a long time. She could be a real bitch sometimes, but . . ." His expression darkened. "I'm going to kill that McKinney motherfucker."

"You think McKinney did it? But I thought you shot him."

"He was wearing a vest," Ed told me. Then he thumped his chest with his fist. "So am I, for that matter."

Blinking in surprise, I took a closer look at him. Yeah, now that I was looking for it I could see a slightly thicker look to his torso beneath the hoodie. I'd been so distracted by the skulls and other goth or emo stuff that I hadn't even noticed.

Goth ...

"Oooooh," I breathed. Now I knew what K@ScottFH meant and how I knew that phone number. "Sofia was two-timing."

"What are you talking about?"

"She was playing both sides of the zombie factions. There was a phone number on her desk calendar that looked vaguely familiar, with what I thought was an email address above it. But it wasn't. It stood for 'Kang at Scott Funeral Home.'" Kang, the seventy-year-old zombie who'd always dressed like a twenty-year-old goth.

"Who the hell is Kang?" he asked, sounding slightly exasperated.

"The zombie you killed at Scott Funeral Home." Yeah, sure, Ed had rescued me and seemed to be changing his ways, but I still wasn't ready to pull any punches. "If anyone was a leader of another zombie faction it would have been Kang," I continued, talking it out more for my own sake than for his. "He was old as shit and had a tight hold on the brain distribution from the funeral homes in this area."

Ed was silent for a moment, face stony. "That's how I tracked him down. Two of the others had his name and number."

As sorry as I was for Kang, I still couldn't help but feel a teensy bit of *I told you so.* I'd told the damn man that I thought someone was hunting zombies and that he should be careful, and he'd blown it off as "not his problem." Jerk.

"I need to call Marcus again," I said after a moment. "And Pietro. He needs to know." I frowned. "Shit. I don't have his number."

"I know his number," Ed said. Then he gave me a puzzled look. "But what does Pietro have to do with any of ..." His expression abruptly shifted to one of shock. "Oh, my god. He's a zombie too, isn't he."

"Yeah, he's another Zombie Leader. I think Sofia was playing Kang and Pietro off each other. In fact," I said, musing, "I bet it was Kang's murder that started getting her all freaked out." I considered this for a moment as I fought to get all the pieces to fit together. I was still missing something. "You've known Pietro a long time, haven't you?"

His throat bobbed as he swallowed. "He and my parents were friends."

A horrible suspicion came over me, but I didn't want to say anything just yet. However, Ed wasn't stupid.

"How long has he been a zombie?" His voice was calm, but I had the feeling that if he tightened his grip on the wheel any more it would crumble.

"Um, a pretty long time, as far as I know." I watched him, wary. Dude was about to snap. "He's the one who turned Marcus," I continued. "Marcus got bit by a raccoon or something and got rabies."

Surprise flashed over Ed's face. "I remember that." His shoulders slumped and his death grip on the steering wheel relaxed a fraction. "He ... Marcus told me he got the shots in time."

"He didn't," I said. "He didn't know he was infected until he started to get symptoms. It didn't even occur to him."

Ed shuddered. He was medically trained and knew that it was almost always too late by that point.

"He was going to die," I went on. "So Pietro ... saved him the only way he could."

Ed didn't respond. He stared at the highway ahead as we drove. I didn't ask him where we were going. Right now it didn't really matter.

"He's the one who killed my dad," he finally said in a voice so raw it made me shiver.

I didn't ask him if was sure. He was. I could see that. His eyes were on the road, but memories flickered behind them.

"He killed my dad," he repeated. "But not my mom." His throat bobbed again as he swallowed hard. "He loved her." His voice broke on that, and then it was as if the dam opened up. He began to sob, and I quickly put out a hand and took hold of the steering wheel. To my relief he slowed down, retaining enough control of himself to pull over to the side of the road and put the truck in park before completely breaking down.

"I used to hear my parents fight," he managed to get out as he leaned his forehead against the steering wheel, his body shaking.

I blew out my breath as it all clicked together. Pietro and Dawn Quinn. Pietro didn't kill her. Her husband shot her in a fit of jealous rage. *But why didn't Pietro turn Dawn into a zombie to save her?* I thought, but then realized the answer. She was probably already dead, and it was too late. And then Pietro killed Sam Quinn in revenge. . . .

Jesus fucking Christ, it was a zombie soap opera.

And I didn't know what the hell to do with Ed while he cried. *Ah hell, should I try and comfort him or hug him or some crap like that?* I mean, the guy had obviously been through a ton of shit, but he *had* tried to kill me not all that long ago.

Fuck it, I thought with a sigh and pulled him to me so that he could cry on my shoulder. First Marcus, now Ed. What the hell was it about my bony little shoulder that made it so easy for men to cry on?

He regained control of himself after a couple of minutes—to my intense relief—scrubbed a hand over his face, put the truck back into drive and pulled back onto the highway. "Let's find you another pay phone," he said.

We didn't want to go back to the pay phone we'd used before, since we both had our paranoia meters pegged on *Everyone's out to get us!* However, it turned out that pay phones were rarer than phone books, and it took almost fifteen minutes of driving around to find another. We eventually located one at a decrepit gas station in an unspeakably dicey area of town, where I knew damn well we were being watched and sized up. I'd been in the drug scene long enough to know that if I'd ever wanted to switch from painkillers to crack or meth, this was the area to find it.

Ed parked and got out, then kept a scowl on his face and the gun in his hand while I scrounged quarters from the floor of the truck.

"Shit," I heard Ed breathe even as the crunch of gravel warned me that someone was pulling into the lot. I straightened and stuffed the quarters I'd found into my pocket as I got a look at the newcomer.

"Shit," I echoed.

"That's a cop," Ed muttered as he leaned against the truck in what looked like a completely casual pose. I didn't see the gun. Both his hands were in plain sight, thumbs tucked into his front pockets. He looked bored and mildly impatient, as if he was waiting for me to finish up what I had to do so that we could get the hell out of there.

It would have worked great in any other location, most likely. But here his gothed-out look made him look like he was in the neighborhood trying to score drugs.

Then I got a good look at the car and my mood sunk even more. "Not just a cop," I groaned, doing my best to keep from looking guilty or furtive, though I was probably managing to look even more so simply by trying to look all innocent and shit. One thing I certainly *wasn't* was innocent. "That's my probation officer." *Damn it!* I could get into trouble just for being in a high-crime area if my probation officer wanted to be a jerk about it. And what if he happened to recognize Ed as Ed? Hanging out with a suspected serial killer probably wouldn't look too great either.

Probation Officer Garza's mouth was pressed into a thin, tight line as he got out of his car. He sure as hell didn't look like he was too pleased with me. He gave Ed a long and measuring look as he approached us. I fought the urge to glance at Ed to see what he was doing. I could only put all my faith in the fact that he'd worked around cops for years and knew what to do—and what not to do—to keep from arousing suspicion.

"'Sup?" Ed said to Garza. "Y'got a light, man?" He slurred his words ever so slightly, and when I finally risked a peek at him I saw that he seemed to be having trouble focusing on the probation officer.

A sour look settled on Garza's face. He ignored the question and turned his attention to me, apparently—

hopefully—pegging Ed as a stoner who was too high to worry about at the moment.

"What are you doing here, Angel?" he asked. I could have sworn he looked disappointed in me.

I gulped, suddenly feeling oddly guilty even though I had no reason to. But, damn, he was intimidating. "It's not what it looks like," I said in a rush. "My car got busted up over on Highway 191, and I had to call my buddy for a ride. And then I lost my purse, and I wanted to call my dad to let him know I was all right so we stopped to use the pay phone. That's all."

He blinked, then frowned. "I see. That's pretty far from here."

I gave a sigh. "Have you ever tried to find a pay phone? There aren't too many of them."

He considered that for a moment. "True." He cast a sweeping look around, eyes narrowing. "You need to finish your business up here and get out of here." He delivered a scathing glance at Ed before turning back to me. "And be careful of the company you keep."

I nodded emphatically. "Yes, sir. I will. Promise."

"And don't forget about Wednesday."

"Wednesday?" What the hell was . . . shit. "Right! Wednesday. Our meeting."

"Yes," he said, mouth twisted sourly. "Please don't miss it."

"I won't," I said as fervently as I could. Cripes, with all the other shit going on, this was the last thing I needed to deal with. And how would he react if he knew I broke into a house and found a dead body tonight? I had a sudden cartoonish image of his head exploding, and I had to press my lips together to keep from busting out an entirely inappropriate laugh.

He let out a low snort, shook his head, then—to my immense relief—turned around and climbed back into his car. I hurriedly dug the quarters out of my pocket and moved to the phone so that he'd believe what I'd said about the phone call. Well, it was partially true.

I started feeding quarters into the slot, relieved beyond all reason to hear the crunch of tires as he backed up and turned around.

"He's gone now," Ed muttered. "Jesus, that was close."

"I am *so* going straight back to jail," I moaned as I fumbled with the coins.

Ed let out a snort of laughter. "Yeah, probably." I shot him a glare, but he lifted his chin toward the phone. "Don't tell Marcus about Sofia on his voice mail."

I paused mid-number-punch. "Why?" Then I grimaced. "Oh, right. That would be evidence that I'd been there."

"Exactly."

Well here's hoping he picks up, I thought, but of course he didn't. No, that would be too easy. I hung up without leaving a message.

I asked Ed for Pietro's number, amused that the last four digits were the same as my ex-boyfriend Randy's, and was completely unsurprised when that call also went to voice mail. "Pietro, this is Angel. I'm trying to reach Marcus. I know you don't like me, but I just want to warn him—and you, I suppose, as well—that Walter McKinney, the head of security at NuQuesCor shot me and tried to kidnap me tonight. I'm worried that y'all might be targeted as well." I paused, trying to think of some way to tell them about Sofia. "I think he killed Marianne. And . . . someone else. Someone you both know." Shit, this was pointless. "Tell him to watch his back," I said, then hung up.

"I think you did better when you were spouting incoherent babble," Ed said mildly as he continued to scan the area.

"I think you're right," I muttered as I fed more quarters into the phone.

"Who are you calling now?" he asked with a frown.

"My dad," I replied. "If the cops find my car on the side of the road they might call him or come to the house, and I don't want him to worry." I paused before dialing. What the hell was his cellphone number? I had him in my contacts as "DAD." I never had to actually dial the damn thing. Cursing under my breath, I checked my watch. Nine p.m. I knew the home phone number but at this hour on a Sunday there was no way he'd be home. He'd be down at Kaster's watching football with the rest of his buddies.

But at least I could leave a message for him.

I jerked in surprise as the phone rang before I could punch the first number in. Ed and I exchanged a wary look, then I picked up the receiver. "Hello?"

"Angel? This is Pietro. I'm sorry for not answering, but I always screen calls from unfamiliar numbers. What's going on?"

I frantically waved Ed over so that he could listen in. "Sofia's dead, Pietro. We're pretty sure that Walter McKinney killed her. Oh, and—"

"Hold on, Sofia's dead? How do you know? And who's 'we'?"

"Yes. We went to her house and saw her body. She'd been shot. And 'we' is Ed. And me."

"Ed Quinn?" he asked, shock and anger in his voice. "Angel, this is ridiculous. You're not thinking clearly and now you want to get Marcus involved in—"

"Shut up and let me talk!" I yelled. "I'm trying to protect Marcus! Look, it's complicated, but that's not the important thing right now." I quickly explained about Zeke the zombie who was beheaded and then grown back, and my theory that whoever was doing it was escalating their experiments using Sofia's fake brain research.

He was silent for a long moment. "You're absolutely certain Sofia is dead?" he said, voice so even that it was obvious he was holding back a great deal of emotion.

"Yeah," I said. "She was shot in the head. I'm sorry."

He let out a long exhalation. "I see. As to your dead zombie, I'll admit that it does seem that he was somehow, as you say, grown back. But that hardly means there's some sort of secret lab doing covert experiments."

Somehow I resisted the deep urge to shriek in frustration. "Y'know, I'm not a fucking moron," I told him, unable to keep the anger out of my voice. "Look, I'm real sorry Sofia's dead, but it's pretty clear that she was playing both sides, and I don't mean that she was bisexual." Then I shrugged. "Then again, I suppose it's possible that she was, but that's not my point." I took a deep breath to get myself back on track. "You weren't the only one she was giving info to," I told him. "And then McKinney shot me several times earlier tonight during an attempt to kidnap me. Ed was the one who fucking saved me. He was duped into killing zombies and turning over the heads to whoever is doing this shit."

"I'm relieved that Ed was there to assist you," Pietro said. "But I have a hard time believing Sofia would do that. We had intel that the other faction was after Sofia's research. And, clearly, tonight they chose to kill her rather than allow us to have it."

Intel? Seriously? I opened my mouth to argue then closed it before I could say something that would forever ruin my chances of getting any help out of him. He was up to something, the fucker. Meanwhile there was a thought trying to work its way loose from the back of my head.

"Angel," he said before I could speak. "It's obvious you're in trouble. I can help you. Tell me where you are."

"Nah," I said absently, still trying to think. "I don't trust you."

He let out a low snort of amusement. "At least you're honest. Are you still injured? Do you need brains?"

"No, I'm cool." Injuries. Brains. Was that it? I covered the receiver and whispered to Ed, "Your mom—she was friends with Dr. Kristi Burke, right? Was she a neurologist too?"

"They worked in the same practice," he said, still looking confused. "But she's not Dr. Burke anymore. She divorced and took back her maiden name. She's Dr. Charish now."

I stared at him, suddenly feeling as if my brain was one of those old-fashioned boards at train terminals in old movies where the little tiles cascaded down to form words or a picture. Because, finally, a coherent picture was starting to form.

I smiled thinly. "She changed her hair color too, right?" At his nod I continued. "And did Pietro know her as well?" I already knew the answer to this one since I remembered she'd been at his little soirée.

Now his mouth twisted into a wry smile. "Most definitely."

Grinning, I uncovered the mouthpiece. "Okay, Pietro, I'm pretty sure you're full of shit. Well, maybe not completely full of shit, but I think that maybe Sofia wasn't the only scientist on your payroll. Dr. Charish also works for you, right?"

There was a moment of silence before he spoke. "Yes, Kristi also works for me, but on a different project than the one Sofia was working on."

I scowled into the phone. "Yeah, well I think your good doctor knew exactly what was going on in her lab. And I'm pretty sure she was the one who duped Ed into chopping zombie heads off." But I still couldn't shake the feeling that I was missing something. Was this whole thing really just about developing better fake brains to make money off zombies? Or was it some kind of zombie war? But if so, why the hell did they now need a live zombie? And why *me?*

There was another extended silence on Pietro's end. "There are dire consequences for harming or interfering with anyone under my protection," he finally said, voice low and dark. "Whoever is responsible for these murders, you can be certain that I will deal with it."

I didn't trust Pietro, but I also knew I wouldn't ever want to cross him. I was pretty sure that all of my comments about the Zombie Mafia were closer to the mark than most people suspected. So, in a way, this was almost reassuring. Almost.

"I have to make some calls," he said abruptly. "Call me again as soon as you're in a safe place."

I scowled as the line went dead. "Asshole," I muttered. I hung up the phone then blinked at the sound of quarters dropping into the change return. Oh, right, I'd been in the middle of calling my dad. I quickly put the quarters back in and dialed the house number, mentally framing what message I was going to leave, in the hopes that it wouldn't be quite so much incoherent babble.

It picked up after the second ring. "Hello, Angel," said a familiar voice that wasn't my dad's.

Chapter 22

"Are you fucking kidding me?" I shouted into the phone. "Get the fuck out of my house, you cocksucking ass-tard!"

"My god, you're a foul-mouthed thing, aren't you."

"Yeah, well, get over it. So what the fuck is this?" I said. "Is this where you have my dad and offer to trade us or some equally lame bullshit? Are you working from *Evil Plots for Dummies* or some shit like that?"

"That's pretty clever," McKinney replied. "I may have to write that someday. But yes, I have your father, and I'm willing to make a trade, him for you. Very simple: you cooperate or your dad dies."

I felt my mouth twist into something not quite a smile. "Uh huh. First off, I don't believe you really have my dad. Second off, go fuck yourself."

To my surprise he chuckled. "Ah. You require proof. Fair enough."

I heard some rustling, then, "Angelkins?"

"Oh my god, Dad," I groaned. "What are you doing at home?"

"What the hell are you talking about? I live here, remember?"

"But it's football night! Why aren't you down at Kaster's?"

"Because it's a goddamn bar!" he shouted back. "And I'm trying to not go to bars any more, 'cause when I go to bars I drink, and I'm trying not to drink any more 'cause it's pretty much the only way to get sober, goddammit!"

"Oh," I said in a small voice. "Okay. That makes sense."

I heard him take a shuddering breath. "What's going on, baby?" he said in a somewhat more normal tone of voice. "Are you in some kind of trouble with these people? You can tell me, honey. I'll love you no matter what."

My chest squeezed so tight I wasn't sure I could even breathe. "Daddy, it's okay. I'm not in trouble. I mean, not like drugs or shit like that. This asstard wants some information I have. This'll all be over real soon."

"Okay, baby. I trust you. You do what you gotta do, y'hear?"

"Oh, I will, Dad," I replied fervently. Damn straight I would.

More rustling, and then McKinney came back on the phone. "Enough jibber jabber. Here's what you're going to do."

"Did you just say 'jibber jabber'?" I asked. "Seriously? What bad guy says 'jibber jabber'?"

He sighed. "You're going to be a complete pain in my ass, aren't you?"

"You started this."

"So I did. Fine. You're going to go to the East St. Edwards High School football field and stand in the middle of the fifty yard line. You know where that is?"

"I know it." Did I ever.

"As soon as you are there—alone—I'll release your dad, let you two wave to each other in passing, and then he will walk out the gate by the north end zone, where he can get into a car driven by your sidekick—"

"My sidekick?" I gave Ed a sidelong look.

"Yes, the knight in shining armor who rescued you from my dastardly clutches."

"Dude, you read *way* too many romance novels. Fine. You let my dad go, my sidekick wonder boy takes my dad far away from cockwaffles like you, and then ... what, I keep standing in the damn field?"

He chuckled. "Yes. Out in the open. And alone. I'll give you half an hour to get your pieces in position." The line went dead.

I hung the phone up. "Could you hear all that?" I asked Ed.

"I got the gist," he said, voice quiet.

"So now what do I do?"

Ed was silent for a moment. I could almost see the thoughts ticking behind his eyes. "Your dad said, 'these people,' which tells me that McKinney probably isn't working alone anymore. I'm betting that he'll have a sniper in place who'll simply shoot you until you can't fight back, and then they'll grab you."

I nodded agreement. "And the stuff with my dad is to

get you out of the way and make sure that you aren't set up to snipe *his* ass."

"Sounds about right," he said, grimacing.

"Why the hell does he want *me*?" I growled.

"Easy target? War between the zombies? Hostage?" he offered, shrugging. "Or perhaps it's something completely unrelated to this power struggle between the factions, and these people somehow found out that you're a zombie, and they need a zombie for some other nefarious purpose, ergo they're after you."

"Sofia knew I was a zombie," I said, grimacing.

"She was definitely involved in all of this somehow." He took a deep breath. "All right then, whatever the reason, somehow we need to figure out a way to make it where being shot won't be so, um, debilitating for you."

"I could wear your body armor," I suggested.

He stepped back and sized me up. "We could try," he said, but he sounded awfully doubtful.

"What's the problem?"

"Well, you're awfully skinny, and I can't exactly put a couple of tucks in a Kevlar vest in order to make it fit you." He shook his head. "I think it'll be really obvious that you're wearing it, which will only encourage a decent shooter to go for places that aren't covered by the vest."

"Well, that sucks," I muttered.

Ed's eyes narrowed thoughtfully. "I have an idea that might help . . . but I don't think you're going to like it."

"Lay it on me," I said. "It's not like I'm brimming with brilliance right now."

I listened as he laid it out for me. He was right. I didn't like it. I kinda fucking hated it.

But it was brilliant enough that I also loved it.

Chapter 23

I lost my virginity to Randy on this football field, in this exact spot, though I didn't remember it being quite so creepy back then. Tonight the lights were all off, and there was enough of a fog to make me jumpy as all hell, certain that any number of unnamed threats were about to jump out at me from the shadows. *I'm the monster*, I tried to remind myself. There was only one threat that I had to worry about, and his name was McKinney. And whoever he had with him, of course.

Didn't help. Still completely freaked out.

On the other hand, I was tanked up on brains darn near as high as I'd ever been. Even though it was dark, I could see every blade of grass, hear the buzzing of the mosquitos, feel the low thrum of the engine of Ed's truck from where it was idling farther down the street. A slight shift of movement from behind the bleachers caught my attention as surely as if the man back there had stood up and waved a flag. He had a rifle pointed at me. I was definitely going to get shot again. But with any luck the combination of zombie super-speed and the reserve of brains I had on hand would be enough to counteract the damage.

I sure as hell hoped so, because right now that was the only plan we had.

A breeze swirled past me, and I lifted my head, nostrils flaring like an animal as the wind brought the scent of two people. They were by the south end zone, and I recognized both scents. *My dad and McKinney*. So Ed was right, the sniper behind the bleachers was a new player. How many others were nearby?

Turning slowly I extended my zombie super senses as far as they could go, seeking out scents and movements. At least one more—over by the opposing side bleachers, and also with a rifle. Possibly more but the light wind wasn't cooperating. Probably one rifle trained on me and one on my dad to keep me from simply grabbing him and bolting. Even with zombie super strength and speed I wouldn't be able to avoid bullets while also shielding my dad.

Which meant that I was back to depending on the Power of Brains.

I clenched and unclenched my hands. A creak of metal alerted me, and I spun toward the south end zone to see my dad and McKinney walking through the gate. They paused at the goal line, then my dad continued toward me alone, shuffling in his usual gait but clearly doing his best to hurry. I breathed shallowly, straining my ears for anything unusual—the click of a trigger or a muttered order to fire.

Nothing but the shuffling of my dad's feet over the

grass. It seemed to take forever, but he finally made it across the field to me. I seized him in a hug. God, he felt so frail.

"You okay?" I asked, releasing him and raking my gaze over him.

He nodded, swallowed harshly. "Yeah. I'm fine. Now let's get out of here, baby."

"No, you have to keep walking," I said, gesturing to the other end of the field. "A friend of mine is going to pick you up, and y'all have to get the hell away from here. Understand?" I could hear Ed's truck rev as he began to ease toward the pick-up point.

He scowled. "I ain't leaving you. You fuckin' kidding? I'm your dad, goddammit."

"Yeah, and I'm your daughter who needs to kick some ass but has to know you're safe first, okay?" I gave him a hard look. He hesitated, and I knew he was re-membering the time it was *his* ass I had to kick—or threaten to kick, at least.

"Please, Dad, you have to go," I said urgently. "I have to know you're all right."

He hesitated, clearly agonized. He wanted to be there for me, help save the day. He'd dropped the ball too many times to count in the last few years, but he'd been there for me when it had counted most, when he had to make the choice between his wife and me.

"It's okay," I whispered. "You have to go. It's the right thing. I can't . . . do what I have to do if you're here."

Swallowing hard, he pulled me into another fierce hug. "Love you, Angelkins. I'm so proud of you." He let me go, gave a nod. "You go kick whatever ass needs kicking."

"I will," I said with a shaky smile. "Now please, go get to safety."

It had to have been the hardest thing he'd ever done, but he did it—kept walking and left me there in the middle of that field. I watched as Ed pulled up right by the gate and my dad climbed into the truck. I braced myself, and as soon Ed gunned the engine to get the hell out of there I broke into a sprint.

I knew I was fast, but the snipers must have been damn good. I felt two hits in my lower back, but I simply peeled my lips back in a feral smile and kept running. Sure, two shots would slow me down some, but . . .

I stumbled and went to my knees. My legs didn't want to work properly. *What the hell?* I was so high on brains that should've barely caused a hitch in my stride. I fumbled to reach the bag in the side pocket of my pants, but my arms didn't want to work either. Fear slammed through me as I slumped heavily onto my side. Numbness swept through me, but it wasn't anything like the other times I'd been shot.

Not shot—tranqued, I realized in horror as I watched a white van speed across the field and stop in front of me. I had no choice but to watch since I couldn't move or turn my head. *If I've been drugged the parasite will take care of it*, I tried to reassure myself. But I knew, with a growing sense of horror, that it wouldn't be quickly enough. My senses were fading, and I felt the first stirrings of hunger, but that was probably my parasite doing its best to simply keep me alive. Why should it care if I couldn't move right now?

McKinney and another man exited the van and approached. McKinney crouched in my line of sight while the other moved behind me. I could feel the second guy putting handcuffs on me or something similar. It was tough to be sure, since I had a Novocaine-type numbness throughout most of my body.

"Hello, sweetie," McKinney said with a grin. "See? I kept my end of the bargain. And now you're pumped full of enough animal tranquilizer to kill an elephant. I had a feeling that would be more effective—and so much less messy—than shooting you. My new partners are bringing a great deal to the table." He gave a nod toward the other man and then gestured to—I assumed—the two snipers.

I couldn't even blink, but apparently I was still able to glare daggers at him because he chuckled. "Fun times ahead, Angel. Fun times."

Chapter 24

Once I was safely handcuffed and leg-shackled, they made a fairly thorough search of my person. If I'd been able to curse—or even breathe deeply—I would have when they located the bag of brains in my side pocket. Instead I was absolutely shrieking in terror on the inside.

"Jesus," I heard one of them mutter. "Is that . . . ?"

"Brains?" McKinney answered. "Yes. And it's the last thing we need to let her have right now."

"That's disgusting," the first one said.

McKinney's response was a bark of laughter. "Well, you'd better get used to it fast."

After that, they put me in some sort of large metal box or container. It had plenty of air holes, though, so apparently they were easing up on me in that they weren't going to let me suffocate. I lost track of time, but it didn't seem to take long before a lesser sort of numbness began to take over my limbs, and I could wiggle my fingers and toes again. But as the paralysis faded the hunger grew. Whatever I'd been drugged with had clearly forced my parasite to use up a lot of resources, and now it wanted to be fed. Badly. The hunger clawed at me, telling me to break the chains and get out of the box by any means necessary. The air holes allowed me to detect two people with lovely, edible brains in the back of the van with me. I wanted them both. I could take them—I knew that.

I clenched my teeth, breath hissing as I fought the urges. Even if I could break the chain on the handcuffs and shackles, I doubted that I could get through the metal of this box. It looked like the kind of container used to transport dangerous animals, like tigers and stuff. In fact, it probably was, now that I thought about it with the few brain cells still under my control. And if this thing could hold a six-hundred-pound tiger, there was no way my barely one hundred pounds would be able to break free, even with a zombie parasite on my side. I'd only damage myself more.

On the other hand, I had the advantage of being a scrawny little thing, and adequately limber enough to wiggle around and get the handcuffs in front of me. The air holes didn't let in much light but there was enough for me to see that the skin of my wrists beneath the handcuffs was torn and I could see through to the bone. I'd lost a few fingernails as well, but I was used to that. My breath came in slow, rasping gurgles, and I made no effort to control it. Might as well see if I could freak out the men with me in the back of the van. It was insanely tempting to say something like, "I want to eat you," but I didn't want to risk them shooting or tranquing me again. I was in a bad enough state as it was.

Instead I curled up into a ball in the corner of the container, squeezing my eyes shut while I tried to focus on anything except how insanely hungry I was. When that didn't work, I shifted my thoughts to what I would do when they opened the container. That would be my chance.

But if I break free, won't they just come after me—or my dad—again?

My lips curled back in a silent snarl. Right now I was willing to take that chance. And if the hunger got any worse, I wouldn't be able to control what I did when that door opened up.

But it did get worse. It was all I could think about. My entire existence narrowed down to an excruciating need to find brains. I had no idea how much time passed as we drove. I thought it was probably longer than half an hour, but beyond that I couldn't be sure. I could barely hold onto rational thought, much less keep track of the passage of time. After a while I was aware of a low huffing growl, then realized it was coming from me. Not long after that, I was aware only of the hunger and the need to reach the two who were just out of my reach.

And then, brains. The scent filled the container, and I dove onto the chunks that dropped through one of the air holes, cramming them into my mouth one-handed as fast as I could. There was something wrong with my other hand, but I couldn't figure out what just yet. Whining, I scrabbled at the hole and was rewarded with several more gobbets, dimly aware of conversation outside the box as I gulped them down.

"Are you fucking kidding me?"

"You were at the briefing. We went through what would happen."

"Yeah, but—"

"But nothing. Give it another couple of minutes, then it'll be safe to take her out."

Shuddering, I pulled myself into a crouch as the warmth spread through me, so painful in its intensity that a gravelly wail escaped me. I wasn't handcuffed anymore, or rather, the handcuffs now dangled from only my right wrist. My left wrist and hand were a mangled mess of bone and shredded skin, though they slowly pulled back together as I watched. I didn't remember yanking my hand out of the cuff, but it was pretty obvious I'd done exactly that.

I took a deep breath—still a little raspy, but much improved. "I need more," I croaked. "Please," I added. "I'm ... damaged, and still really hungry. I ... I don't want to hurt anyone."

I heard a snort, wasn't sure if it was contempt or disbelief, but a few more chunks dropped through the hole. I snarled silently as I scraped up everything I could from the floor of the container, but the snarl had nothing do with my more animal instincts and everything to do with the fact that I officially hated these motherfuckers with every fiber of my being for essentially making me eat off the goddamn floor and for doing all of this to me, and by fucking god I was going to make them pay somehow.

I took a deep breath and fought for calm. The one silver lining of going into total "monster mode" with the hunger was that I'd forgotten about the ace in the hole Ed had come up with. Good thing, because I wanted to save that for when I knew I could take maximum advantage of it.

And I could already tell that now was not that time.

I tried to see what I could through the air holes and realized with a start that I wasn't in the van anymore. Couldn't see much—just enough to let me know that I'd been moved while I was still out of my head. Some white walls. Several black-fatigued men who I assumed were my guards now. Four, maybe five. I couldn't be sure.

Someone slapped their hand down on top of the container, and I let out a startled yelp.

"All right, sweetheart," McKinney said, crouching down so that I could sort of see his face. "Here's how it's going to work. I open the container, you come out all nice and easy, I remove the shackles, then you get some time alone to clean up." I saw his mouth spread into a hard smile. "If you do absolutely anything that looks like an attack or resistance, your guards will shoot you—with bullets and tranquilizers, and this time I'll make you wait until you're a rotted pile of bones before I give you what you need. Do you understand?"

I swallowed to work moisture into my mouth. "Yes," I said, voice shaking slightly to make it sound like I was scared.

Oh, who the hell was I kidding? I *was* scared. Terrified out of my goddamn wits and second-guessing every decision that had led to this point.

Metal squealed as the front of the container swung open. I blinked as light flooded in, then shivered at the sight of the bloody streaks along the walls where I'd obviously tried to claw my way out. I crawled out as quickly as I could with my legs still shackled, but I stood too quickly and had to grab at the container as a brief surge of dizziness sent me swaying. I could feel the tension in the room go up a notch, and I was suddenly hideously aware that each man had a weapon trained on me.

I wanted to laugh. I weighed less than a hundred pounds, and they were acting like I really was a six-hundred-pound tiger.

The dangling handcuff slapped against my leg and my humor vanished. No, they were reacting with exactly the right amount of caution. I straightened as the dizziness passed, took stock of where I was. *A public bathroom?* At least it probably had been at one time. White room with tiled floor, an overhead fluorescent light that buzzed annoyingly, and an odd mixture of smells—fresh paint and old mildew. Along the walls and floor were ghostly outlines of plumbing that had apparently been ripped out and spackled or tiled over. One toilet and sink were left, as well as one stall partition and a lone shower stall with a curtain so new it still had that fresh plastic smell. Against one wall was a narrow bed, looking utterly out of place in the bathroom setting. As a holding cell, it made a certain amount of sense. No windows, a heavy door, and even a drain in the floor in case . . .

I shuddered and yanked my thoughts into a different direction. At any rate, this wasn't quite the "secret lab" I'd been expecting.

McKinney approached with latex-gloved hands. I stood absolutely motionless as he removed the handcuff and shackles. After he straightened he placed them on the top of the container, but kept his gloves on.

"Now take your clothes off," he ordered.

"The fuck I will," I shot back.

He narrowed his eyes in a sneer. "No necrophiliacs

here. No one here is going to rape you. But you will be searched."

Necrophiliacs? The fuck? I made a quick scan of the other guards. All wore equal expressions of mild disgust and disdain. It threw me briefly for a loop—not because I wasn't used to being regarded that way, but because I *was*. Yet this time it was for something that I had no control over, not for the way I acted or dressed or because of anything I'd done. It was weird and awful and humiliating, yet at the same time a sick relief coiled through me at the realization that, out of all the horrible shit that could possibly happen to me here, at least rape wasn't something I had to fear. At least not right now.

But my hands still shook as I lifted them to my shirt. Whether they looked at me with disgust or not, this was still a bunch of strange men who were going to see me naked.

"Don't you have any women guards?" I asked, hating that my voice had a quaver in it. "Please."

"No," McKinney said flatly. "Take your fucking clothes off or I'll shoot you and leave you starving."

I stared at him for a couple of seconds, but it was clear he meant every word. I yanked my shirt off, trying to be angry and fierce about the whole thing, but it didn't work. Not one bit. I couldn't even turn away from the guards. They were all around me so I kept my head down and didn't look at any of their faces 'cause I knew that if I saw anything other than disgust or disdain I'd fucking lose it. I pulled my bra off then kicked my shoes off and shoved my pants and undies down, kicked it all away and stood there naked with my arms clamped down by my sides 'cause I didn't want to do that pathetic thing of trying to cover my chest and privates and all. And I tried my fucking damnedest to stay angry, and even thought about how much I hated Clive, and hated the fucker who'd drugged me and was gonna date rape me, and how much I fucking hated McKinney and these others.

But none of it worked. I could feel myself crying and saw the fucking tears plopping on the floor while I kept my head down and let that motherfucker do what he felt he had to do to search me.

"Towels and clothes are on the bed," he told me when he finished. "Get cleaned up and changed."

I didn't respond and he didn't wait for one. He left with the guards, leaving me standing naked and shaking in the middle of the white room.

Chapter 25

I finally forced myself to shower and change into the t-shirt and sweat pants that had been left for me, knowing that if I didn't, McKinney would come back and do it for me, in as horrible and humiliating a way as possible. After that I slept for awhile—no idea how long—and woke up at the sound of the door opening. I didn't move except to open my eyes and see a guard step in and set a tray down on the floor. I stayed where I was on the bed until he left and closed the door, and only then kicked the blanket off to see what had been left for me.

The tray was a plastic cafeteria tray that looked like it had been purchased at a public school garage sale. For that matter the food looked like it as well—rubbery pizza, lukewarm chocolate milk, and green beans swimming in an oily liquid dotted with something that was probably supposed to be bacon or ham. And—to my utter shock—brains as well. Two neat slices, like a couple of pieces of pound cake. I gave them a dubious sniff, but as far as I could tell they were the real thing.

I attended to some necessary bodily functions, then picked up the tray and brought it over to the narrow bed since I didn't feel like sitting on the floor to eat.

I ate everything, including the nasty green beans, since I figured my parasite needed to save its efforts for other stuff instead of having to give me a boost because I was malnourished.

The door opened as soon as I took my last bite, confirming my suspicion that I was under constant surveillance. McKinney stood in the doorway with two other guards behind him. I couldn't tell if they were the same ones who'd watched me get strip-searched earlier. They all looked the same to me. *I need to pay attention to this stuff though*, I told myself. If I ever got the chance to make a break for it, knowing the number of people I was up against would prove pretty darn useful.

"Let's go," he snapped.

I stood up, silently followed him out. I got a good hard look at the guards and did my best to memorize details about them. One had acne scars and a sharp cleft in his chin. The other had oddly perfect eyebrows, and I suspected that he had them shaped.

I wasn't at NuQuesCor. That much I could figure out. Even with the smell of new paint, it was tough to disguise the fact that this was an old building. It also didn't feel like it was very big. The hallway ended at a heavy door about thirty feet to my right, dead-ended at about the same distance to my left, and I thought I counted eight doors along its length. Not that I had much time to count, since we were only going across the hall.

McKinney gestured me in to the open door across from mine. I entered to see . . . a completely empty room. White walls and tile floors, with the same faint new paint smell over old grime. And only one coat of paint to judge by the thinner patches where nebulous patterns of graffiti peeked through. Another bathroom, this time with outlines of urinals on the wall—which reinforced my suspicion that this had once been a public place. There was no toilet, shower, or bed in here. Instead, one wall was almost completely filled with a big-ass window. They weren't even bothering with two-way mirrors or any shit like that. Nope, apparently these people couldn't care less that I knew they were watching. I glanced around, unsurprised to see surveillance cameras in every corner of the room. Whatever was about to happen, they intended to record it thoroughly.

Behind the window was a small room—a former office, perhaps?—with two long tables covered in computer equipment. Two men in guard outfits sat at one table, eyes shifting between their monitors and me. Behind the other stood two people. I didn't recognize the first one, a stocky middle-aged man wearing a dark blue suit and a dubious expression.

But I recognized the other, even though we'd never officially met.

"Hi, Doctor Charish," I said, giving her a tight smile as I fought to hold onto my ragged composure. "Did you kill Sofia?" Sure, McKinney might have been able to go straight from the failed ambush to Sofia's house, but it made more sense that he had someone else working with him that night.

Dr. Charish leaned forward and touched a button in front of her. "Why, yes. Yes, I did." Her voice came from a speaker above the window, yet I could also hear it, muffled, through the glass. That glass was thick, but it wasn't bulletproof-thick. Was it thick enough to keep out a pissed-off zombie? I sure as hell wanted to find out.

"Why? Because she was playing both sides and working with Kang?" I shook my head, baffled. That didn't make any sense.

The woman smiled. "No. Although, yes, she was indeed briefly involved in a rather pathetic series of talks with Kang regarding her pseudo-brain formulation. She always was too altruistic for her own good. But that, of course, ended when Kang died."

Sudden understanding swept through me. Now Sofia's reactions over at Marcus's house made sense. *Sofia had no intention of giving Pietro a monopoly on the fake brains, so she approached Kang to let him know he wouldn't be cut out.* But then Kang was killed, and not long after that it looked as if Zeke—a zombie—had tried to sneak into the lab. No wonder she was freaking out, thinking she was at the heart of some sort of conflict between zombie factions. I was beginning to wonder whether there really were any zombie "factions" at all, at least not in the way that Pietro made it out to be. Perhaps Kang had been the de facto "leader" of the zombies who bought brains from him, but there was no way he had as much influence and power as Pietro.

"So why kill her?" I asked.

"Sofia suspected that I had a pet project of my own." She made a sweeping gesture around her. "And I knew that once she heard you'd been attacked, she'd go tattling to Pietro." She nodded toward McKinney. "That being said, we need to get started."

Still baffled and off-balance, I turned as another man walked in. The two guards left, leaving just me, McKinney, and this new guy in the room. The exiting guards pulled the door closed, and a shiver ran over me as I heard it lock from the outside.

The newcomer looked like he was in his late twenties, blond and blue-eyed, with a short haircut and muscular build to match the other guards here. He had on a simple white t-shirt and grey sweat pants like mine—though obviously much bigger—and he held himself so stiffly that I had a feeling he was holding down fear by the sheer force of his will. Fear of me? What the hell was going on?

I jerked as a beep sounded in the room. "Now recording contagion series one point one," Dr. Charish said.

"Angel, this is Philip," McKinney said. "He volunteered for this study.

Baffled and wary, I gave Philip an awkward wave. "Um, hey, Philip."

He gave me a tight smile and short nod in response.

"And now, Angel, if you would be so kind," McKinney said, "please turn Philip here into a zombie."

I could only blink at him stupidly for several seconds. "Wait, what?" I said once I found my voice. "I can't do that! I've never done that before!"

"I suggest you figure out how," McKinney said, tone mild.

I looked in horror to Philip. "You volunteered for this? To become a zombie?"

He lifted his chin. "I'm a volunteer for the enhanced soldier protocol."

"Enhanced soldier ..." Suddenly I understood—at

least part of it. *They want to make zombie soldiers. This has nothing to do with zombies vs. zombies. It probably never did, or at least certainly not to the degree that we all thought.* Dr. Kristi Charish had taken this whole thing to another level entirely. Well, that explained the whole secret lab thing and the team of mercenary guard types. Zombie soldiers . . . ? Would the government be interested in something like that? Probably. Or maybe a private contractor like those Halliburton people in Iraq. I peered at the man in the suit behind the glass. He looked soulless enough to be either government or corporate.

But they haven't fully committed, I thought as I looked at the slight frown on the man's face and the tension on Dr. Charish's. Not yet. *They want some proof that this is real and that it'll work.* That explained why this whole scenario seemed rather low-budget. Why sink a bunch of money into a project that sounded like a shitty late night movie? No, Dr. Charish had to prove she wasn't giving her sponsors a line of bullshit. She needed to show them what a zombie could do, show them that more could be made.

And *that* was why they now needed a real, live, fully functioning zombie. Me.

I looked at McKinney. A hint of a smirk curved his mouth, and I abruptly realized that he *had* recognized me when I went to the lab to pretend to apply for a job. Anger at myself swept over me. I thought I'd been so damn clever. They needed a zombie, and I'd been the logical choice since I'd been doing my best to become a pain in their ass.

Didn't matter. I had no intention of doing what these assholes wanted. I turned to the window. "Y'all are completely fucking batshit insane," I said, crossing my arms over my chest defiantly. "No. I won't do it."

McKinney shrugged. "I rather expected you would say that."

And with that he pulled his pistol and fired two rounds into Philip's chest.

The sound of the bullets slammed through the room while I cried out in horror. Philip staggered back, then slid down the wall, gasping for breath as he clutched at his chest.

"It's simple, Angel," McKinney said. "Turn him into a zombie, or he dies."

"You fucker," I breathed, moving to Philip on shaking legs. Dropping to my knees beside him, I struggled to remember what Kang and Marcus had said about how zombies were made. *A simple bite isn't enough. There's some mauling involved. So . . . what the hell does that mean? Do I simply bite him and keep biting him until he's a zombie?*

Philip's eyes met mine. "Do it," he gasped. "Please."

I felt strangely ridiculous and self-conscious doing this with all these people watching, especially knowing that the whole thing was being recorded, monitored, videotaped, and anything else that could be done. Talk about the ultimate performance anxiety.

"I'm so sorry," I whispered, then pulled his shirt aside at the collar, leaned over, and bit down hard on the junction of his shoulder and neck. He stiffened as I increased the pressure. I tasted blood, and nausea rose at what I was doing . . .

But only for an instant. Hunger abruptly surged, but far different from what I was used to. This hunger urged me to bite harder, to rip the flesh away. I dimly felt him struggling against me, but I was strong—far stronger than he was, and I held him pinned down while I literally mauled his neck and chest, tearing the shirt away, biting and ripping until even the gunshot wounds were lost in the damage and resulting gore. Yet I didn't feel any sort of urge to get at his brains, only the overwhelming need to mangle him as much as possible.

And then as soon as it had started, the urge was gone. Philip lay still on the floor in front of me, blood flowing from a dozen wounds, though so sluggishly that I knew it would be over for him soon.

"God *damn*," I heard McKinney mutter.

"Brains," I rasped through the blood and flesh in my mouth. I turned and spat a gobbet of who-knew-what onto the floor. "He needs brains right now," I said, louder. I heard the door open and close, but I didn't take my eyes away from the bloodied man in front of me. A second later something cool and slippery was pressed into my hand. I didn't need to look down to see what it was. Right now my parasite was working overtime, doing what needed to be done. I was a passenger in my own body at this point.

I put a large hunk of brain into my mouth, then leaned over Philip and started biting him again—but this time not trying to damage him. Somehow I knew what was going on—now I was transferring the necessary proteins over to Philip along with the colonizing spores, using the previous wounds as pathways. I felt like a mother bird, chewing the brains up to mush then spitting them out into Philip's body. A part of me knew how unbelievably disgusting this was, but I kept going, chewing, biting, spitting.

Philip took a sudden gurgling breath, and I paused. The bites were starting to close up. I shifted to where I was sitting against the wall and pulled Philip to me, cradling him against me. Now I began to feed the brains to him directly, placing small hunks into his mouth. He shuddered as the first piece hit his tongue, but then his own newfound instinct took over and he swallowed it down. I continued to feed him, watching as the wounds healed before my eyes like some sort of time-lapse film.

His eyes blearily opened after the last bite. "Now you gotta sleep," I told him, or rather, my parasite told me to tell him. Because that was how it worked, I instinctively knew now. Infect the new zombie, feed it, then let it sleep while the parasite does its thing and gets all happy and settled in its new home.

An oddly content smile curved his mouth, then his eyes drifted closed again. He leaned his head against my shoulder and slept like that while I held him, the two of us surrounded by a pool of his blood.

I must have dozed off, because the next thing I knew someone was trying to pull Philip from my grasp. I jerked awake and clutched him tightly to me.

"No," I gasped. "Get away. He needs to stay with me."

The guard didn't release Philip's arm. This was the one with the too-perfect eyebrows. "I need to take him. Get him checked out."

"He's fine!" I insisted, curling my lip. "They can check him out right here."

His eyes hardened. "That's not going to happen." He tried again to pull Philip's limp body from me, and I let out a growl—a deep throbbing sound I had no idea I could make.

The guard dropped Philip's hand and jumped back, but then his mouth tightened into a thin line and he pulled a Taser from his belt. *Ah, shit, this is gonna suck.* Marcus had once described being tasered—which he'd had to experience in order to carry one on duty. His words: "That shit fucking hurts. If anyone ever tells you to comply or be tasered, you'd better fucking comply!"

But I wouldn't . . . couldn't . . . comply with this. All I knew was that Philip needed to stay with me a while longer.

I squeezed my eyes shut and braced myself for the feel of the metal probes shooting into my skin, but before the guard could fire, Dr. Charish's voice came over the speaker. "Stand down. Leave the subject as he is. We'll come in to get our samples."

Relieved, I opened my eyes and resisted the urge to stick my tongue out at the guard with the Taser. He looked more than willing to "accidentally" tase me. However, he stepped back, eyeing me with undisguised distaste. For the first time I realized that Philip and I weren't exactly a pleasant sight. None of the blood had been cleaned up, and it was starting to congeal to a sticky mess. I swiped at my face with the back of one hand, grimacing as a thick smear of drying blood came away with it. I definitely looked like a monster now, I was sure of it.

Dr. Charish entered, flanked by two more guards. I quickly catalogued them—one had gorgeous blue eyes, and the other had a nose that had clearly been broken a few times.

"Angel, that was absolutely amazing," she said, eyes shining with a fervor that seemed obscene considering the level of gore present in the room. "The way the parasite works is a study in brilliance. This . . . this is the work of a lifetime." She dropped to a crouch beside me, ignoring the *fuck off, bitch* look I gave her. "I need to get samples from you both now." She tilted her head. "Tell me, is your reluctance to let Philip go driven by the parasite? Does it feel like an instinctive need, or do you simply not want to be left alone in here?"

"Get the fuck away from us, you psycho bitch," I snarled.

She reached a hand to Philip, then had to backpedal as I took a swing at her. "Fascinating," she said with a breathless chuckle. "An attachment between parent and child would explain a great deal, such as why Marcus is so taken with you."

I set Philip down and leaped over him in an explosive move that could only be accomplished with zombie super speed, and in the next breath I was on Dr. Charish with my hands around her throat.

Aaaaanndd . . . the next breath after that, I learned just how much it hurt to be tasered.

An eternity or so later the searing pain stopped. I moaned on the floor, distantly aware of a guard helping Dr. Charish to her feet. Shivers of pain echoed through my body, and I could still feel two sharp points where the probes had embedded themselves into my lower back.

"Angel, please," Dr. Charish said, coughing a bit as she straightened her clothing. "I don't want to hurt you."

I let out a dry laugh. "A bit late for that, don't you think?" Before I could think about it too much I grabbed the two wires and yanked the probes out of my skin. Pain flared briefly, but thankfully settled within a couple of seconds as my parasite worked to repair the damage. *That's a good little parasite*, I silently crooned. Too bad a mild jab of hunger came along with the decrease in pain.

"Here's what I don't understand," I said as I crabbed my way back toward Philip. "Why'd you have Ed kill those other zombies? Why not kidnap them the way you did me?"

"I had to prove my research had merit before I could get investors to commit the sort of risk and resources that holding a live specimen would entail," she explained. "And, if you must know, I had actually intended to have Ed obtain a live zombie for us. But he inexplicably decided to drop out of sight before I could do so."

I narrowed my eyes. "You called in the anonymous tip about him being the serial killer."

"Yes. I couldn't be sure what he was up to, and it was necessary to keep him out of the way. But, in all fairness, he *was* the serial killer," she pointed out. "Now hold still while I get samples from both of you." She cocked her head and gave me a thin smile. "Unless you enjoyed the Taser?"

I grudgingly extended my arm.

"You regrew the bodies from the heads he gave you," I said.

"Just the one so far," she corrected absently as she slid the needle into my vein and carefully drew the syringe until it was full of blood. "It takes an enormous amount of brains—and time—for the parasite to regenerate that much tissue." She pulled the needle free and stuck a piece of gauze on the puncture site.

"Oh, I see," I said. "You just did the one, but you didn't have enough real brains, so you tried to use Sofia's fake brains," I said. "But something went wrong. That's why Zeke looked so old and why he died when he fell."

She let out a soft sigh as she repeated the blood-drawing routine on Philip. "That's right. It mutated the parasite to where it couldn't survive. The subject would have died soon even if he hadn't fallen. But I've since modified the brain substitute formula to remove the chance of that sort of mutation happening again."

"Zeke was trying to escape, wasn't he?"

Her lips pressed together in annoyance. "Yes, which is why I've completely changed the protocols."

Ha! I was right! Not that it made any difference at this point. But, still, Ha! I was right! "And what happened to the real Norman Kearny?"

She gave me a blank look. "Who . . . ? Oh, right, the janitor. Quite dead and disposed of. Unfortunately for him he was the one person in our personnel files who was the right age to take the fall, so to speak, for the dead zombie, and who likely wouldn't be missed." She shrugged. "We didn't have time to make up a whole new personnel record. Easiest to simply do a bit of identity-switching."

Well, that explained why the guy at the lab had said there was an opening in the custodial department when I'd pretended to apply for a job. Poor Norman. The really shitty part was that he died for no reason since we figured it out anyway because of the wristwatch.

"At any rate," she continued, "despite the problems, the regrowth of the zombie was enough to prove that the program had potential."

"You used Ed," I said. "You convinced him his parents had been killed by zombies so that he would start hunting them. You didn't want to get your hands dirty hunting down zombies on your own." I curled my lip in my best contemptuous sneer.

"Angel, I'm not much bigger than you. I don't have the brawn, so I had to use the brains." She tapped the side of her head. "Besides," she said with a shrug, "it wasn't a total lie. His dad *was* killed by a zombie."

"Yeah yeah, I know," I retorted. "Pietro was banging Ed's mom, his dad found out, shot her, and then Pietro killed his dad. Then, since you worked with his mom, you had access to her notes and research."

Dr. Charish sat back and regarded me with something that almost—*almost*—looked like respect. "My goodness. Marcus said you were clever. Perhaps I was wrong about why he wanted a relationship with you."

Right then I silently vowed that at some point I would slug this bitch in the face, hard.

She spread her hands. "Anyway, yes, I approached Pietro and told him what I knew, convinced him that I wanted to continue Dr. Quinn's research. I could see the greater potential even if he could not." Her smile was chock-full of self-satisfaction. "Then I bided my time, waiting for the breakthrough that would make my plan possible."

"Sofia's artificial brains," I said.

"Did you know Pietro paid for her entire education?" Dr. Charish asked. "Sofia had an interest in medicine, but he convinced her to go into neurobiology. Supported her the whole way, while making sure she specialized in fields that would benefit him."

Okay, that was more than a little manipulative, but I already knew that about Pietro. "And you hired her to make sure you could keep an eye on her and what she was doing."

"Of course," she said. "And with Pietro's blessing as well, since it kept her close." She chuckled. "That made things much easier all around, since it can be unwise to cross that man."

"I can't wait to see what Pietro's going to do to you," I said.

She lifted an eyebrow at me. "Do to me? For what?"

"For crossing him," I said. "He told me he'd never allow any of the zombies under his protection to be harmed in any sort of research."

"Angel, I didn't cross him." She leaned in close and smirked. "He simply made an exception in your case."

She chuckled at the stunned look on my face. "Can you blame him?" she asked with a tilt of her head. "He's been grooming Marcus for bigger and better things for a long time now, and it didn't take much persuasion on my part to convince him that the last thing he wanted was to see Marcus hooked up with barely literate trash."

I felt as if a fist had closed around my chest. She stood and raked her gaze over me. "Let's get you cleaned up and fed, shall we?" she said with a bright smile. "We need you at your best!"

With that she left the room, leaving me to stew in my hate and fear.

Chapter 26

Food was brought in for Philip and me, once again on plastic cafeteria trays. Cheeseburgers and fries this time, and, of course, a side of brains.

The amount of brains they were giving me was generous—which either meant they didn't know how much I needed, or they expected me to burn them off. Considering how much Dr. Charish clearly knew about zombies, I had a bad feeling it was the second reason.

Philip twitched then went still again, eyes remaining closed. I had a feeling he was awake and was trying to get his bearings without giving himself away. And he'd have probably pulled it off if I hadn't been paying close attention—also known as "bored out of my mind."

"Hey, Philip," I said. "There's no one else in here or the observation room, but I'm sure they're still monitoring us."

He opened his eyes and looked at me. I allowed myself a moment of self-congratulation that I was right about him being wide-awake. He sat up, eyes flicking around the room, taking in the blood that covered the floor and us.

"There's some food for you," I said with a nod toward the second tray. "Brains too, which you'll want to eat, I'm sure."

A flicker of disgust passed over his face, and I almost laughed. "Yeah, I know," I said. "But your instincts will take over quickly enough."

"He shot me," he said in a low voice. Frowning, he pulled his shirt up, but even through the dried and congealed blood it was obvious he was unwounded. He ran his hand over his chest. "That's amazing."

"Yeah, it's fucking miraculous . . . as long as you're tanked up."

"Tanked up?" He gave me a puzzled look.

"Well fed on brains," I explained.

"Ah. Well that shouldn't be a problem," he said.

I lifted an eyebrow. "Uh, right. Well, here's the deal. The more you exert yourself, the more brains you'll need. So your days of weight training and ten mile runs are over."

His brows drew together as he opened his mouth to argue, but I cut him off. "You still don't get it, do you?" I said. "You don't *need* to do all that training anymore. The zombie part of you takes care of being strong and fast, and all it wants in return is brains."

He considered that for a moment. "But if I had sufficient brains, I *could* train to improve, right?"

Frowning, I shrugged. "I guess. Honestly I have no idea. I've never been much of a fitness chick. And I've never had so many extra brains that I would've been able to test it out." Not that I'd want to. I still had nightmares about high school phys ed class. I pulled the second tray over to him. "Here. You need to eat."

He lifted the plastic fork, hesitated, then dug into the brains.

"Jesus," he mumbled, an expression of bliss crossing his face.

I grinned. "Yeah. Crazy shit, huh?" I let him eat for a few minutes. "Why on earth would you volunteer for this?" I asked him when he was nearly finished with the contents of the tray. "Did you know what you were getting into?"

A faint smile twitched the corner of his mouth. "Well, I didn't know I would be shot and then . . ."

"Eaten?"

"Well . . . yes." A bit more of a smile revealed itself. Maybe this guy had a personality after all. "We were told it was an experimental program with a high risk of death."

"Again," I said, "why the hell would you volunteer for something like that?"

"Because we were also told that if the procedure succeeded we would be unstoppable." He ran a hand over his chest again. "Invincible."

I sighed and leaned back against the wall. "Dude, you really should've read the fine print. It's all candy and roses as long as you have the brains, but just see how you feel after you've been without for a few days." I picked at a flake of dried blood. "This is all about making super zombie soldiers or some shit, right?"

He frowned and didn't answer, which was all the answer I needed. I smiled thinly. "You look like the kind of guy who's been in the military."

"Three tours in Iraq," he answered gruffly.

"Okay, well, I imagine there's lots of exertion, right? Now can you see yourself lugging a cooler of brains around with you . . . ?" I trailed off. God, I was slow sometimes. Dr. Charish had found a better use for fake brains than feeding civilian zombies. Zombie super soldiers. Unstoppable and invincible.

Philip didn't seem to notice my shift in mood. "They'll take care of me. I have no doubt about that."

The door swung open, and the man in the suit came in. "Yes, we'll take good care of Philip," he said, confirming my suspicion that they were constantly listening in. "In fact it's time for him to come with us so that we can see what he's capable of." Philip scrambled to his feet and stood at attention. I rolled my eyes.

"Take him," I said dully. "Happy fighting. Rah rah, and all that shit."

They took me back to "my" room, let me shower the blood off, gave me fresh clothes to change into, then left me alone. I didn't know what time of day it was or how much time had passed since I'd been taken, but I curled up on the narrow bed and fell asleep as soon as I closed my eyes.

It might have been half an hour or ten hours later that I woke up, but either way I felt fairly rested. I lay there quietly, ignoring my need to pee while I listened, doing my best to get some sort of clue as to where I was.

The place smelled like new paint, but beneath that there was a faint scent of rust and brackish water. My first instinct was to wonder if I was on a ship or barge or something, but if that was the case, I thought that surely I'd be able to feel some sort of motion or rocking, even if it was docked. Instead I could hear and feel an occasional low rumbling, as if a truck was driving by. *Great, so I'm close to a road. Yeah, that really narrows it down.*

It didn't matter. The important thing was to break the hell out however I could. Then I could figure out where I was and how to get to safety.

And warn Marcus.

A fierce ache squeezed my chest at the thought of him. I still wasn't completely certain of my feelings for him, and I knew it was far too soon to think about whether I was in love with him or anything like that. But I did trust him. We had issues to work out, but I was absolutely certain that he would never throw me under the bus. Pietro was the one who'd betrayed me. I didn't fit into his bigger plan for Marcus and whatever schemes he had going.

I let out a low laugh. His bigger plan was tiddlywinks compared to what Dr. Charish was up to. I couldn't imagine that he had any idea. He loved his power too much. There's no way he'd want to have to answer to some government or corporate type.

The light abruptly increased. They knew I was awake. I sat up and raked my fingers through my hair as a guard I didn't recognize entered with another tray. *Brown eyes, mole on his chin.* I mentally tallied the number of different faces I'd seen so far. At least half a dozen, plus Philip. Maybe not so low-budget after all?

There was a slice of brain on the tray again, which didn't fill me with a warm fuzzy feeling. If they were feeding me so much it had to mean that they had more tests or other bullshit planned.

I ate quickly, then attended to my various personal needs. McKinney and two guards came in as I finished and marched me across the hall again. For an instant I thought perhaps it was a different room, because every speck of blood had been cleaned up. But no.

Dr. Charish was on the other side of the big window, of course, as well as two other lab-coated people I hadn't seen before. The blue-suited man wasn't there. Beside Dr. Charish was a new observer: mid-forties perhaps, dark-skinned with an angular face, wearing a black suit that was a somewhat nicer cut than blue-suited guy. I got the unmistakable impression that *this* was who Dr. Charish was working with. Or for. This was who was really interested in this whole super zombie soldier thing.

"Morning, Doc," I said, baring my teeth at her. "Who's your new pal?"

"Good morning, Angel," her voice came through the speaker above me. "I trust you slept well?"

"Like the dead," I answered.

She chuckled low in her throat. "Funny. Well, let's see what you can do for us today."

The door opened. A sick feeling began in my gut that increased to near panic levels as McKinney and a black man in white t-shirt and grey sweat pants walked in.

Clenching my fists by my sides, I watched in helpless rage as McKinney pulled his gun.

"No, not again," I pleaded. I looked over at the doctor. "I can't do this again!"

"Well, you'll need to give it the old college try then."

The doctor's voice chirped from the speaker. "Oh, wait. You didn't go to college, did you?"

Fury burned through the sick feeling. I'd never killed anyone in my life, but I was more than ready for her to be the first. "Don't shoot him," I pleaded with McKinney. "You don't have to do that. I swear I'll try." I turned to the new dude. "You do know that's what he was going to do, right? He shot the last guy on the gamble that I could turn him into a zombie."

The new guy's expression didn't shift, but I saw a muscle in his jaw leap. "Yeah," I continued. "That's right. You have to die for this to work."

McKinney lifted his gun, pointed it at my head. "He knows how the soldier program works. Just do it." Except he slurred the word soldier oddly.

"Wait . . . are you saying soldier with a *Z*?" I asked. I laughed despite the horror of the whole situation. "Oh my god, seriously? You're calling it a 'Zoldier program' because it's zombie soldiers? That has got to be the dumbest thing I've ever heard!"

To my surprise, McKinney shrugged and chuckled, though the gun didn't waver. "On that I have to agree with you, but unfortunately it wasn't up to me."

Jesus, this guy was a fucking psycho with his weird mood swings. Scared the ever living shit out of me. I shot a look toward the window. Black suit dude was scowling. I had a feeling "Zoldiers" had been his idea. Figured. A name that stupid could only come from the government. Besides, if they were with an Evil Corporation, their suits would be nicer.

I took a deep breath and turned back to the new guy. "What's your name?"

He flicked a glance at McKinney and received a whisper of a nod in response. "Name's Aaron Wallace, ma'am," he told me.

"I'm Angel." *And I'm going to be your Angel of Death today, one way or the other,* I thought miserably. "You, um, should probably sit down," I said, waving in the general direction of the wall. I gave a nervous gulp. "I . . . I'm sorry. This is going to hurt."

Aaron moved to sit and leaned against the wall, still keeping his back straight and stiff. "It's all right ma'am. I've been injured before."

I knelt down beside him, met his eyes. I wanted to tell him that he needed to run, get the hell out of here. Tell him that he had no idea what he was getting into. "There's no going back from this," I whispered. "There's no cure."

He gave me such a sweet smile that it almost brought me to tears. "It's all right. I'm ready."

I wished I was.

Taking hold of his shoulders, I leaned over and bit him hard, the same place I'd bitten Philip, right on the meat of muscle of his traps. Aaron let out a soft hiss as I tightened down, but didn't twitch at all. I bit harder, tasting blood, then released him, swallowed uncertainly, and bit again. *C'mon, killer instinct,* I silently begged the parasite. *I can't do this on my own.* Blood filled my mouth on the third bite. I could feel tears leaking down my cheeks as I tried to pretend I was simply eating a really tough piece of steak and did my best to tear the flesh.

I sat back on my heels and looked up at McKinney. "It's not working," I said, trying to keep my voice steady.

"I swear, I'm trying. I swear. Maybe it's too soon. Let me try some other time. Please!"

McKinney regarded me, mouth twisted in thought. "I'm not ready to quit trying yet. There's one thing that's different." And with that he lifted the gun and shot Aaron twice in the chest, in an almost exact duplicate of the wounds on Philip.

Aaron jerked, eyes wide as he fought to get breath.

"No!" I screamed. "It's not working. I'm not going to be able to save him!"

"Philip was dying when you tried to turn him," McKinney replied, utterly calmly. "Perhaps being near death is a requirement. Now, try again."

I struggled to catch my breath. Could he be right? I'd been close to death when Marcus turned me. And Marcus said he had rabies . . . but surely he hadn't been actually *dying* when Pietro turned him? Would simply having a fatal disease count?

Aaron met my eyes as he fought for breath. Blood bubbled at his mouth, but then he gave me that same sweet smile. How could a seasoned soldier like this be so . . . innocent? I struggled to give him a smile in response, but I knew it was a sickly effort.

I leaned forward once again and bit down, silently praying with everything I had that this would work. I bit, I chewed, I even forced myself to swallow a small hunk of Aaron's flesh in case that was what would trigger the mauling instinct.

But the only thing it triggered was nausea, and it wasn't long before Aaron let out a low sigh of breath and went still.

"Fascinating," I heard Dr. Charish say. "Though annoying," she added. "It seems the parasite has a built in population control, which makes sense considering that human brains are a limited resource."

I got slowly to my feet, turned to face her. I knew I still had blood around my mouth but I didn't wipe it off. She stood with her hands on her hips, looking between me and Aaron's body with undisguised impatience and aggravation. The black-suited man didn't looked very pleased either.

"And how, pray tell," he asked, "are we supposed to build a unit of Zoldiers if we can't make more than one?"

"I can fix that," Dr. Charish snapped. "The limitations are there because of the shortage of food supply. Once the parasite is introduced to the pseudo-brains it should adjust accordingly. I've given the new formulation to Philip, and there are none of the issues that were present with the previous batch. Which means we're in business." Her gaze went back to me, eyes narrowing. "And which also means that we don't need to waste resources on this one anymore. Take care of it, McKinney."

I crumpled as McKinney's rounds hit me in the chest and stomach. God damn it, I was getting really fucking tired of getting shot. I made sure to fall so I was facing away from the group, though. Because Ed's brilliant idea was hopefully going to pay off now.

"Do you want me to finish her off?" McKinney asked.

Dr. Charish laughed. "Oh, heavens, no! This is an excellent chance to see how the zombie parasite reacts when it doesn't have the brains it needs." I couldn't see her, but I could practically hear the bitchy smile spreading across her face. "I want to see her rot. Let's see how cocky she is when her tits are falling off."

The government guy made a disgusted noise in his throat. "You're a sick woman, Kristi. But I suppose that's necessary for this sort of research."

"Just wait until you've been around the zombies for a while," she said with snort. "Besides, this way if it turns out we still need her, we can just throw some brains at her and she'll be good as new." She chuckled. "I can keep her as a test subject forever, if need be."

And that's when I stood up.

See, Ed's idea had been brilliant and disgusting. He was a paramedic who knew anatomy and how to stitch wounds; I was a zombie with the ability to heal without a scar. And the perfect place to hide a stash of brains was, of course, in my abdomen.

McKinney's stomach shot had actually helped me out by piercing one of the sausage casings of mushed brains that Ed had stuffed inside me—which, for the record, had not been a fun experience *at all* since anesthesia didn't work on me. But oh, it was all so worth it now. After being shot I'd had to curl in on myself and do a bit of quick digging to pull the other tubes open and squeeze the brains out before the parasite could repair the damage, but while Dr. Charish and the others were yammering, I was busy getting tanked up to the max—three brains worth. I didn't even need to eat the brains. The parasite didn't give a shit how it got what it wanted. This was a sure-shot delivery system.

And *I* was the motherfucking predator now. I'd felt this way when I'd saved Marcus from being killed by Ed, and it had taken all the will I had to hold back and keep from doing everything I could to stay this way.

But right now I had no intention of holding back. Sweet zombie Jesus, I *was* fucking invincible.

They could see it, or sense it in their puny little hind-brains. Pure panic filled Dr. Charish's face, and even McKinney went pale. She stabbed at a button on the keyboard in front of her and an alarm started hooting in the hallway.

My lips curled back from my teeth in a feral grin. "Zombie Super Powers, activate, you fucking bitches."

I went for McKinney first. Even though I desperately wanted to smash through that window and take down Dr. Charish, I was a smart predator and knew that Mc-Kinney was the one who posed an immediate threat to me. Plus, I didn't want to waste energy on smashing things too soon.

McKinney had enough training to go for the "fight" instead of the "flight," but it didn't matter. I got to him before he could squeeze off a shot and wrenched the gun from his hand with an adorably sweet sound of breaking bones. Okay, so I *might* not have actually pulled the gun from his hand before doing the wrenching.

He was tough—I had to give him that. He let out a choked cry of pain, but a snarl of determination curved his mouth. His other hand was already going for his an-kle, where I figured he likely had another weapon.

I punched him hard in that determinedly snarling mouth, crushing lips and teeth. He staggered, but before he could fall I seized him by the side of his head. He tried to swing at me, but I batted it aside easily. I gave him my best evil-predator-bitch smile as he struggled to focus on me.

"Yeah, I'm a zombie, you motherfucker. And I'm also

a person." I slammed his head hard into the window. "I'm a woman." I slammed it again. "And a daughter." And again. "And a really fucking cool chick!" Oh what the hell, one last time, for good measure.

I let him drop and grinned at the bloody spiderweb of cracks in the glass. The room beyond the glass was empty and a distant sound of running footsteps echoed along the hall. The predator inside me keened in pleasure. A hunt. This would be fun. But first . . .

I crouched over the body of McKinney. His skull came apart easily since it was already fairly shattered, and I quickly gulped down the contents. While I ate I yanked off his belt and looped it around my waist. It was far too big but I threaded it through his holster and managed to tie the long end around the buckle so that it wouldn't fall off. He also had a phone—unfortunately, with no signal. Either we were in the middle of nowhere, or we were in a big metal building. Or both. I clipped that onto the belt as well. I probably looked ridiculous but I didn't give a shit.

My gaze shifted to the body of Aaron. "Sorry, sweetheart," I murmured as I smashed his skull against the floor. "Just think of this as me avenging your death."

After I finished I wiped my mouth with the back of my hand. It came away bloody, and I stood. Time for the monster to bust herself out.

Chapter 27

McKinney had another gun in an ankle holster. It was a small thing that only held eight rounds, and I used them all to bust through the thick window. My room was locked, but the door of the observation room stood wide open. I kept McKinney's other gun with me. I wasn't much of a shot, but since I figured I was up against at least half a dozen guards I needed every edge I could give myself.

Right now my senses were at superpower levels, and I could literally scent the direction they'd gone. Unfortunately, Dr. Charish and Suit Dude had a good head start, and that damn hooting alarm was apparently the *grab-everything-and-get-the-hell-out* signal.

I came out of the observation room and saw Dr. Charish by the door at the end of the hallway, urging two guards loaded down with computer equipment to hurry the hell up. She turned and saw me, then gave a little shriek of horror as she dove through the doorway and put her shoulder to the door to get it closed. I dug in hard, running faster than I'd ever run in my life, but it clanged shut just seconds before I reached it. I slammed hard into it in the hopes of forcing it open again, but only managed to do something unpleasant to my shoulder as a heavy click told me the door had latched and locked.

Scowling, I rotated my shoulder while I assessed the door and the surrounding frame. I briefly thought about trying to shoot out the lock, but then grudgingly admitted that shooting the lock probably wouldn't work at all the way it did in the movies. Besides, I'd seen something through that heavy door before it closed. It was all clean and white and new paint where I was, but outside that door was another story entirely—rust and grime and broken windows.

And I knew exactly where I was.

I could hear voices beyond the door, so I leaned close and listened.

"She won't get through that," Dr. Charish said. She was breathing hard, but she sounded calmer. Apparently she was pretty confident that I was stuck. "It doesn't matter now. We intended for this facility to be temporary. That's why we built it out in this shithole. We have Philip. It's time to move on to the next phase."

The government dude responded, but they were moving off, and I couldn't quite make out what he was saying. Unfortunately, my busy little parasite was fixing up my shoulder instead of keeping me in super zombie mode. Damn it.

I wasn't getting through that door or the walls, I knew that. But there was another way out that these assholes probably hadn't counted on. At least I sure as hell hoped they hadn't.

I ran back to the observation room and yanked at the edge of the carpet. I didn't know a lot about computers, but even I knew that a super secret government lab wasn't going to advertise its presence or risk being hacked with a wireless network. And, perhaps they'd even use the conduits that were already in place.

I grinned as I saw the floor panels beneath the carpeting. As I'd suspected and hoped, the cabling for the computers and cameras and stuff had been strung through the service tunnels beneath the floor. And they'd even been nice enough to not screw the floor panels back down again. I was sure they'd never imagined that their prisoner would know about those tunnels.

Damn good thing I'm a skinny little bitch, I thought as I shimmied through the narrow tunnel. And also a damn good thing I wasn't claustrophobic. Or afraid of the dark, since it was black as utter pitch in the tunnel. I continued to listen hard as I slid myself along while doing my best to ignore the dirt, dead bugs—and live bugs—and occasional dead rat. After a few minutes I was pretty sure I was beyond the section where I'd been held and which was now locked down. Now I simply had to keep going until I could find a way out.

Gradually I began to hear voices, and I slowed, not wanting to give away my position. *Give away my position,* I thought with a silly grin. *Heh.* Boy, didn't I sound like a secret agent?

"We're not going to simply leave her to rot," the suited dude was saying. For an instant I thought that maybe he was having a moment of compassion, then he continued. "Too much risk of someone coming here and finding her. We're all set to ..." Then he moved off, and I couldn't hear the rest of the conversation.

Oh well. So much for compassion.

I saw light ahead and breathed a sigh of relief. They'd never bothered to replace the section of flooring that had been removed to get the dead copper thief out. I edged ever so cautiously to the opening and peeked out. Dr. Charish was there along with Suited Government Dude. Four guards were quickly packing computers and boxes into the back of a familiar white van. Two other guards were lying crumpled on the ground, yet everyone seemed to be ignoring them. Had they tried to rebel or something and been killed?

After a few seconds of scanning, I located Philip sitting on the steps to the foreman's office, and in almost the exact spot Marianne had been the last time I was here. I slid back into the tunnel and pulled the phone out. I had a signal now. But who to call? Ed didn't have a phone, and I couldn't remember Marcus's number ... But I *did* remember Pietro's since it was so similar to Randy's.

And, man, did I ever have some things to say to that motherfucker. I scooched further back into the tunnel and dialed Pietro. I was about to leave him one fucking hell of a voicemail.

"Yes? Hello?" Pietro said.

He said he doesn't answer if it's an unfamiliar number, I remembered. *Which means ...*

"McKinney?" Pietro said, sounding annoyed. "What the hell is going on? Why are you calling me?"

I pushed aside my brief shock. "Hello, Uncle Pietro,"

I said speaking low and cupping my hand around the phone. "You probably figured you were well rid of me, right? Guess I'm not so easy to kill, even for a zombie."

I heard his intake of breath. "Angel? Where are you? Marcus has been going crazy with worry."

"Oh, really? And did you tell him how you threw me under the bus and told Dr. Charish that I was fair game for her experiments? Did you know she's screwing you over too and working with the government to make zombie soldiers?" My voice shook with anger, and I had to fight to keep speaking quietly.

"Angel, I . . . wait, *what?* What the hell have you gotten yourself into?"

The shock in his voice was genuine, and I would have laughed if I wasn't still so pissed. "Me? Oh, no, you're not putting that shit on me. You started this, pal, when you unleashed your pet, Charish, on me. But now you have bigger problems than free-market fake brains. Why don't you come to the old Ford factory on the Kreeger River and see for yourself. Then we can have a nice long talk, 'kay?"

"Wait, Angel," he sounded truly frantic. "You don't understand. I never—"

I disconnected, quite pleased with how upset he sounded. Good. He deserved that much and more, the fucker.

I dialed 911 next. "Oh my god, please help!" I babbled in a hoarse whisper as soon as the dispatcher answered. "I'm in some big warehouse thing by the Kreeger River. There's a huge drug deal going down, and I think a gang war is about to start. They already killed two guys. There are guns everywhere. Please help!" There, that should be enough to get a few units sent.

"Ma'am, please remain calm," a woman responded. "Can you be more specific as to your location? Your phone has its GPS disabled."

"I heard someone say something about Ford?" I said, trying to sound panicked. "Does that sound right?"

"Yes, ma'am. I know where you are. I'm dispatching units to you right now." I heard the click of a keyboard. "How many suspects are there?"

"Twenty . . . maybe thirty?" I lied. "I don't know. They kidnapped me but I got away, and I'm hiding right now."

"It's going to be all right," the woman said in a calm voice, though I could detect an edge of excitement. It wasn't everyday that the St. Edwards Parish sheriff's office had an excuse to call out their SWAT team. "I need you to tell me everything you can about what's going on. What's your name? Are there any other hostages?"

"I'm, um, Charmaine, and I think there are some others," I said, warming to my story. "I saw a—" I let out a squawk of alarm and dropped the phone as the floor above me gave a massive shudder.

"Ma'am?" I heard the dispatcher say. "Charmaine? Is everything all right? Talk to me."

Light flooded over me, and I looked up to see Philip pulling the entire section of flooring away. One of his eyes was clouded over and his right ear hung oddly on the side of his head. His cracked lips peeled back in a grotesque smile.

"Hello, Mother."

Chapter 28

I let out an unholy scream—totally for the benefit of the dispatcher, of course—then braced myself since I knew what was coming next. Sure thing, Philip grabbed me by the front of my shirt, yanked me out and held me up with one hand. I screamed again, but this time purely for my own sake as Philip turned and tossed me a good dozen feet. I landed hard in a sprawling slide that managed to scrape several layers of skin from my hip and shoulder and sent a sharp jab of pain through my chest. One of these days I probably needed to learn how to tuck and roll and all that crap.

But I had to deal with a pissed off zombie-baby right now. I staggered to my feet and yanked the gun out of the holster. Philip paused in his approach, then let out a dry, rasping laugh. "That can't kill me. You should know that."

"I know, but I need you to listen to me for just a few

seconds." Holy shit, I sure as hell didn't want to try to actually fight this guy. I'd burned through most of my excess brains and, judging by my growing hunger, I'd suffered more injury than just a few scrapes from being thrown. Plus, Philip actually *knew* how to fight.

"Look, there's something wrong," I said urgently. "You shouldn't be rotting so quickly. It's the fake brains that Doc gave you. They . . ." I trailed off, only now seeing the two guards that I'd thought were dead. They were slowly getting to their feet, and had gaping bites on their neck and shoulders. And the look in their eyes . . .

"Oh, that's not good," I breathed.

"Forget her!" Dr. Charish yelled from the van as she brandished something in her hand that looked like a protein bar. The two new zombies turned and began loping toward her. "Let's go, Sergeant! We're about to blow this place. There's no way she'll get clear in time." She grinned nastily. "Now get your ass in the van!"

Ah, shit. Now I saw the little tan chunks placed around the factory next to barrels that probably had something flammable in them, especially around the section I'd just managed to break out of. I'd watched enough *Mythbusters* to know what C-4 looked like. I heard sirens in the distance, and I knew there was no time left. There was no way these assholes were going to leave any evidence lying around.

I didn't wait to see what Philip was going to do. I turned and started sprinting, but not in the direction of the door like she probably expected. I had no doubt they'd shoot me if I tried to get past them, and I figured I had at least a minute until they could all pile into the van and get clear. There was no way I could run fast enough to make it out before they did, but if I could just remember correctly ...

There. Just past the foreman's office was a bank of windows that overlooked the river. Many of them were broken, but most weren't. I risked a glance back and saw that the van had cleared the broad doors and was accelerating fast.

Any second now ...

I wasn't stupid enough to try and dive through the windows since I wasn't sure I had enough mass behind my scrawny ass to actually break through. Instead I snatched up an abandoned chair mid-stride, then swung around in a big arc like one of those hammer-throwing dudes in the Olympics, and let it fly at the windows.

It smashed through with satisfying ease and a few seconds later I heard a muted splash. But I was already moving. I sort of expected the place to blow up right as I was diving through the hole that the chair had made in the glass—because that would have been insanely awesome and dramatic. But instead I simply hit the water in an awkward splash with no explosion to propel me.

The water was cold enough to make me gasp for breath—which sucked ass since I was still underwater at the time. I wasn't the best swimmer in the world by any stretch, but I finally managed to get my head above water, cough out the nasty river water, and start doggie-paddling away from the edge of the building with everything I had.

The place blew not even five seconds later, and the force of the blast shoved me underwater again. Instinct screamed at me to get my head above the surface, but I fought back and stayed underwater, even doing what I could to get deeper. As I expected, debris began to rain down into the water almost immediately. I barely missed getting clipped by a large section of a brick wall, but I did get smacked hard in the shoulder by a twisted hunk of metal. It bore me down several feet before I could wriggle myself free, all while I hovered right at the edge of full-blown panic. I didn't want to think what could happen to me if I somehow got trapped at the bottom of the river.

My lungs were bursting by the time I started paddling my way back up. A brick or something equally hard and heavy whacked me on the head right before I surfaced, and I had to tread water for a moment while I fought the dizziness and gulped air. *C'mon, little parasite*, I numbly urged. *I know I've been asking a lot of you lately. I promise I'll give you a nice big brain as soon as we get out of this.*

I heard more sirens now, and lots of people shouting. I started paddling again, nice and slow, toward the far end of the building in the hopes that I could get out of the water over there without anyone seeing me. 'Cause I had *no* idea how the hell I could explain why I was there and what had happened.

I couldn't feel the cold anymore—couldn't feel much of anything, which I knew was a damn good thing and a bad thing all at once. But my arms and legs kept moving and the combination of the current and my sloppy paddling finally got me down to the rocks that formed the bank on the south end of the factory.

It took me several tries to clamber up out of the water and onto the rocks. Everything was so numb that I couldn't get a decent grip and I slipped several times. The hunger was getting damn serious, but at this point I could only hope to maintain enough control not to attack anyone. I didn't really have a choice. If I stayed in the water it would only make it worse.

Breathing through clenched teeth, I eased my head up over the edge of the bank and peered at the activity. The outer walls of the factory still stood—but smoke poured from what was left of the roof, and flames licked out of the gaping holes that had once held windows. At least half-a-dozen police cars were there, but they'd clearly shifted their mission to keeping everyone clear of the scene until firefighters could get there—which wouldn't be long to judge from the sound of more sirens and the honks of approaching fire engines.

The wind shifted, sending clouds of acrid smoke over me, but for the moment I welcomed it. At least the smoke drowned out the smell of everyone's brains, which meant I might actually stand a chance of controlling the hunger for a while longer. I decided not to think about what I was going to do after I got away from here. I didn't have the faintest damn clue.

Another car pulled up just as I was about to climb the rest of the way up. I hunched down, waiting, then stiffened as the driver got out.

Pietro Fucking Ivanov.

I seized a rock, but before I could carry out my not-very-well-thought-out plan of "run at him while screaming like a maniac and then bash his head in a lot over and over" Marcus exited the passenger side, staring in naked horror at the burning factory. My shock doubled as Ed climbed out of the back seat.

Wow. Apparently a lot had happened while I was gone.

I staggered up over the low wall, hoping that none of the firemen or police were looking toward the river. "Marcus," I croaked, but there was too much noise. Scowling, I pitched the fist-sized rock still in my hand at Pietro. It missed by several feet, but it did hit his windshield, making a marvelous spiderweb of cracks. All three men turned in unison.

"Hi, boys," I rasped. "Miss me?"

Marcus ran to me, scooped me up in his arms before I could do more than twitch, then hurried back to the car as Pietro pulled the back door open.

"God almighty, Angel," Marcus said, sliding in with me and then clutching me close. "I thought I'd lost you."

"Here," Ed said, thrusting a blanket at Marcus. "Wrap her in this."

I lifted my head to look at Pietro as Marcus tugged the blanket around me. His eyes met mine and his face crumpled.

"Angel, I swear I didn't know that this . . ." Pietro gestured vaguely in the direction of the factory. "Any of this . . . I had no idea. I swear."

I opened my mouth to tell him he was full of shit, to tell him I knew he'd thrown me under the bus, but all that came out was, "Braaiinns."

Yeah, I was kinda hungry.

Pietro handed me a brain smoothie and then we got the hell out of there. A roadblock had been set up, but Pietro showed the deputy something in his wallet, and was waved on through without any further questions.

I finished the first smoothie and was still in pretty lousy shape, but the other two zombies had apparently planned for the possibility of a high need for brains and had a cooler packed full of smoothies and baggies. The hunger started to fade by the time I finished the third smoothie, but it took me downing two baggies of straight-up brains before I felt even close to "okay." Damn good thing that Pietro owned some funeral homes.

"We need to talk," I finally said, relieved that my voice was normal again. "Especially, you, Pietro." I glared at the back of his head while he drove. "But first we need to go to NuQuesCor."

"No problem, Angel," Marcus said. He still had an arm around me which I didn't mind one bit. "What's at the lab?"

"Heads," I said. Ed stiffened and flushed. "I don't know how many—if any—are still there, but I want to get them back."

Marcus exhaled and didn't argue. Not that I expected him to. "It'll take about fifteen minutes to get there."

"I'll take care of it," Pietro said, pulling out his cell phone.

I narrowed my eyes. "What do you mean? If any of the heads are there, I want them back."

"And you'll get them," he replied, dialing a number. "But you're looking to break in and take them back by whatever means necessary, right?"

I scowled. "Pretty much. I'm a little tired of playing nice."

He put the phone to his ear. "Dominica five-oh-four." A pause. "NuQuesCor in Colomb, Louisiana. Retrieval of any human heads matching the victims of the decapitation murders that occurred in St. Edwards Parish in the last four months. Most likely from the labs of Dr. Sofia Baldwin or Dr. Kristi Charish." Another pause. "One hour." He clicked off and set the phone down. "Do you mind if we try it my way first?" he asked me.

"I'll believe it when I see it," I muttered, leveling a black glare at the back of his head.

"Fair enough," he replied. "Why don't we allow Angel to get cleaned up, and then we can say everything that needs to be said over coffee."

Chapter 29

When Pietro said he wanted to give me a chance to clean up I figured we'd stop at a convenience store where I could wash the worst of the grime off in the bathroom and then buy a vastly oversized shirt that I could wear as a dress until I could get home. It's what I'd have done.

That, however, was not how Pietro Ivanov handled such situations. No, instead he rented a room at the only Hilton in St. Edwards parish, handed me the key card, and informed me that if I wanted a shower I should go on up, and that he would obtain clothing for me.

I stared at him for a few seconds, then silently took the card, went on up to the room, and took the hottest shower of my entire life.

He must have made another one of those mysterious phone calls while I was scrubbing blood and river grime off me, because, laid out on the bed when I emerged was a selection of clothing, various toiletries, and even an assortment of makeup—in my damn color palette even. And, finally, a note on the bed that said that the others were down in the hotel café and to please join them when I was ready. I was tempted to take my damn sweet time, but I knew that this whole mess was far from over, and everyone needed to know what was going on.

In the end it took the four of us talking it out to piece together just how the hell everything had gone down.

First, I found out how Ed came to be there with Marcus and Pietro. It was simple, really. After Ed got my dad to his little safe house in the woods, he went straight to Pietro and said, "You fucking owe me." And, yes, he used those exact words. To his credit, Pietro did agree that yes, he did fucking owe Ed.

I held back on saying the same damn thing to Pietro. I could tell by the way he looked and acted around me that he was fully aware of that fact. It simply remained to be seen how much he'd truly known about, and what he intended to do about it. And what I intended to do about it, for that matter.

I told them what had happened to me, how I'd been forced to turn Philip into a zombie and how the sweet-faced Aaron had died. Told them how Ed's plan had paid off, and how I'd escaped. Also told them what I'd seen—Philip rotting far faster than he should have, and the two guards who'd appeared to be turned by just a couple of bites. And, finally, told them that Kristi and her pet pseudo-zombies had escaped and were now dust in the wind.

No one looked happy about any of that.

As for the rest, Pietro explained that Dr. Charish had

been good friends with the Quinns as well as being Dr. Quinn's partner in their neurology practice. After the pair had died, Kristi Charish had taken possession of all of Dr. Quinn's notes and research, some of which dealt with theories of how a "zombie" parasite could operate. Curious as to why on earth Dr. Quinn would have been pursuing such a subject, she broke into the Quinn's residence before their possessions could be packed up, and stole or copied as many notes and papers as she could find. Among the stolen papers was a notebook of rambling entries written by Ed's dad, and under any other circumstance, Dr. Charish would have likely dismissed it as a rather amateurish attempt at writing fiction. But paired with everything else she found, as well as the circumstances of their death . . .

Pietro gave a heavy sigh. "Kristi is not a stupid woman. She initiated a romance with me, and eventually 'discovered' that the zombies were real."

"Which she'd suspected the whole time," Marcus said, frowning. "That was merely a way for her to confirm and get the inside scoop."

"Precisely," Pietro said, mouth turned down in a grave curve. "And even when the romance fizzled, she made sure to remain close to me. We were friends, or so I foolishly believed."

"Why didn't you have Dr. Charish do the fake brain research?" I asked him. "Why Sofia?"

A sardonic smile touched his mouth. "I did. But none of Kristi's attempts worked, and I eventually banned any further experimentation on any of the zombies within our faction."

"And this was before I came along," I said, super

sweetly, "so you didn't have a convenient zombie you wanted to get rid of to throw her way."

He flushed, shoulders slumping. "I swear to you, I thought the worst that might happen would be that you'd feel sick."

"Yeah, whatever," I said. I didn't buy that for a second, because otherwise why not allow any of his other zombies to be guinea pigs? But I wasn't going to pursue it right now. I had other shit to take care of first. "Please, go on," I told him.

He didn't look at me, which was probably a very good idea on his part. "Sofia was a brilliant girl," he continued, "and came up with a protocol that would allow her to test her formulations without risking any 'living' zombies. About six months ago, she told me she was close to a breakthrough. I'm confident that, given a bit more time, she would have perfected it. She was meticulous. Did not wish to cut any corners or take undue risks."

"Six months ago was when I started getting mystery packages in the mail," Ed said, expression bleak.

"Exactly," I said. "I think that the darling Dr. Kristi Charish has had plans for the zombies for quite some time. But it all depended on being able to develop a dependable and plentiful food source."

"You mean making super soldiers?" Ed asked. "She'd worked on enough government grants to know who to go to with her idea. But, of course, first she had to prove she wasn't totally full of shit."

I leaned forward, tapped the table. "I bet she told them she had something that worked. She jumped the gun, and then got impatient when Sofia was taking her sweet time. So she copied Sofia's research, got Ed to grab some zombie heads for her to experiment on, and told the government dweebs she was good to go."

It was Ed's turn to flush in shame, but I reached out and put a hand on his shoulder. "Dude. She's a world-class manipulator."

"I know," he said in a low voice. "But I'll never forget how close I came to killing the two of you."

"Just means you have to buy my beer until the end of time," Marcus said with a grin.

Ed laughed weakly. "Sounds more than fair."

"But why did she want only the heads and not the whole zombie?" I asked.

"She didn't have the funding, support, or facility to house captive zombies," Pietro stated. "To store heads, all she needed was a cooler. And, at the time, the heads—and brains—were all she required for her research."

"Oh, right," I said. "Makes sense." I cocked my head. "But we can't forget that the darling Doctor Charish is on the loose now and god-only-knows where with live zombies of her own."

"I have many connections," Pietro stated. "She will not slip my net."

"Oh, really?" I retorted. "She worked under your nose for how long? Pardon me if I don't trust your 'net.'"

Pietro grimaced and didn't respond. Ha! Point to Angel.

"Okay," I said. "So she got the heads and regrew at least one zombie that we know of using the fake brains." I looked at Marcus. "By the way, dude, I think it's insanely cool that it's possible to do that."

"I never knew it was," he admitted. "It's probably never been tried before because of the huge amount of brains it no doubt takes."

That was a good point. It had taken quite a few brains to heal me up from a number of injuries that were only mildly life-threatening.

"And yes," Marcus continued, "you apparently were right, and Zeke *was* trying to escape from the lab. But the fake brains screwed him up somehow, and he didn't grow back properly."

I grinned. "Now was that so hard? You need to accept I'm right a lot quicker in the future."

He chuckled and gave me a squeeze. "I'll do my best."

Pietro cleared his throat awkwardly. "It was not long after this that Kristi came to me, again asking for a ... volunteer."

I scowled. "I still don't understand why she felt the need to come to you for this. Why didn't she simply go out and kidnap the first zombie she could find? I mean, why did she need your permission? She was already way over the line, right?"

Pietro was silent for a moment. "I am very old," he finally said. He looked up at Marcus. "Far older than you suspect, I am certain," he told Marcus. His gaze shifted to me for a fraction of a second, but in that instant it was as if he dropped a veil. Suddenly I could feel the immense weight of years and experiences and accumulated triumphs and grief. Then he looked away and the sensation was gone.

This dude has been a zombie a helluva lot longer than thirty years, I realized.

"Over the years I have been careful to cultivate influence," he continued. "Kristi was right to be wary of my anger, and I'm certain that she was careful not to 'cross the line,' so to speak, until she was positioned with influence that she hopes can match mine."

I kept the icy look on my face and didn't respond.

He let out a soft sigh. "Yet having experience and influence has not saved me from doing some colossally foolish things." He met my eyes again, but I didn't get the "holy crap, he's been around a long time" vibe this time, to my relief.

"I behaved utterly heinously to you," he said. Then his mouth twisted in a grimace. "Marcus has expressed his displeasure quite vehemently." He paused. "*Quite* vehemently. But he has stated that his forgiveness of me is entirely conditional on you, and whether you can accept my apology."

Well, whaddya know. Marcus was letting me control my own damn life. I slid a look toward him, but he was doing that stony-impossible-to-read face thing. He was so damn cute when he did that.

"I'm a lot like my dad," I said to Pietro. "I can hold a grudge like nobody's business. And as much as it would be great and awesome for everyone to forgive each other, and we all have a big group-fucking-hug, I can't tell you I forgive you until I actually feel it and believe that you really do regret what happened and that you're not just blowing smoke up my ass."

The barest hint of a smile curved the edge of Pietro's mouth and he gave a grave nod. "That seems eminently fair." He turned his attention to Ed.

Ed held up his hand before Pietro could speak. "We'll talk later," he said, eyes dark and haunted.

"Of course," Pietro replied, subdued.

"So, um, here's what I don't quite get," I said, eager to bust up the sudden weird tension. "How did she get the head of security at the lab to do all of her dirty work, including killing several people? And why didn't she simply get McKinney to get the zombie heads she needed?"

"I did some research on him after he snatched you," Ed said. "With the help of Pietro I found out that his real name is William Rook and he's, well, like an evil Jason Bourne-type. Super spy, assassin, mercenary type of dude, rumored to be involved in any number of covert government operations. In other words, he pretty much specializes in doing the dirty work." He paused as the waitress came by to refill coffees. We all gave her friendly smiles, then immediately leaned in close again as soon as she walked off. "And Dr. Kristi Charish hired him less than a month ago. *After* she was able to prove that her zombie soldier concept had some merit."

"Oh, I get it," I said. "He wasn't doing *her* dirty work. He was keeping an eye on her and doing what was needed for this whole government conspiracy zombie project thing."

"Correct," Pietro said. "He is a very dangerous man." A pained look flashed over his face. "I wish I'd thought to have him checked out sooner, but Kristi assured me that she'd investigated him thoroughly and that I could trust him." He didn't say more, but it didn't take a genius to figure out that Pietro had used McKinney for some dirty work of his own.

"Yeah, well I ate his brain." I leaned back and laced my fingers behind my head. "Motherfucker shot me. I couldn't let that shit slide." *I killed a man. Shouldn't it bother me more than this?* Yeah, sure, he was a really bad man, but still . . .

I straightened abruptly. "Shit. What day is it?"

Marcus tipped his wrist to look at his watch. "Well, in about an hour it'll be Tuesday."

"Oh, whew," I slumped back in relief. "I didn't miss it."

"Didn't miss what?" he asked.

I gave a rueful smile. "My meeting with my probation officer."

Ed snorted. "Seriously? You've just survived a secret government zombie lab and that's what you're worried about?"

"Exactly!" I shot back. "I just survived a secret government zombie lab, so it would suck pretty damn hard to go through all that and then end up back in jail because I missed a simple meeting, right?"

He blinked. "I can't argue with that."

"Don't, man," Marcus said fervently. "Don't argue with her. It's much better that way."

I smiled and sipped my coffee.

Chapter 30

And then Marcus took me home. My dad and Ed had retrieved my car and someone had paid to replace the tires. Considering that the old tires had been dangerously bald, I was pretty pleased at how that worked out. I suspected Pietro had something to do with it, since I knew my dad didn't have that kind of money. Also, miraculously, my purse and its contents were still in the car, which saved me a buttload of hassle.

Dad gave me such a long embrace that I wasn't sure he was ever going to let me go. I didn't mind.

"Someday you'll tell me what that was all about, right, baby?" he muttered, voice rough.

I gulped and nodded. "I will. I promise."

He finally released me and gave me a wavering smile, then lifted his head and looked to Marcus. "Thank you for keeping her safe and bringing her back."

"She kept herself safe, Mr. Crawford," he replied. "She's a tough chick. All I did was give her a ride."

"Yep," I said as I rummaged through my purse to make sure everything was really there. "Just call me the Angel of Kicking Ass." I gave him a wink.

My phone was dead, but as soon as I plugged it in it lit up like a Christmas tree with missed calls and text messages—almost all from Derrel, with the others from Nick and Monica. I skimmed through the text messages, confusion growing. From Derrel I had: *Call me.* And: *Where are you? You need to watch the news.* And: *Call me! Where the hell are you?* From Monica simply: *Yay! I'm so happy for you!* Then, from Nick: *You're late for work.* And finally, from Derrel again: *I'm going to kill you if you don't call me!*

The last text message from Derrel was from only twenty minutes ago, so I went ahead and called him back.

He answered with, "Don't you ever check your messages?"

"Um, I've been a little busy. I was sorta out of town. What's going on?"

"You need to watch the press conference Dr. Duplessis gave yesterday. It was on channel five news and it's on their website."

I started to remind him that I didn't have a computer at the house, then spun to Marcus. "You have a smart phone, right?" At his nod I told him, "Derrel says I need to watch the coroner's press conference from yesterday on channel five news."

"Okay," I said to Derrel after Marcus pulled up the video and started it. "I'm watching it . . . Wait. What the hell?"

Derrel chuckled. "Keep watching."

Dr. Duplessis was standing in the conference room behind a lectern, still wearing the damn bowtie.

"When Angel Crawford was nineteen years old she made a mistake—an error in judgment. No one was hurt, and any damage to property was minimal. In due order she was brought before a judge where she received a suspended sentence and probation.

"Our justice system is intended to rehabilitate offenders, and if we do not allow these people who wish to improve themselves the opportunity to do so, then we have failed them and failed ourselves as a society.

"Angel Crawford is a dedicated and hardworking employee who was the victim of a crime. She was held up at gunpoint and told to turn over the body bag containing a decedent. In most professions employees are told that, if they are robbed or threatened, they are to comply with the perpetrators demands in order to protect their own lives. This office is no different. And to imply that her prior record somehow contributed to this terrible incident—especially without knowing any of the details or reasons for the theft—is as vile an accusation as when a rape victim is blamed for somehow inviting their attack.

"Therefore I wish to make it perfectly clear that I refuse to bow to any of the political games that my opponents and the press are playing, because in this scenario, as in most political games, the pawns we so casually toss around are real human beings and our petty maneuverings have real consequences for them. Suspension or dismissal of Angel would not

only rob this agency of one of its finest workers, but it would also give credence to the idea that this office was at fault or somehow negligent. And, I tell you now, it was not."

There were still several minutes left on the video but I hit stop. "Wow, he sure loves to talk, doesn't he?"

"Yep," Derrel said. "He pretty much says the same thing four more times in different ways. I figure he's going for the 'Vote for me or I'll keep talking' tactic."

"So I still have a job?"

"Damn straight." I could hear the broad smile in his voice.

"Hang on a sec," I said, then covered the receiver. I gave Marcus a probing look. "Did you or your uncle have anything to do with this?"

A smile played over his face, but he shook his head. "I swear, neither of us had anything to do with this." I thought he had an odd inflection on "this" but I couldn't be sure. I uncovered the receiver. "Seriously," I asked Derrel. "What gives? I mean *I* know how awesome I am, but why would the coroner go public like this?"

"Dr. Leblanc," Derrel replied. "I mean, don't get me wrong, the rest of us rallied around you too, but he was the one who went into Dr. Duplessis's office and told him that if the coroner caved to the pressure to put you on leave or fire you, then not only would he quit but he'd throw every ounce of his support behind whichever of the coroner's opponents had the best chances of beating him." Derrel cleared his throat. "There might have been some other stuff said behind closed doors. But whatever was said worked."

"Wow." And then because I didn't know what to say, I said, "Wow," again.

"You cool with coming back to work Thursday morning? Oh, and you've been on *paid* leave these past few days. Just FYI."

I grinned. "Yeah. Totally cool."

"Thank god," Derrel said fervently. "I thought I was going to end up partnered with Nick."

"Well, at least he can type," I teased.

He made an inarticulate sound. "I'll see you Thursday," he said.

I laughed and disconnected. "Looks like I have a job again." I gave my dad and Marcus a quick rundown on how it all came about.

My dad sighed and shook his head. "Weird fucking job," he muttered, but there was no disgust in his eyes anymore.

Marcus gave me a hug. "I'm happy for you. But I should let you get some rest now."

"Let me walk you out," I said.

I accompanied him out to his car. He smiled and moved to kiss me, but I planted a hand on his chest, stopping him. "Here's the thing, Marcus," I said. "I like you. A lot."

His mouth twisted. "This is where you say 'But I don't think this is working and we should just be friends,' right?"

"Oh, no, not at all," I said, amused as his eyebrows drew together in confusion. "I do think we should go out on dates. I just don't think we should leap into being boyfriend and girlfriend the way we did. Because, really, we never did *date*." I took a deep breath. "I want to see if we have more in common than simply being zombies. And great sex. Because, dude, if that's the only reason we're together, then that's kinda fucked up, and can't possibly end well."

"Okay," he said slowly. He reached and rubbed my shoulders. "I like you, too. A lot." He looked like he was about to say more, but then apparently changed his mind and simply gave me a rueful smile. "I'd like to date. Get to know you."

I tipped my head up and gave him a light kiss. "I don't think I'm the same person I was three months ago. I'd like to get to know me, too."

He looked a bit lost, so I pulled him into a hug. He gave a little shudder then relaxed against me. Part of me felt awful and sick, but at the same time I knew that this was the right thing. I deserved to be with someone who wanted to be with me, whoever the hell that was.

I gave him a squeeze then released him. "Call me tomorrow?"

"Will do," he said, smiling again. It was probably fake, but he was putting in a damn good effort.

I kissed him again, sent him on his way, then turned to head back inside. Maybe he and I really would work things out. In fact, I realized that I rather hoped we would. But at least now I knew that it wouldn't be the end of the world if we didn't. I was stronger than I'd ever dreamed. And I had plenty of people in my life who had my back, no matter what.

Chapter 31

The next morning I headed to the probation and parole office, arriving with plenty of time to spare before my meeting. I sat stiffly on the hard plastic chair in the waiting room, legs crossed and arms folded, as I stared at the cheesy motivational posters on the dingy wall and avoided making any sort of eye contact with the other two people in the room.

I heard footsteps coming down the hall, and I straightened, noting with mild amusement that the others did as well. Officer Garza came around the corner, and the two slumped back again.

He gave me a slight chin lift. "Come on back, Angel."

I followed him down the hall and into an office that might actually have been spacious if it hadn't been crammed full of furniture and filing cabinets. He motioned me toward a chair while he took a seat behind his desk, an odd expression lingering on his face.

"Is everything all right?" I asked.

"I think so," he said, pushing the papers away from him and leaning back. "See, I was going to talk to you today about your GED studies and tell you that as soon as you passed it I was going to put you in for early termination of your probation."

I stared at him in surprise for several seconds. "Seriously? All I have to do is pass it, and then I'm done?"

He snorted. "Well, I *was* going to say that. But then something happened this morning that changed those plans."

Elation shifted to terror. Had someone seen me at the factory? Was I about to be charged with arson or some shit like that?

"I got a phone call from the governor's office not half an hour ago," he said. Then a bemused smile came over his face. "You've been pardoned."

"I . . . Hunh? What?" I blinked. "What the hell?"

He shrugged. "Don't ask me to explain it. But there's no mistake. Trust me, I checked. Three times. Full pardon. Record expunged. I've never seen anything like it." Then he leaned forward, expression fierce again. "I don't know what the hell this is all about, but I swear to god, Angel, if you blow this and get into trouble again, I swear I'll throttle you."

I grinned. Then I laughed. Pietro Fucking Ivanov. "Don't you worry about me. I'm not going to screw this up."

I was even going to go ahead and take the damn GED. After all, I had a feeling that pretty soon I was going to need all the smarts I could stuff into my brain.